Forge Books by Janice Law

The Night Bus
The Lost Diaries of Iris Weed
Voices

Janice Law | **Voices**

A Tom Doherty Associates Book
New York

VOICES

Copyright © 2003 by Janice Law

This book is printed on acid-free paper.

Book design by Michael Collica

A Forge Book
Published by Tom Doherty Associates, LLC
175 Fifth Avenue
New York, NY 10010

www.tor.com

Forge® is a registered trademark of Tom Doherty Associates, LLC.

Library of Congress Cataloging-in-Publication Data

Law, Janice.
    Voices / Janice Law.—1st. ed.
        p. cm.
    ISBN 0-765-30275-6
    1. Kidnapping victims—Fiction. 2. Birthfathers—Fiction. 3. Connecticut—Fiction. 4. Young women—Fiction. 5. Amnesia—Fiction. I. Title.

    PS3562.A86V65 2003
    813'.54—dc21

                                                                        2002045461

First Edition: June 2003

Printed in the United States of America

0 9 8 7 6 5 4 3 2 1

For Marianne Santo Domingo, who plays a sweet piano, and Reg Upsall and all the nice folks at Fife Park and Albany Park, St. Andrews

Acknowledgments

Many thanks to Kay Kidde, my
invaluable agent

Part | **One**

Spring 1990

After she lost the names, the voices began. Names, voices: facets of memory held in mysterious balance. The voices came as compensation for the awkwardness, the embarrassment, the forgetfulness.

Do you remember? the voices asked. A certain summer morning with the shadows near the woods black as ink, impenetrable, the meadows wet and fresh, and the air smelling of wild roses. The roses, you remember. Red ramblers on a picket fence, dew spangling their leaves, a hum of bees in the branches. You remember that! And the others, the wild roses, some as small and white as the flowers of the brambles, but sweet, breathing perfume over the roadsides and the tangles at the edge of the wood, and especially the pink ones, single flowered, that filled the rough pastureland—there is no scent like them. June roses, June, roses, the dark shadows that edge the wood, the smell of meadows with wet grass and roses. This is dangerous ground, June a dangerous month; even roses would be dangerous if there were anything specific, if there were a name, a date.

But the names have gone, erased by the anesthesia or carelessness or too little oxygen, gone forever, and so now the voices start, now they say, But you remember the roses. The wood. The road. You remember the road: dirt, potholed, fern and bracken and white roses along the edges, and right where it joined the tarred state road, a meadow. You remember the meadow.

But you could remember, the voice says. One voice now, young, like the ghost of her younger self, like the girl in the meadow, picking wild geraniums and dandelions, picking flowers like Persephone and, like her, about to be dragged into the underworld.

Of course, she'd suspected for some time. That was to be understood, but with shock, blood loss, anesthesia, and emotional reaction there were so many variables. "Emotions distract from concentration, from the concentration needed for memory," the doctor said, and Leslie, meek, sedated, convalescent, had agreed and kept her reservations to herself. When she came home, she was exhausted; homecoming itself, passionately anticipated, was exhausting. The relief of survival, the comfort of familiarity, who'd have thought those debilitating? She had to develop stamina and relearn the normal defenses so that she didn't burst into tears and strain the enormous surgical scar with weeping. Enormous and, as it had turned out, excessive, unnecessary. She'd had the wrong symptom for an ectopic pregnancy: insufficient pain. The exploratory scar was the result, an ugly double row of horizontal stitches like the teeth of a sinister zipper that had opened to reveal one of nature's little anomalies, a ruptured fallopian tube. There had been insufficient pain, too much blood and, sometime in the course of a long, and probably messy, operation, too much anesthesia or too little oxygen. She'd forgotten the names.

Not Doug's, certainly, nor Heidi's, the neighbor from two houses down who brought them homemade lasagna and a macaroni casserole after she got back from the hospital. Nor Dylan's, the cat's, nor the butcher's at the local store, nor the crossing guard's near the paper, though she did draw a blank with one of Doug's uncles, a complete blank, and then called him by the wrong name. But that was covered over, laughed off. She'd felt the moment of panic, a sensation of sudden precipitous instability, the old cliché of the ground opening under her feet, then social rescue and Uncle Al saying, "You've made me ten years younger, Leslie, darling," and giving her a hug.

"I'm still so stupid from the drugs," she'd said, and the aunts agreed that it was terrible, what an ordeal, and it was no wonder if she was a bit muddled up still.

And Doug had been wonderful, had done everything possible; she was so lucky. If he grew impatient when she neglected a chore or forgot an errand, he was apologetic as if he, not she, were at fault. Sometimes she cried—though she couldn't stand people who were weepy—or got only half the things at the store or drove past the dry cleaner or left the banking slips on the desk. "You're trying too hard, trying to do too much," Doug would say. Leslie could feel that he was worried, worried and frustrated and a bit angry, but at fate, not at her. He continued to do the shopping even after she was strong enough to drive, and when, resentful, she found fault with his purchases, she wanted to bite her tongue. "I'm sorry," she'd cry. "I don't know what's wrong with me."

But increasingly, Leslie did know, and she was not back at the paper very long before she realized the true dimensions of the problem. She could even pinpoint the day. It was a hot Tuesday in April. Outside, the brilliant Florida sun fired the street; inside, a full-throated air conditioner blew unnatural breezes over the newsroom. The stocky figure of a leading local developer stepped from the blinding glare that curtained the glass facade, waved to the newsroom in general, and advanced with a bundle of plans, some skillfully glamorized sketches, and a handful of Polaroid snaps. Leslie knew that he had been married three times, had a son in college, a history of tax troubles, and at least one unsavory associate. She knew, too, that his latest project, around a small lagoon off the inland waterway, was on hold because the city was refusing the water hookups. In fact, the last story she'd written before she went into the hospital had concerned the zoning board deliberations on that project. But Leslie didn't know his name—or, rather, she found that she couldn't say his name, though she knew that she *had* known it, maybe knew it still. She had an almost physical sense of the name, like a bulky, necessary but irretrievable object, elusive as a disobedient dog. She felt the sweat on her forehead as he said, "Hi, Leslie. Good to see you. Feeling better?"

"Surviving," she said. "Surviving, thanks."

"Surviving is numero uno," he agreed.

Late as usual, Harvey, her news editor, breezed in, a Styrofoam coffee container in his hand. "Hello, Al," he called.

"Hey, Harvey! What are you doing up at this time in the morning?"

So Al was his name, Leslie thought, while the developer launched into an effortless flow of persiflage. Al what? She began trying letters, Al *A*—, not *A*, definitely not. *B*? Bond, Brown, Bates? No, not *B*. She saw an *S*, definitely an *S* before Al said, "I gotta talk to Leslie, I know you never do any work," and Harvey laughed and headed to his office.

"It's important to get our side out," Al told her, his smooth round face conveying equal amounts of shrewdness and geniality. It was weird, Leslie thought. She knew how to handle him and just how far to trust what he was saying, but she still didn't remember his name.

"It's only fair to let the public know that we'll be a multimillion-dollar addition to the tax roles. Hell, there's water all over this state if there's the will to develop it. That's the key."

"But only so much of that water is under city control," Leslie said automatically, though she was still thinking *S*. Something with an *S*. Maybe "swine"? With his short, broad nose, small eyes, and round forehead, Al suggested a very elegant and well-brushed porker. "You do want the development to be part of the city, don't you?"

"Certainly. Though there are other arrangements possible." Al pursed his lips and nodded sagely, as if there were municipalities all over the county eager to host his latest cheap and dubious development. "We aim to conserve our resources. Low-flush toilets in every model, standard. Ditto the showers."

"And lawns?" Leslie asked. Doug was always preaching against lawns, and now those water-gobbling sponges slid into her mind, although she wasn't really interested in lawns or in Al or in his project or in anything but the fact of his name. Even her own voice seemed distant, a stranger's voice, as she asked, "What about lawns? The Sun Coast homeowner's pride and joy?"

"Too much fuss made over lawns. These will be small, anyway," Al said and winked. "You read this. See if you're not impressed. I know you'll be fair." He beamed at her, genuinely charming and amusing. In certain moods, Leslie could see how he'd thrived despite the reports of shoddy construction, weak cement, and inadequate drainage. He had buoyancy, that was it; his energy and pleasure were borne up to the surface, and all his sly and dubious deals were somewhere far down in the nasty currents below. At the moment, she sure could do with a little of that buoyancy, with an infusion of Al's bubble and confidence.

"Right," she said, but the papers were trembling in her hand. She couldn't wait for him to be gone, couldn't wait to reach down into her file, to flip through the cuttings, to find the headline, "Water Commissioners Nix LeSeur Estates." LeSeur. Al LeSeur. Even in print, it looked as strange as the name of some exotic reptile, as a location beyond the moon. She opened her narrow reporter's notebook. Yes, Al LeSeur. Interview, February 3. "I'm the most forward-looking developer in the region and what the hell are they giving me but grief?" That was in her handwriting. She'd written that. The developer with the tax troubles, the smile, the two ex-wives, and the big alimony bill was Al LeSeur.

And the water commissioners were? Leslie's heart expanded, pressing against her lungs, contracting her stomach. The water commissioners? She could see their faces, the brown jacket one favored, the diamond rings armoring the fingers of—what was her name—the capable secretary who sat to the right of the chair and took the minutes? Leslie impatiently searched her notebook. Water Board meeting, January 9. Muriel Wisnocki in the chair. Hugh Meredith had spoken about inland wetlands policy. She'd made a note about the subject but remembered nothing. That had been the first meeting on Al, Al—she felt panicky again—Al S—. Al LeSeur. Yes, that was it. Al LeSeur, developer. Muriel Wisnocki, water commission chair. Commissioners, Meredith. Meredith and . . . But though she closed her eyes and bit her lip, Leslie couldn't bring up the other names and had to consult her notes. Then she sat down at her desk and got acquainted with disaster.

On Thursday, she went into her editor's glass-walled inner office. Harvey Whistler was tall, heavy, and blond with a pallid face and a languid manner that some of the old-timers saw as aristocratic and Southern, but that Leslie had always found affected. Whenever Harvey began laying on his drawl and his just off the plantation manners, she thought of her Uncle Mac, who'd had a keen nose for pretension. But though Uncle Mac would have pegged her editor as a slacker and dubbed him, "Harvey à la posh," Leslie was grateful for his underpowered nonchalance.

"I'm not sure I can cope yet, Harvey," she replied when he

asked how she was doing. "Stairs, walking, driving: I just didn't anticipate feeling this wiped out. Even half-time is a killer when I'm out doing beat stories."

"Hmmm," he said. "I thought you were looking tired. I've been meaning to ask if you were okay." He lit another cigarette and fiddled with his ashtray. "We certainly don't want to do you in for the sake of a LeSeur boondoggle. He is up to something, isn't he?"

"He's always up to something," Leslie said. "But I think the water hookups are going to be a real problem for him this time."

"We'll keep on top of that," Harvey said, making a note. Though indolent, he was not a bad newspaperman. "What about rewrites and copyediting for you temporarily? I'm afraid it's the best we can do." He waved one long, pale hand half dismissively, half apologetically, and Leslie felt herself flush with relief. She would have time to corral those strange mental objects she had once taken for granted; she would have time to relearn all the social and political labels of the city. "There's a lot of useful stuff off the wire that needs to be selected and edited," Harvey continued as if she might need persuading.

"Rewrites and copyediting sound ideal. I appreciate this, Harvey. Really. I just came back too soon, the doctor says."

"Dedication," he said. "We could use more of it here at *Sun Coast*." He gave a lazy, condescending smile, which irked Leslie despite her gratitude. It was easy for him to be laid back and superior to it all. Scion of a wealthy Virginia family, Harvey had attended a string of exclusive schools from kindergarten through college. For him, the *Sun Coast Times*, even in an editorial role, was a contraction of expectations and entitlements. Leslie had arrived from a different direction entirely. After a succession of underfunded schools, she'd attended the community college, then nights at South Florida and an internship with the paper. For Leslie, the *Sun Coast Times* with its grainy photos, astrology predictions, recipe exchanges, tide times, and local seniors column represented a solid achievement that she was determined to retain even if she had to write messages to herself like an old lady. Day after day, Leslie took compulsive notes for every phone call, every message. She opened up her notebooks and struggled to associate the assorted developers, glad-handers, council members, appointed VIPs, and community airbags with their proper names. She read back newspapers, too, and studied her old pieces, fighting down the panic that lurked just under her smile whenever she hit a patch where the names meant nothing, where she'd forgotten the meetings, where mysterious events appeared under her byline.

Rebuilding her memory was no fun. Success merely restored the status quo, and failure made her depressed and nervous, feelings she tried to hide under as much good cheer as she could muster. In contrast to this discouraging mental rehab, work with the feature wire was almost always fun. The lighter news of the day was a distraction from her own struggles, and Leslie found herself looking forward to the strange romances, cures, scandals, and triumphs that showed up on her screen. She read the collected oddities with a sense of wonder and curiosity, as if they were modern-dress versions of the stories Aunt Flo used to read her out of a big green clothbound *Grimm's Fairy Tales*.

This pleasure in the bizarre and the unexpected surprised Leslie. The accident that had damaged her memory seemed to have opened other doors in her imagination, for she discovered a newly vivid sense of odd lives. She was enchanted with the World's Greatest Elvis Impersonator, a fearless self-promoter who'd escaped a humdrum office job into ersatz rock royalty. And with the California bigamist who'd embezzled from his university to pay for his exponentially increasing family, and even with the lonely moose that had wandered down from the Maine woods to become hopelessly enamored of a Holstein heifer.

In this flood of human—and animal—interest items, the

Eden story was one of the least sensational. "Twenty-five years later a family, and a town, remember" was the cutline. Below was a short piece about Ruth Eden, a lost Connecticut child still untraced after almost twenty-five years. Some enterprising, if callow, journalist had unearthed her story on the eve of the sad anniversary and had interviewed a number of the townspeople for a feature.

Touching, Leslie thought, but hardly relevant to *Sun Coast*'s readers. She was about to kill the article, when she was transfixed by one short paragraph: "Several people saw Ruth Eden near the country road that June day. They remember a small, dark-haired girl picking flowers at the edge of the meadow. All of them assumed that her parents or playmates were nearby, and no one thought to ask what she was doing so far from home." The letters wavered on the blue screen, and Leslie felt a lurch of shock, a dislocation touched with fear.

". . . picking flowers at the edge of the meadow . . . reported the child missing shortly after two P.M. . . . . older, black or dark blue Chevrolet sedan in the area . . . meadow a mile from the Eden home, a neat Cape Cod cottage . . . through the wood toward the country road . . . picking flowers at the edge of the meadow . . ."

Leslie could see the meadow, wet with insect spittle and dew, noisy with bobolinks, cowbirds, and sparrows. The grass, very tall, shoulder high; the sun, hot overhead; the woods, dark green with blacker shadows, a dangerous place, frightening with the trees creaking overhead, with the mossy rocks, with the brush where an evil devil lurked or bad elves. She looked up at the screen, astonished, half expecting to see the tangle of vines and weeds around the fallen trunk, its bare roots sinister above the somber, peaty pool of water that collected where the tree had been wrenched from the earth. She had seen that. She had been frightened by that. She had remembered and forgotten, and now, in the great effort of remembering and relearning, there it was again. The fallen tree, the belief in devils and elves. Where had they come from? And the wood. The wood was dangerous. The meadow was full of sunlight and safety and flowers. Flowers for a daisy chain. She knew how to make one, and it came to Leslie suddenly that her mother had taught her, that she had been shown, that she had sat on grass, fingers sticky from the dandelions' milky sap, and slit their stems and inserted the soft, slippery stalks, one into the other, to make a bright, limp, pollen-smelling circlet that slipped down over one ear, that she had sat and laughed with a woman with black hair, not like Aunt Flo at all. Someone different. A woman forgotten or hidden: her mother, who had lost a child, too.

Leslie was staring at the computer screen, still seeing not just the lighted dots of the letters but also a wood, a lawn, a meadow—vivid, yet contracted, like the memories of someone without peripheral vision, when Betty and Marianne, photographer and women's page editor, respectively, came clacking into the newsroom in their heeled sandals, their bags slung over their shoulders, their as yet unlit cigarettes at the ready.

"So, Leslie, going to lunch?"

"Skinny gals never eat," Marianne teased.

Leslie looked up at their tanned faces and took a moment to return from the mysterious space that had opened in a few inches of type. "God! Is it that time?"

"Five to. Lost in the feature wire again? Latest serial killer?"

"Or the lovesick moose?" Betty asked, for long ago they had discovered that Leslie was too good-natured for serious gossip. Her contribution to lunchtime amusement was to keep them up to date on the most interesting developments from the feature wire. "I'm rooting for the moose," Betty added, as she fanned out her newly frosted hair, an innovation courtesy of an experimentally minded hairdresser down on the bypass.

"A slow day," Leslie said, saving the story and abruptly logging off. "The moose is fine, and we've got 'Eighty-Year-Old Woman Covers House with Bottle Caps,' 'Neighbors Protest Obscene Sculptures on Beverly Hills Mansion,' and 'Elvis Impersonators Meet for Annual Conference.'"

"No wonder people keep reporting Elvis sightings. He's all over the place," Betty said.

"Elvis is a saint for our times," Leslie said in her best news commentator voice. "Our rock of salvation."

"I can't stand theology," said Marianne.

"Especially with bad puns. You'd better stay in the AC," Betty told Leslie.

"You want us to bring you back something?" Marianne asked. "No problemo if you're tired."

"No, no, I've been at the computer long enough." Though the trip down the hot bypass would be tiring, Leslie was eager to get out, to laugh a little, to be healthy again. "Just a quick stop at the john and I'm ready."

But in the lavatory, she loitered before the mirror. Her face looked different, thinner, with signs of strain around the eyes like one of those dreary "before" shots in the fashion makeover pages. For the first time, Leslie thought that she looked older, a creepy sensation in itself, and when she pulled back her dark hair, memory unexpectedly rose and wavered, then flashed away from the surface like a wary fish, leaving a queasy fear in its wake. This is nonsense, Leslie told herself. I'm losing my mind along with my memory. I've got to avoid stories about children, about disappearances, about catastrophes in general . . .

"Hey, Leslie! Come on!" Betty and Marianne began shouting and pounding comically on the door. Two good office buddies, easygoing, pleasure loving, profane, they'd been kind when Leslie was in the hospital, told her funny stories, brought the office gossip, sent her a teddy bear. Now they were trying to pull her back to normal life, whatever that was, and Leslie knew she should be grateful. She *was* grateful. She took a deep breath and told herself that she was fine, that everything was okay, that everything was under control.

"Where're we going, guys?" Though she was smiling as she spoke, Leslie realized that her voice was a little too loud, a little too hearty. Like a singer unable to find the right key, she felt that she'd mislaid her social pitch and had to struggle to find it again with jokes and wisecracks.

"The Burger Beast," Betty said.

"Vomitus," was Marianne's reaction.

"Food writers are such snobs," Betty said. "I gotta go to Kmart. Okay?"

"Sure. I'll stop at that discount swimsuit place. I need some new suits," Leslie said. "No more bikinis for me."

"Listen, you gotta ignore conventional wisdom," Marianne said as they left the building for the torrid glare of the parking lot. "You wear a bikini if you feel like it."

"I don't feel like it," Leslie said. "I'd feel like the Bride of Frankenstein in a bikini." What she really felt like was crying, and it took a certain amount of willpower to quash the impulse for tears.

"I have an appendectomy scar," said Marianne, who favored suits in the micro-mini category.

"You have a rakish scar," Leslie said, making an effort to keep her voice light. "Mine is in the slasher attack category."

"We're going to get lunch," Betty said. "Can we stop with the medical discussion?"

"You're just jealous," Marianne said. "No 'distinguishing marks.'"

"The hair must count for something," Leslie said.

"I think I need some green in it," Betty said. She could always be drawn into a discussion of hair and style.

"You'll scare the retirees."

"Naw. Just keep your eyes on the green bits, please. Or maybe purple. You go this far"—she fanned out her straw-colored locks—"you can maybe go a bit farther."

They speculated on this, Marianne suggesting a rearrangement of Betty's spectacular but much tortured hair. The sun was shimmering on the cars, and when Marianne unlocked her Mustang, its hot vinyl and metal breath made Leslie's head throb.

"You need one of those windshield shades," said Betty. "My brother got one."

"Yeah?"

"With some overdeveloped babe printed on it."

"Your brother's sexually retarded," Marianne said. She put the car in gear and turned on the air conditioner. The hot wind roaring through the vents gradually turned dank and cool, and the heavy tinting at the top of the windshield damped the blue-white sky to indigo. Marianne whipped down the palm-lined boulevard and out onto the white-hot commercial strip with its cornucopia of fast food, fast beer, fast shopping, fast banking—even fast death, Leslie thought, as they passed a huge funeral home billboard emblazoned, "Did you think to pray today?"

Everywhere there were new condos, new parking lots, new concerns of every type, selling cars and boats and housewares and eyeglasses, books new and secondhand, clothes expensive or cheap, gifts and souvenirs, plus those Florida staples: homes, land, and dreams with nothing down. Leslie had always approved of this dizzying and ephemeral profusion. The vulgarity and newness that were fashionably deplored were precisely what she liked. She felt at ease with change, with development, with the tides of commerce that turned a corner lot first to a clothes shoppe, then to a burger stand, a package store, a pizzeria, or a surf shop. Doug could bemoan the rape of the state, the rampant greed, the shortsighted, suffocating overdevelopment, but she liked cruising down the highway in the cool, artificial air, the car stereo thumping out U-2 or Kim Wilde, shuttled from one air-conditioned, fluorescent-lit, pastel-decorated, Muzaked stop to another. Someday, Leslie fancied, they'd come out to lunch, and all the music systems would be tuned the same, one song all the way, a continuous melody that would carry them along and give them the illusion that the world was all in sync.

But at the moment, things were definitely out of sync. Driving back to work with Marianne and Betty in a fog of cigarettes, chicken nuggets, and fries, Leslie found the commercial strip disorienting, the very image of sudden, inexplicable, and unwelcome alteration. She wished that she'd never been pregnant, that she could somehow erase the last five months, that she could return to a life that now seemed not only happy but effortless, a life, that is, where she did not have to be obsessive about names and where she didn't have to remind herself of what to feel or how to react.

Back at her desk, Leslie folded a particularly vapid press release into a hat for her get well teddy, sharpened pencils until their needle points began to break, and watered the spider plants, the cactus, and her little jade tree—the usual resources of a procrastinating writer. The other side of her nervousness was this sporadic indolence, and instead of finishing up with the feature wire, she read through the Eden story again and then sat wondering why she had always felt at home on the Sun Coast. The answer was not long in coming: It was because almost everyone had arrived from somewhere else. Leslie could say that she "grew up in Syracuse and north of Orlando" and was raised by her Aunt Flo and Uncle Mac. That was enough amid the refugees from cold and snow, the arthritis exiles, the compulsive golfers and tennis players. There was no need here for the small-town interrogations. "Raised by Aunt Flo? Parents dead? Where? How? Aunt on your mother's side? Your father's?" It had been easier as a child to refer to them as "mom and dad," which pleased Aunt flo, surely, but which had left a residue of uneasiness, a faint nausea at the heart of family relations.

"You're called Leslie, now." She remembered that day,

standing small and angry in the square, old-fashioned kitchen with the cracked gray-green linoleum, the yellow plaster walls, the pendant ceiling light like a flying saucer. She was stamping her feet and crying, as the overhead light soared away from Aunt Flo with her thin, anxious, obsessive face, and left Leslie with the strangeness, the smell of floor polish, and the slow, rich smell of stewing beef.

"You want him to come back? Leslie lives here. Not ___. Just Leslie. No one else." She remembered that, but not the name, which was forgotten, repressed, a dangerous name, just as June was a dangerous month; roses dangerous flowers, woods dangerous, and, at last, even memory itself threatening. Now Leslie wondered if Aunt Flo had said, "Not Ruth." And "him"? The "him" who might come back, who would come back for the unknown name, the forgotten name, but not for Leslie, not for this strange new girl living in a strange new place with Aunt Flo? Leslie didn't know, didn't remember, though the knowledge must still be hidden somewhere in her bones, because she felt her heart contract and, angry with herself, collapsed the accordion folds of the printout. All stupid speculation. Stupid and dangerous, especially in her present state of mind. At certain times you are vulnerable to coincidence, that's all. I'm a sensible person, she told her haggard image in the washroom mirror. Then she took a couple of Tylenol and went home early, filled with sweet reason and common sense.

Less than a week later, having convinced herself that she'd feel better if she knew for sure, if she were busy, if she did something she really felt like doing, Leslie queried the wire service for any follow-up or supplemental material to the Eden story. When there was none, she impulsively took the afternoon off and drove up to the university library in Tampa. She checked the *New York Times* on the microfiche for June 1965, the month Ruth Eden disappeared, and then asked the location of the nearest holdings of the *Hartford Courant* and the *Hartford Times* for

1965. She started a file, the wire story first, then photocopies of the short news items from the *Times* and the longer pieces from the Hartford papers, complete with a tantalizingly fuzzy photograph of Ross and Kate Eden, a handsome young couple frozen by tragedy. The man was square faced, sober, his eyes stunned. The woman was holding her son, her hands tense on his thin shoulders, her face a terrified, passionate, protective mask.

And behind it? Was this the woman who had sat on the grass threading dandelions into a chain? Leslie stood before the bathroom mirror and held the photo up to the glass, but the mirrored oracle gave her no satisfaction. Something about the forehead? The eyebrows were right, as thick and straight as her own, but the nose was different, and the woman's expression was so strained that Leslie couldn't tell about the mouth. Kate Eden had dark hair, darker than hers, Leslie guessed, though the boy was fair and so was Ross Eden. She put the clipping back in the folder, where it worried her like an untold secret. One day at the office, she photocopied a recent snap of herself for comparison, but she could not decide if the loss of halftones increased or decreased the likeness.

The more Leslie thought about the Edens, the less she seemed to know, and the more fluid memory and information became. At last, she stopped relying on speculation, and, like a good reporter, set out the dossier. Ruth Eden, age five, had disappeared on a June morning, after she went out to play in the backyard of the Eden home on Kennels Road in Woodmill, Connecticut. Woodmill was a small western Connecticut town, largely rural, with an early Congregational church, a Revolutionary War–era cemetery, and a consolidated school that took pupils from several neighboring towns. It was a safe, isolated town, a place where Ruth Eden could certainly be allowed out alone to play in the backyard. Her mother, Kate, twenty-six, housewife, part-time worker at the newsstand in the village, was making brownies for the PTA bake sale. According to Mrs.

Eden, Ruth was still in the yard at eleven when Paul Schott, a friend from the local drama group, stopped with information about the costumes that would be needed for the upcoming production of *Carousel.*

He'd brought some of the cast measurements, and after he arrived, Kate looked out the window and checked the yard. Ruth was playing on her swing set, alone because her brother was in school and Patty, the nearest neighbor's girl who usually came down mornings, was in bed with chicken pox. Kate Eden sat at the kitchen table and had a cup of coffee with Schott, who was on his way to Millerton for a house inspection. They went over the costume requirements, and Schott left before eleven-thirty. Kate Eden walked him to his car, checked her mailbox, and went around the side of the house to find the swing set empty. She had been worried, but not too worried. Ruth sometimes wandered into the pasture at one side of the house and had gone as far as the woodlot on occasion. Kate Eden called her daughter several times, then thought that she might have walked up the road toward her friend Patty Nolan's house. Mrs. Eden returned to the front yard, but the road was deserted.

Believing the child was on the other side of the hill, Kate Eden started up the road, and Leslie, who had covered a number of missing children cases, could imagine her mixture of exasperation and fear. Halfway up, Mrs. Eden had suddenly realized that she was wasting time and ran back to her house to telephone. Ruth was not at the Nolans'. Alarmed, Kate Eden checked the backyard again, then set off through the field toward the woodlot. She estimated that she left the yard around noon but said that she could not be sure, because she had waited a short time, hoping to hear from Mrs. Nolan that Ruth had, indeed, arrived. Mrs. Eden had gone quite far into the wood, and she estimated that she had gotten within a hundred yards of where Ruth had last been seen.

And there was the odd thing, the odd thing that Leslie picked up on: The last witnesses claimed to have seen Ruth Eden shortly after one P.M. in the meadow on the other side of the woodlot. Wouldn't the child have heard her mother calling? There was no mention of deafness, of disturbed behavior, of dis-function in the family. Aunt Flo suddenly whispered in her ear that "you never know with kids, you never know what the hell they're going to do." Leslie's journalistic experience confirmed that. But Kate Eden was in the woodlot sometime after noon, and Ruth was still in the meadow after one o'clock, and it was bad luck, bad luck of the sort that Leslie now recognized, that prevented Kate Eden from scooping up her tearful daughter and bringing her home with a story to amaze the relatives and amuse the neighbors.

Instead, bad luck: Kate Eden gave up too soon, or panicked, or felt that she'd better get help at once. She returned to tele-phone her husband at his liquor store. He came home with the car, and they drove up and down the road and searched the field and the woods again. The police records showed that they'd reported the child missing at two P.M., forty-five or fifty minutes after she was seen by George and Mabel Zinsser, a retired couple returning from a routine checkup at the local hospital. Five other people had seen the child between noon and one, including a farmer bringing a load of hay in for a horse farm two miles down the road from the Edens. Later, there were some reports that a strange car had been in the area, or, rather, Leslie could see from the original stories, several strange cars, variously black, dark blue, green, or maroon, older models of Chevys, Fords, or Buicks. The most promising was a "dark, older Chevrolet," which had been seen at the local carnival, but all the carnival people had subsequently been cleared, and none of them owned a car that matched that description.

With that mysterious, half-described car, the trail ended. A suitable vehicle was never discovered. For several months, "Ruth Eden" was sighted in various New England localities, but

A breeze came up off the Gulf to set the palm fronds, the jasmine, and the oleanders rustling against the screens, as Doug and Leslie finished the dinner dishes. Indigo clouds had already extinguished the sunset and darkened the pine-shaded yard, and Leslie felt the damp electrical anticipation that promised rain. Against the early dark, the intimate yellow glow of the kitchen lights turned her husband's tanned arms to gold and sank into the khaki of his faded shorts. Doug whistled softly as he put away the plates and moved his feet in time to the merengue beat issuing from the local Cuban station. He is always so graceful, Leslie thought, a person at ease within his body. That ease and grace was what she'd liked about him from the first day at the community college. She'd have to admit she'd noticed how attractive he was right away.

"You're looking thoughtful," he said.

"I was thinking how handsome you are."

His fair, open face flushed, but it was true. Doug was tall and robust with even features, gray eyes, and large, well-shaped hands. He had wavy light brown hair and the efficient, rather than overdeveloped, physique of a man who employs his muscles for useful things, for building cabinets and hefting boards, driving nails and cutting mortises. Even more important was the air of candid cheerfulness that made people trust him. "You have the nicest husband," any number of his customers had said, and there'd been at least a few who'd have been happier without a Mrs. Austin in the picture at all.

"Well," he said now, "my handsomeness is a welcome topic at any time." And he gave her a kiss.

Leslie could have let things run in a pleasant direction, but instead she said, "I'll tell you what else I was thinking. I was thinking about what I can remember."

"The names, you mean?" Doug asked cautiously. He knew, without really understanding, her struggle with names. In his business, the names and addresses of people who wanted kitchens went right into his order book. His suppliers were in the Rolodex, and clerks at the various lumberyards were not offended if they were greeted simply with an easy, "How's it going?"

"No," Leslie said. "I've been trying to think what's the very earliest thing I can remember. Farther back is supposed to be better—you know, a sign of intelligence."

"Oh, my memory goes very far back, then," Doug teased.

"So," she said, "what's the earliest thing you can remember?" He stopped polishing the dish he was drying and thought for a second or two.

"I remember having a little Boston Bruins jacket," he said, smiling reminiscently, "and going out on my bicycle and hearing the neighbors say, 'Here's Bobby Orr.' I was maybe four, maybe five."

"And from then on, you remember?"

"What do you mean 'remember'?"

Leslie had already asked Marianne, Betty, Heidi, and several others. It was a desperately important, if unscientific and informal, poll. "I mean after that you remember your life in sequence—going to school, joining a team, meeting various friends. You remember one thing, and, in back of that, there's nothing, you were too young to remember. But on the other side, there's regular memory."

"More or less. Though I don't remember a lot about going to elementary school. Or junior high, for that matter. Probably a blessing."

"Junior high is purgatory at the very best," Leslie agreed.

"Amen. Towel fights, that's what I remember." He playfully snapped the dishcloth at Leslie.

"Don't be Neanderthal," she said and retaliated, giggling. But though they got their dish towels soaked and almost upset the coffeepot, she couldn't quite leave the topic. "Still," she said, when they stopped laughing, "you remember being Bobby Orr. You remember being a really little kid and then growing up."

"Sure."

"See, that's what kind of bothers me. What I remember first is sitting in Jennifer Bayheim's living room listening to an old Beatles record because neither of us had gotten invited to a birthday party. I must have been eleven, ten at the youngest. Before that—nothing. Nothing at all. Or rather just a few odd things. Things that don't make any sense."

"The Beatles," Doug said reminiscently and whistled "Can't Buy Me Love." For someone who didn't sing or play an instrument, Doug was surprisingly musical. He could convey a lot in a few whistled bars.

"Our favorite was 'Yesterday,'" Leslie said. "We were romantics at heart." She made an attempt at the tricky intervals of the opening, and Doug joined in, more accurately, with a whistled accompaniment.

When he went back to the dishes, a few bars of "Yesterday" hanging, sweetly nostalgic, in the air, Leslie thought that he should really have asked, What things? What odd things? When he did not, she said, "Like the meadow. I remember a meadow on a June morning. I know the month."

"You read it was June," he replied, too quickly, and she knew that telling him about the Eden story had been a mistake.

"I knew it before. That's the one thing I'm sure of. There were roses. I remember roses and the smell of roses near the meadow."

"Okay, you knew before," he said more abruptly than he intended. The great sadness he sometimes sensed in her made him feel guilty and helpless. It worried him, because he had no idea of what to do.

"There were no meadows in Syracuse," Leslie said.

"Maybe you were taken to a park or something. What's a meadow to a little kid? Or not so little. You say the first thing you really remember was at ten or so."

"The grass was over my head," Leslie said patiently. "And I was frightened. I'd been frightened by the wood."

"What wood?"

"The wood behind the meadow."

Doug began putting the plates in the cupboard, rattling them emphatically into place. "So what happened then?" he asked. "What comes next?"

"That's what's odd. There is nothing else." Was that true? Sometimes the voices, the strange, new subliminal voices, whispered that there was more, that she did know, that she could remember if she tried, a proposition that alternately frightened and attracted her.

"You know you can have vivid recollections of something you've seen or heard. I remember some of the crazy stuff they showed us in Sunday school, like the stoning of St. Stephen. Scared the hell out of me."

"All right, forget memory for a moment. Forget the subjective side altogether and look at the facts." Leslie smoothed out a coffee filter and set it into the basket. "I grew up with Aunt Flo and Uncle Mac. Where were my parents? What happened to them?"

"You said they were dead." He sounded almost suspicious, and Leslie realized that one of the undesirable by-products of her search for memory was that a lot of things she'd said or assumed might not be so.

"Yes, but I've no proof. No obit, no death certificates, nothing. I was just told, 'They're dead.' But not right away. First it was, 'They're away for a while.' "

"That's odd, but it doesn't have to mean any more than that she didn't know how to tell you."

"I never had a birth certificate, either."

"Of course, you did. You needed one for your passport when we went to Mexico."

"Yes, I called Aunt Flo and said that I had to have one. I absolutely had to have one. And I would, wouldn't I, if I wanted to change jobs. With all this crazy proof of citizenship stuff. I told her I absolutely had to have one."

"So?"

"So she got me one. Don't ask me where. I was supposedly born in Orlando. Doug, we moved to Orlando when I was in junior high."

"You could still have been born there. As you say, you don't know anything about your parents."

"I do know that Aunt Flo made a big deal when we moved about going somewhere entirely new. Somewhere none of us had ever been. And I remember Uncle Mac telling me that we had to 'learn the ropes,' learn the 'Southern way of doing things.' "

"Still, she had the certificate."

"Doug, I expect she bought it. Just as if I was some illegal."

"I don't see Aunt Flo . . ."

"Aunt Flo knows how to survive; she's as tough as they come. Listen, here's something else. She was supposedly Dad's sister, but she doesn't have a single picture of him. Not even a wedding photo."

"Not everyone takes as many photos as my family."

"We didn't take any at all. Which is something I've just realized since the surgery. Maybe it's just from the strain of trying to remember all the useful stuff I've forgotten, but I've started to remember other things. Like no school photos. I was usually kept home on one excuse or another, and if I *was* in school on the day, she never bought any. They were never 'nice enough of my girl.' In junior high, I bought some on my own to trade with the other kids. I thought she'd be angry, but when she found them, she just said, 'Very nice.' Why do you think that was?"

Doug shrugged.

"Don't you see? I was too old for it to matter anymore if there were pictures. Before that—not a single one. You know, for our yearbook we were supposed to bring in a baby picture. I asked her. 'Oh, we never bothered much about pictures,' was what she said. I stole one of Jennifer's and put it in as mine. And Aunt Flo wasn't happy when I got my picture in the paper graduating from community college, either. She tried to pretend she was, but she wasn't."

"All right, there's something funny about your Aunt Flo and photographs. But it's no proof that your parents are alive. And it's no proof that you're that Eden girl, either."

"No one said anything about Ruth Eden. You're the only one who's mentioned her." Leslie knew that she sounded defensive.

"I know what this is all about," Doug said, as if he did know. Or thought he knew. Leslie found herself getting irritated. She didn't know; she didn't have a clue.

"What's it all about?"

"Look, honey, you've had a rough time. Everything's been difficult. It's natural that you should . . . well, wonder about Aunt Flo and so on. I mean after the baby."

"I never thought of it as a baby. It was just a pain in my side. We didn't even know." Nonetheless, she started to tremble.

"Yes," said Doug, putting his arm around her shoulder, "I know that, but . . ."

"Yes." Leslie bit her lip, near tears. She hadn't particularly wanted children, hadn't worried about having a child until now. Now that she hadn't had the child, now that her chances were reduced quite radically, now she wanted a baby.

"Once you get feeling better, there's no reason why we can't try again."

"No reason at all."

"So you've got to rest and not upset yourself. Right?" He gave her shoulder a little shake as if to wake her from a bad dream.

Leslie knew she must smile now. She could feel his anxiety and knew she should agree, as she usually did, as she was usually willing to do. Why not now? What was wrong with her?

"Right?"

Leslie smiled at his blunt, kindly face, then pressed her cheek against his T-shirt. The reassuring warmth of his body and the familiar line of his rib cage brought her almost to tears, because, even in that moment, she could feel the great gap that was opening between them.

Just the same, her intentions were good; she understood Doug's point and agreed completely. She must rest, she mustn't upset herself, she must resist the siren song of what might have been—so much more poignant and seductive now when everything seemed so unsatisfactory. Really, Leslie understood just what she should do, and she tried to do it. She went with Doug to see the local high school play slow, inept games of baseball. She met for lunch every day with Marianne and Betty and stopped at the strip malls with them and feigned interest in the new clothes on the racks and the new novels in the bookstores. She sat with Heidi's kids for an hour every day, so that her neighbor could visit the hospital where her husband, Dwayne, was recovering from back surgery. The kids were a boy and a girl, four and five, respectively. They had boisterous sessions in their green plastic wading pool that left Leslie soaked and laughing, or else they all lay on the floor together in the air-conditioned living room, eating fruit and pretzels and watching Bert and Ernie on *Sesame Street*. Though Heidi was always apologizing for them, the kids were all right. Kevin and Erin made Leslie laugh even if she was tired, even if she had to change her clothes after they'd all played around the pool.

It was the adult world that was the real problem, and there, Leslie knew, she was just going through the motions. But at least she was up and moving; she was going to work, making the dinners, feeding the cat. Maybe the emotions would come. Maybe one day she'd wake to find herself efficient and happy again, set to juggle the roles she'd once managed so effortlessly. Maybe that would happen.

There were times when she felt hopeful, when life would suddenly and unexpectedly break through the sensory flatness that surrounded her. One mild afternoon, she and Doug took a picnic down to Casperson's Beach. The Gulf was a lovely milky green with pelicans coasting in strung-out files just above the surface. They had a swim and floated on the warm water, buoyant and carefree. Afterward, Doug retrieved his binoculars, and they walked inland through the back side of the park, looking for herons, egrets, and rails around the swampy lagoon between the beach and the golf course. They saw skimmers and lots of snowy egrets, and though Leslie didn't have her husband's passion for birds, she caught some of his quick delight in the flash of wings and the lunge of a fishing heron. The sand was pleasantly warm underfoot, and the bright sun whitened the sky overhead.

Everything felt not just pleasant but natural, as if her nervous system were again fully operational. Later, after they ate their picnic dinner on the sand and sat enjoying the shore breeze and watching the tiniest curls of surf darken the gray sand, Leslie felt her social pitch returning and, with it, the possibility of happiness. She leaned her head on Doug's shoulder to watch the sky turn watermelon pink and the fading sun drop toward the Gulf.

"Want to take a look along the waterway?" he asked.

"I think I've walked enough," she said. "Go ahead. I'll just be lazy."

"You don't mind?" he asked, though he was already reaching for his binoculars. "Buddy's seen an eagle the last few days on his way to Port Charlotte. I thought I might spot one along the waterway." The low sun reddened Doug's tanned face and turned his thick, curly hair to bronze. Looking at him, Leslie smiled a little to herself. Certain things, certain feelings were, indeed, coming back to her.

"Good luck," she said. He scrambled up to the strip of cracked and potholed tarmac, a relic of the last few hurricane seasons that had chewed the beach all the way back to the abandoned coast road, leaving a miniature sandy cliff striped with layers of bone-white shells. A thin band of palms and palmetto scrub clung precariously to the top; behind them, a little dry savanna ran to the rock-lined sides of the inland waterway.

Leslie lay flat on the sand and watched the evening clouds gather into monstrous, doughy shapes: white turning lavender, lavender turning pink, and pink declining to slate gray. Perhaps she fell asleep momentarily, or perhaps it was only her unaccustomed concentration on the sky, on those vast columns of suspended water vapor, that made her dizzy. She realized that she had not been outdoors very much, had not been alone, had not felt quite this exposed to . . . what precisely? She couldn't say, but she was suddenly aware of the emptiness, of the inhuman scale of the towering clouds, the curling water, the long expanse of beach. She felt as if Doug and her whole ordinary world had vanished into mystery. "Nothing is certain," the waves whispered, while the shadowed palms and the surging clouds, darkening markedly now that the sun had set, seemed the very image of sudden and unpredictable change.

Leslie stood up, uncontrollably alarmed: Her emotions spiked unpredictibly like a virulent fever. She put on her shoes to scale the sandy slope that came away beneath her feet, revealing the dry, tenacious roots of the palms. At the top, she missed the path and had to push through brittle-leaved palmettoes that rustled with displeasure. She picked up her feet in case of snakes and swatted bugs at every step. Descending a little gully, Leslie thought that she'd lost her way completely, but a dozen yards farther on, she spotted the sandy track, white in the coming night, and followed it onto the dry grassland that always made her think of the ancient African savanna and of early primates armed with sticks and frightened of the vast plains and fierce animals.

Leslie had not gone very far before she began to recover herself. The moment of exposure and isolation faded; common sense resurfaced. How silly could she be! She might already have missed Doug. While she was thrashing about in the bushes, alerting every mosquito in the county, he could have walked back on the path, expecting to meet her at the beach. The dry, grassy expanse ahead was empty. An early star hung over the earth berm that rimmed the waterway, and she noticed an old, listing sedan crouched near a clump of trees. Her wayward imagination kicked in again, conjuring trouble for Doug, strangers, the thunderclap violence of modern life, before a shadow stirred from behind a clump of palmettoes, and her husband waved.

"Two of them," he called. "Beautiful. I wish you'd come. No doubt at all; you could see their heads and tails, so white. I forgot the time."

"It's all right," Leslie said, although she was shivering. "I walked in this far and then I was afraid I'd missed you."

"We'll come back earlier one night," he said. "Or maybe drive to Port Charlotte. The Red Sox are playing there next week. Buddy says he regularly sees eagles along I-75 near Port Charlotte."

"I've never seen a bald eagle," Leslie said, trying to be enthusiastic, trying to cover the remnants of her anxiety.

"We'll go," Doug said, putting his arm around her. "Birds and Sox, okay?"

"Sure. We'll bring the Sox luck if anyone can." She hugged him, taking comfort from the familiar, steady thump of his heart.

"I love the Gulf at night," Doug said as they strolled back along the shore toward the parking lot, but Leslie gave a shudder. So many things she had once liked—or simply not noticed—had acquired a newly sinister character. Something inside of her had been lost, stolen, or mislaid—she didn't know which—but the result was that the universe was suddenly too big for her, and her life, stretched and distorted like an old sweater, didn't fit neatly anymore.

There were pieces missing, loose ends, a general truncation of personal history, and, in this mood, the Eden family represented not just a distraction but an almost irresistible alternative. A week after the evening at the beach, Leslie gave in to the Edens' siren song and called the Woodmill Consolidated School. She described a story in vague but ambitious terms and sent off a check; ditto to the local Woodmill paper, a thin weekly with good back files. She had the material sent to the office, and when she brought the packages home, she hid them in her underwear drawer.

The first afternoon she beat Doug home from work, she took out the old yearbooks and the photocopies of birth announcements and society notes. The Birch-Eden wedding had gotten a lot of space and three photographs, including one of the wedding party in front of a pretty stone church. The bridal party looked terribly young; Ross Eden, handsome; Kate, vivacious. Leslie went over the pictures with a magnifying glass, bringing up the features of parents and grandparents, of the flower girl and the ring bearer, searching for resemblances, for the family trait that would strike an unmistakable chord. Then the yearbooks: Kate with the cheerleaders, chunky in a heavy letter sweater, not pretty but vital and attractive, full of the energy that would end in that mask of fear, anger, and desperation a dozen years later. And there she was in the drama group, as Emily in *Our Town*, another young woman bound for grief over maternity. Ross Eden belonged to an earlier volume, lazily overseeing the Electronics Club's array of tubes and wires and posing, self-consciously handsome, with the baseball team. The youth of Ruth Eden's parents—of her parents?—emerged out of the silly "favorite sayings," capsule biographies, class wills, and predictions, out of the parties and proms that, at a distance of almost forty years, seemed nearly as exotic as entertainments among the pharaohs.

Though they were married within a year of her graduation, Kate Birch was not with Ross Eden at these affairs, but with a taller, thinner boy with short brown hair and bony, expressive features. Leslie made a face and reproached herself for facile assumptions. Childhood sweethearts, early marriage, the ideal couple struck by the caprice of fate: that was the scenario Leslie had secretly wanted. If these were her parents, she wanted them to be as happy and perfect as a lonely, troubled child had once imagined them. Instead, Ross Eden smiled blandly from a clutch of photos, each with a different girl, and three years later, Kate Birch attended proms and formals and skating parties with the lean boy whom Leslie discovered in the roster of the Class of 1955: Paul Schott, Drama Club, 1, 2, 3, 4; Glee Club, 3, 4; Cross-Country Team, 1, 2, 3, 4. Ambition, draftsman. Favorite saying, "I gotta check my trapline." Paul Schott, who had visited Kate Eden the day Ruth disappeared, a man who knew the woods, Leslie thought, and she felt her heart jump without knowing why she felt uneasy or why the information made her anxious. She closed the folder, irritated with herself. Doug was right. This was foolish and needlessly upsetting.

But though Leslie resolved to go back to work full-time and keep her mind on the *Sun Coast Times*, she discovered that Woodmill and the Edens had insinuated themselves into an imaginative life that showed hitherto unsuspected vigor. In day-dreams, she constructed an alternate life for Ruth Eden, trying on, in this way, another self, the way she and Jennifer Bayheim used to try on dresses as kids, hoping to glimpse the sort of women they'd become in the look of a flowered skirt or a new style of jeans or a deep-brimmed hat. Leslie imagined life in quiet Woodmill with its pretty stores and green fields, and at Woodmill High with its quaint and curious customs like the Maypole, Senior Reception, and Service Day. There was no harm in that, no harm at all. In fact, she felt better; she felt that once again she had an interest, an unforced, spontaneous inter-est, something to occupy her mind pleasantly, and everything was fine until one day when she went for a walk at lunch instead of riding down to the strip malls and commercial plazas. Leslie was in the tidy, well-planted park that ran between the lanes of the boulevard when she felt the curious mental tickle of memory. In some strange compartment of her mind, a dark car with heavy, rounded bumpers drove along a dirt road with trees on one side and a meadow on the other. Though she had only a vague image of the driver, thin and pinch-faced with light, wary eyes, Leslie had the awful feeling that he was in some sense familiar. The car window was rolled down, and as he drew level, he stopped, pushed open the door, and asked if she'd like a ride, a "little ride" in his car. Leslie remembered that and she remem-bered considering.

When she didn't answer, the strange man asked, "Where do you live?" and the child, that earlier self, had pointed back toward the wood.

"I could drive you home," he suggested, but she shook her head, and it shocked Leslie, the adult Leslie, to realize that she had not wanted to go home, had not wanted to hear her mother calling, had not answered.

The car door opened. The interior was brown, she thought, though the image, in the way of memory images, could not be interrogated. But she remembered the door opening and how the man sat, leaning forward, furtive, appealing, his forehead damp, his hands trembling.

"What about the carnival?" he asked. "What about a ride to the carnival? Wouldn't you like that?"

Leslie felt, rather than saw, the child nod, a quick, abrupt gesture, and then she must have stepped under the wire and gotten into the car, to be driven slowly but inexorably out of Woodmill toward parts unknown. That must have been it, but the tide of memory receded capriciously, returning Leslie to the heat and sun of the veterans' memorial park, where the dazzling light made her dizzy, and the heat, sick to her stomach.

Back at work, Leslie sat distracted and a little frightened. Of course, she was skeptical; like any good reporter, she had learned skepticism. And what was this but what half a dozen fiction writers she'd interviewed had told her? That characters "come alive," that ideas come unbidden, that dialogue, the very breath of the muse, drifts into the subconscious. Leslie knew all that. And Ruth Eden had certainly been on her mind, the focal point of semiserious daydreams and speculations that any fool could have seen were unwise. Still, the troubling memory of the car carried an unmistakable conviction, because Leslie had been imagining Ruth Eden's life as innocent and happy, destined, but for the malignity of fate, to unfold smoothly. Now, unwillingly, she realized that Ruth Eden's life, too, might have had ragged edges. She might have been unhappy at home; the "ideal marriage" might have been uneasy; this past, too, might be tainted, disturbing. Unable to concentrate, Leslie was abrupt at an important interview, snapped at Betty when she asked what was wrong, and quarreled with Doug when he came home and found her sitting sobbing on the edge of the tub.

She felt nervous and tired simultaneously, and when she went to bed early, she couldn't sleep. For a long time she lay awake, and then, it must have been near dawn, for she could hear the doves, she dreamed that she was sitting in an old-fashioned car with brown fabric seats. Outside were the lights and signs of the commercial strip, but, in the way of dreams, Leslie knew that it was not the familiar territory of malls and plazas, but a little carnival of long ago. Someone was stroking the back of her neck and a soft voice was saying, "You've been bad." And she knew she had. The carnival was forbidden territory, a ride with a stranger was bad, running away was wicked. "Bad girls are punished," the voice said. Oh, she knew that was true! She had had for so long a sense of overwhelming, unspoken tension, of the unhappiness of Mommy and Daddy, an unhappiness that, in some unfocused and terrifying way, was her fault. She was bad, and they were unhappy. She began weeping as if her heart would break. "It's all right," the voice said. Kindly, she thought. That was the terrifying thing, the voice was softly kind. "You don't have to go home." She wept, protested, terrified but incoherent. "You've been bad," the voice said, firmly now, with malice as well as persuasion. "Bad girls are punished." The voice was Aunt Flo's but not Aunt Flo's, too. It was Aunt Flo's and the man's, the man from the dark car, who, she realized as she thrashed up out of sleep, had brought her to Aunt Flo's and Uncle Mac's.

It wasn't Uncle Andy at all, though she'd been told that he'd brought her after an accident, after a vaguely described collision. "Uncle Andy was the stork," Aunt Flo used to say. "Uncle Andy brought my girl. Of course, you were upset. No surprise you don't remember about the crash! It's God's blessing you don't!" But none of that was true. "None!" she spoke aloud and woke Doug.

"It's all right," he said. "Leslie, you're dreaming." He was used to having her awaken mumbling and crying in the night. But this was not a dream, not entirely. She had been given the meadow, the car, the man, and she was afraid that eventually either memory or imagination would give her what he'd done and why she had forgotten everything.

But even before that time, life had become intolerable, and she'd made up her mind to see Aunt Flo.

Leslie and Doug were sitting at the kitchen table over the remains of a fried chicken dinner when she told him. She'd cooked the chicken herself, although she'd been exhausted after work—she seemed lately to be getting worse instead of better. But she'd wanted to give Doug a treat, she'd wanted to do something to please him, not just out of gratitude but also in compensation for—she didn't know quite what—something serious, though, something important. So there in the Publix, she'd passed up an assortment of rotisserie chicken and baked chicken parts, thought "to hell with cholesterol," and bought a fryer for Doug's favorite meal. She cut up the chicken, dipped the pieces in egg and flour, and set them to sizzle in the hot oil. She'd gotten a cabbage, too, not the precut stuff, and made coleslaw and stopped special at the bakery for Italian bread, which she heated in the oven, so that when Doug got home, the whole house smelled wonderful.

He was cheerful and appreciative. When he began teasing her affectionately at dinner, Leslie realized that he thought she was making progress, that she had, perhaps, reached the turning point. The knowledge that she was going to disappoint him made her abrupt and awkward. "I'm going up to see Aunt Flo this week," she said.

"What about work?" he asked.

"No problem," Leslie said quickly, although she hadn't

dared ask Harvey yet. "I've got everything done for next week already."

Doug shook his head. "No can do this week. I'm finishing that kitchen in Englewood. She's a good customer, and I promised a rush job. Then I've got that commercial installation over on the bypass. Middle of next week is the earliest I can take time to drive you up."

"You don't need to drive me," Leslie said. "I don't want you to have to take time off."

"Leslie, you're just about able to get to work and back. You should see your face—you're white as a sheet."

"I'm giving my all to the *Sun Coast Times*. That's why I'm taking a few days off." Leslie could hear an unpleasant edge in her voice.

"We're not talking about a trip around the block here. Flo's what?—three, four hundred miles away?"

"I'm not going to do it in one day, Doug! But I've just got to see her. You know I'm not getting better. You know that, don't you? I look awful. I feel awful."

"I wish you'd gone to that Dr. Tarlow, the one Ranson suggested. I think you should still go, I think . . ."

"I don't need a psychiatrist," said Leslie, who had a perfect horror of discussing anything important with strangers. Her Aunt Flo always referred to psychiatrists as "witch doctors," and Leslie agreed one hundred percent. Not even beginning psych had changed her mind. "I just want some answers," she said. "Aunt Flo and Uncle Mac never told me anything. Before it didn't matter, I didn't care. Now, all of a sudden, it does matter. I don't know why, it just does."

"Honey, it's all connected with the surgery, the pregnancy," Doug said. "Dr. Ranson warned you there might be an emotional reaction."

"He was right; there has been an emotional reaction."

"If you understand that," Doug began, "you can start to put it behind you."

Doug said, "put it behind you" and "getting over it" a lot lately. "It" being everything: forgetfulness, exhaustion, sexual indifference, this sudden obsessive curiosity. Leslie knew he wanted to protect her, but she had the feeling that too much in her life had already been put out of sight and out of mind.

"You know we can still have children," he was saying now. "Ranson assured us both of that."

"It's not just children," Leslie said.

"Then what the hell is it, Leslie?"

"It's . . . I guess it's nearly dying. A hundred years ago, I might have died; one hundred and fifty years ago, I'm dead for sure. That makes you think and then it makes you wonder."

"You can't worry about what might have happened to you. You had the best care."

"Except for the anesthesia."

"Even that, Ranson says . . ."

"What does Ranson say?"

"He says it's quite common; even the memory loss is quite common. It's related to anxiety."

"Ranson is just protecting the hospital."

"You have an answer for everything," Doug said. She heard his irritation, although he was trying to conceal it. That things between them were artificial and overly careful was not entirely her fault, but Doug's as well. Doug felt that he should have taken her to another hospital, found another surgeon. Leslie considered these regrets irrational, but she knew her husband still felt guilty.

"Listen," she said, "I know I'm lucky. Things could have been a lot worse, and the doctor did his best. But you felt the same way when Mal flipped his truck. You sat right at this table and said that was the first time you'd ever thought dying was possible. That's the kind of reaction I'm talking about."

"I didn't start turning our whole life upside down."

"I'm not turning our life upside down. I'm just going north and see Aunt Flo."

"And I'll be glad to take you, but I sure as hell can't go on such short notice."

"I don't want you to drive me. Doug, I don't know how to explain it to you, but I feel that I can't get better without knowing—I don't even know what I want to know—but something more than I know now. And I've got to do it myself."

"It's that damn Eden story, Leslie. I wish you'd never seen it. You're not that girl; it's all just a fantasy."

"I want to see what Aunt Flo knows," Leslie said stubbornly.

"And how the hell would it matter anyway? After all this time, how would anything be changed? All you're going to do is hurt her and hurt yourself."

That was a sore point. In some subtle way, Leslie blamed her aunt, but she tried to ignore that feeling. Instead, she had almost convinced herself that Aunt Flo could—and would—tell her the truth. "Maybe I'd like to have a real family," she said, "instead of a couple of mysterious elderly relatives."

"I thought *we* were a family," Doug said, hurt. "We'll have children, I promise, Leslie."

"You know what I mean. I mean besides us. Look at you. You have family."

"Almost too much family," he said. Although he would never have admitted it, one of Leslie's attractions had been that she had come unencumbered with relatives.

"It's not just people. I feel as if I have no past, no substance. I'm like the boy without a shadow," she said, but he wasn't really listening.

Doug was not introspective, and Leslie knew he hated discussing other people's emotions. His kindness was genuine but deeply practical. Had Aunt Flo lived in California and Leslie needed money to fly west, he'd have had a plan, reasonable suggestions, a way to manage. He had ideas now. By next Wednesday for sure—he'd call Jimmy in to help him with the commercial job. They'd get it done early; she could call Flo and set up a visit. But he didn't want to discuss the reasons why Leslie had to go, why the visit was necessary, why uncertainty was eroding their happiness. And he didn't want her to go alone.

He kept on about that while they finished up the dishes, and later, in bed, he stroked her back and asked her to wait until he could take her north.

"All right," she said, against her will, against, even, her better judgment.

"Promise?" he said, as if he sensed her resistance.

"Yes, promise," she said, but at some level, she wondered if she meant it. The streetlight that whitened the thin drapes carved the wide, square plane of his forehead, the blunt nose, and thick, curly hair. Leslie loved him. He was the treasure of her life, and yet, in spite of her new dependence on him, her illness had made her feel detached. She saw his emotions without that intuitive sympathy that had made them close. She loved him, she wanted to please him, but something that had been there was missing. Dr. Ranson, the gynecologist, said this was natural. "The body forgets," he'd said. "The body remembers pain and forgets pleasure and has to relearn it."

And Leslie had shuddered. Everything forgot: The mind lost its moorings, the muscles and membranes forgot, the blood and bones drifted into oblivion before their time. The names were gone and pleasure and sympathy, and in their place was the car and the man with the brown suit that was too big for him, the man with the thin, nervous face, the moist, caressing hands.

When he'd wept, she'd been frightened; she had never seen an adult cry. Crying was for babies and little kids. Adult tears turned the world upside down and showed her that nothing was sure, nothing was safe. He cried that he was bad, that he didn't blame her for wanting to go home. But when she shrewdly seized the moment and demanded to go back, he recovered. "You've been bad," he said. "You know that." He didn't need to spell it out; there was more now. "They won't want you back. Besides, you wanted to come. You didn't want to go home." She had cried then, refused to eat, been genuinely, recklessly naughty.

She remembered a room—a motel room, probably, very poor and quiet with window screens worn thin in patches like an old rug. She had sat at a table playing with a box of kitchen matches, lighting one after another, watching the bluish flare and smelling the sharp, metallic odor. Then she saw her hand reach out, blue at the fingertips, and a piece of paper burst into orange flowers and a tablecloth blossom with black circles.

Then nothing. A curtain came down, and there was only Aunt Flo and Uncle Mac and the family mythology. Like a child in a fairy tale, Leslie had been transformed beyond recognition and given the famous drink that erases memory. But Aunt Flo knew. If not everything, she knew how Leslie had arrived and when. And something else that had drifted into Leslie's mind between the pale gray light and the glaring Florida sun: the resemblance between Aunt Flo and the thin man in the brown suit; Aunt Flo might know about that, too.

At eight the next morning, Leslie got up and called Harvey with apologies to say that she wouldn't be in for a few days. Nothing serious, just a touch of the late flu that had been rolling though the retirement homes and senior centers, pawing a few invalids and convalescents like herself as it passed. Then she threw a pair of slacks, some blouses, underwear, and sneakers in her case, fed Dylan, and left a note for Doug that read, "Darling, I'm so sorry, but I just can't wait. I'll be at Aunt Flo's. I love you. Please don't worry."

At ten, she opened the back door to the humid, faintly sulfur-smelling air and put her bag in the car. Dylan followed. He climbed up the planter, settled himself on the shady soil, and yawned. Leslie went over to rub his tawny head for luck, then picked him up and walked around the yard for a few minutes, telling him that he was a fine cat and wishing human love was as easy as animals'. Dylan was content with two meals a day and a friendly pat; he didn't test the quality of her affection. Because he took what was available today, without, so far as she knew, troubling himself about tomorrow, she was a success with Dylan. With Doug, on the other hand, Leslie felt that there was more she could be doing, more she should be giving.

But rather than explore that idea, Leslie returned Dylan to the shade and set off toward the interstate after Aunt Flo, who had been pointed northward ever since Uncle Mac's death. Mac had been a Syracuse city bus driver who'd retired to Orlando after a back injury. He'd loved the heat, the beach, the semitropical vegetation; Aunt Flo complained of the humidity, the crowds, the traffic. When Mac died, victim of an early, sudden, and massive stroke, she sold their small house and bought a trailer north of Jacksonville. She sold that a year later and rented in north Georgia; then, like a small continental plate, she drifted north again. Flo was outside of Chapel Hill, North Carolina, now, and it was Leslie's opinion that she would keep moving until she got back to Syracuse where she could complain again about the dreadful weather, city corruption, and university expansion.

Aunt Flo liked college towns; she'd worked on and off for the university food service while Leslie was a child. When she got tired of students, she did alterations and finishing for a bridal shop. She had sewed for a similar outfit in Orlando, and Leslie thought that her birth certificate had probably come via some illegal in one of the clothing workshops there.

As she drove up the interstate, Leslie tried to concentrate on her childhood with Uncle Mac and Aunt Flo, but instead she kept thinking about old cars, about sitting in a car as a small child, about the disorienting speed, the dizzying progression of clouds, smokestacks, phone lines, and trees. She'd been carsick as a child. Aunt Flo used to say, "Our girl just needs to look at a car. She just needs to hear that car door slam!" It was a bit of a joke, and Leslie had taken it in good part, though she never willingly rode anywhere. Fortunately, as Aunt Flo loved to point out, "Our girl's a good walker!" And later a cyclist. Leslie rode all over the city on her bike and, sometimes, up front in Uncle Mac's bus. She had liked the bus. With its enormous front windows and long doors, you could see where you were in Uncle Mac's bus and see where you were going. Especially when her bike was on board, Leslie had rarely felt sick on the bus.

She thought now that had been because she'd loved Uncle Mac. And Aunt Flo? Leslie found that question unwelcome and focused on the road for a time. Perhaps she did not want to examine her feelings for Aunt Flo, who was bossy, devoted, uneducated, and shrewd, a tiny, defiant, contentious woman. Leslie remembered her as middle aged, but she was how old now? Seventy-three or seventy-four. Flo was a dynamo, hardworking and determined: Her sewing money had paid for most of Leslie's education, and she'd been set from the first that "our girl" should go on. In that and in other ways, Flo had taken good care of her, yet Leslie was aware of a sediment of anger, a residue of fear, almost, and remembered again being told that only "Leslie" was safe, only "our girl." With a kind of distilled resentment, she felt that Aunt Flo had some things to answer for.

That afternoon Leslie stopped just short of the South Carolina border. Earlier she had considered some old-fashioned cabins, but unwilling to raise more ghosts, now settled for a chain establishment with a bright logo and smoking or nonsmoking rooms. She lay down on the wide quilted spread and fell asleep instantly, waking after strange, inconclusive dreams to call Doug. They had a tense, apologetic conversation. He was genuinely angry that she'd gone—angry with an anxiety underneath that made Leslie feel guilty and afraid.

"I love you," she said. "You know that."

"Yes," he said without a great deal of conviction.

"I just had to come. I thought I'd made you understand that."

"You promised to wait. You know how I worry."

"I felt so well when I got up this morning, I just knew it would be all right. I'll be back in two days."

"I know you'll do what you want to do," Doug said, which Leslie felt was unfair.

She kept trying to explain her conviction that she'd feel better once she saw Flo, but Doug heard only impulsiveness and nerves and said, "I don't know why you couldn't have waited a couple of days, Leslie." By the time they hung up, she was almost in tears, but even then Leslie was impatient to see Flo, the arbiter of memory, and impatient, too, to continue north, as if there were some place, some physical place, she had to reach instead of knowledge, information, answers.

Leslie left the motel parking lot soon after sunrise, and, by midafternoon, she was driving through a pretty but confusing little Carolina town looking for Flo's street. She found it after some difficulty in an area of well-kept two- and three-family houses and frame bungalows. Aunt Flo had the second floor of a nice brown and green shingled house that reminded Leslie of their old place in Syracuse. Aunt Flo was out; she did her shopping in the afternoon, a neighbor said. But Carolina wasn't as hot as home, and Leslie found that waiting on the porch was pleasant. The town had had rain the night before, making the small lawns look green and tender after the coarse Florida grass. The azaleas were in rampant bloom, and even the smallest houses had brilliant patches of their pink, purple, red, or orange flowers. Small children played a couple of yards away, and someone with a trained soprano voice practiced Puccini arias in an upper apartment. Leslie had been sitting for a while before she saw a woman far down the walk, pulling a shopping cart. A moment later, she recognized the small, neat figure, the dyed red hair, the brisk, energetic stride that was now, Leslie realized with a pang, not quite so brisk or energetic. She hadn't seen Aunt Flo for some time, not since the hospital, for Aunt Flo avoided the big Austin family festivals where all Doug's relatives congregated. Instead, Leslie would drive up for a brief visit, sometimes with Doug, more often alone. She was suddenly uncomfortably aware that those visits had been much less frequent since Mac died.

Leslie stood up when her aunt approached and came down to help with the shopping cart.

Aunt Flo kissed her cheek. "You might have called. I have nothing special in." Leslie saw that she was tired, that her lack of preparation distressed her, perhaps spoiled Leslie's visit.

"Don't worry about groceries. I've got the car." She nodded toward the Chevy parked at the curb.

"What's Doug doing?"

"He has the truck," Leslie said. "He had to work."

They carried the groceries up to the porch, and Aunt Flo sat down to rest on one of the hard metal chairs. "You drove yourself? Too much for my girl." She smiled then and leaned forward to touch Leslie's knee.

"My girl"—Aunt Flo's oblique and understated way of saying she loved her, as in "My girl can do it," when Leslie had panicked about her SAT exams, or "Well, for my girl . . . ," when Aunt Flo would miraculously stretch the modest family budget to encompass some treat, some opportunity. How often had she said, "We'll just go into Dey Brothers and get something for my girl," and how often had she repeated proudly, "I always knew my girl would get to college"?

Leslie was uncomfortable. "I'm all right," she said. "I'm fine. Just tired." She felt, however, not tired but disconcerted. All the way north, things had seemed simple, and she had been resentful of Aunt Flo, resentful and suspicious. Now here was her aunt, looking much older and not nearly so brisk and chipper, looking, in fact, like a woman who'd worn herself out providing for Leslie. With a familiar confusion of affection and irritation, Leslie realized that Aunt Flo didn't look as if she'd been withholding all the answers.

"I was sorry," Aunt Flo said after a moment. "Like I told you at the hospital, I was really sorry about the baby."

"It was too early to think about. I mean, I didn't even know for sure I was pregnant."

"Ah," said Aunt Flo, as if considering whether that would make a difference. "But you'd like a child?" She leaned forward a little as if the answer were important. Her thin dry skin was seamed with a fine network of lines.

"Yes, I would. Now that I've thought about it."

"Now that you haven't had one."

"Yes, I suppose that's it. Human perversity at its best."

"I always wanted a child," Aunt Flo said reflectively. "For years and years, but Mac and I never could manage it. I lost one at eight months. That was the closest we got."

Leslie reached out and took Aunt Flo's hand. She did not know what to say about children to her aunt, so she said, "I miss Uncle Mac."

"The best husband in the world," Aunt Flo said. "But for the fact we couldn't have a child."

They sat silent on the porch. A small boy with cinnamon skin and a red baseball cap walked a yellow puppy. A mockingbird began singing in a tangle of old roses. At the bottom of the hill, Leslie could see a traffic light and a steady line of cars glittering in the sun, but the porch cast a heavy shade, cool compared to the golden afternoon light on the lawns and sidewalks. "This is a nice porch," Leslie said. "It reminds me of our old house in Syracuse."

"I like a porch on a house. Though it depends on your neigh-

bors," Aunt Flo added judiciously. She went through the lot for
Leslie. The singer was a music student, an impressive voice but
too many boyfriends. The downstairs tenant worked for the city
and his wife was a teacher. Their marriage was unhappy, Aunt
Flo said, and she predicted its demise. Still, they were pleasant
enough, although she used the downstairs porch only when they
were both out. "It's a rest by the wayside," she said.

"You're feeling all right, though?" Leslie asked anxiously.

"Right as I'm going to be at my age."

"You should maybe get a car. The walk to the store and
all . . ."

"Cars are expensive," Aunt Flo said. "Besides, if I didn't
walk to the store, I wouldn't get any exercise."

Aunt Flo had always been big on walking, on exercise, on
keeping going. "At least it's not too hot," Leslie remarked. "It's
been so hot at home."

Aunt Flo got up. "Makes me think I have some milk I must
put in. You'll maybe need to get more. I wasn't expecting you."

"I know I should have called, but I just suddenly wanted to ·
come."

Aunt Flo smiled. "I love to see you anytime." She unlocked
the door up to the second-floor apartment and added, "I hope
there's nothing wrong, though."

"Not really. Not with Doug or anything."

Aunt Flo gave her a look but said nothing, and Leslie got the
alarming impression that her aunt was nervous. When she
thought of Aunt Flo, Leslie always saw her as tart and brisk, a little terrier of a woman, spunky, confident, and determined. But
Aunt Flo was intelligent, intelligent enough to see that something was wrong, maybe even to guess what it was.

"No, I leave the cart at the bottom," Aunt Flo said, as Leslie
started to bring it up the steep stairs. "I don't usually have someone to carry it."

Leslie collapsed the device and leaned it against the wall.

"I got a chicken breast," Aunt Flo said. "That will do us tonight."

"More than enough. I can go to the store if you need anything else. We can go tomorrow and get you some staples, if you want."

"Only one tomato, so kind of a thin salad. I don't buy much now. Without Mac."

"Uncle Mac liked a good meal," Leslie said, hearing, as she sometimes did, an echo of her aunt's speech.

"He did, indeed. I don't cook the way I used to." She opened the upstairs door, and Leslie set the bag down on the kitchen table and looked around. Aunt Flo had moved just before Leslie took sick; she hadn't seen this latest apartment, which was old-fashioned and dark in the front rooms but with a big, square kitchen.

"Quite nice."

"Preserved untouched since the fifties," Flo said drily.

"Desperately fashionable now," Leslie said. "Doug's actually had to search for some of these old-time ranges."

"Funny what people will spend their money on. But I feel better knowing I'm in style."

"Good cabinets, too," Leslie remarked. Doug's business had given her an eye for quality work. Under layers of gray-green paint, these were solid wood with nice old glass doors.

Flo was more skeptical. "The devil to clean," she said. "All that glass was filthy." The cleaning of new apartments was always an epic undertaking with Flo, and she gave Leslie a digest as they put away the groceries: canned goods, dried beans, tuna, some vegetables, a packet of stew beef, a small bottle of milk.

While she was in the cupboards, Leslie noticed a black *Cats* mug. The golden feline eyes reminded her of the trip she and her aunt had taken to New York City as a graduation present. That had been a happy time, and Leslie had a sudden memory of her aunt's face, relaxed with joy as she watched the dancers. "Do you really like it here?" Leslie asked. "You're so far away."

"I didn't see much of you when I was in Orlando."

"I'd just started at the paper," Leslie said, though she felt a little prickle of guilt and regret. "I was working such long hours."

"I know it was a hard drive for you, and I didn't want you to neglect your work. But what I'm saying is, it wasn't going to matter if I moved north."

"I just didn't expect you would move so far away." In that moment, Leslie understood that her absence had grown out of uncertainty and suspicion.

"I've been restless without Mac," Aunt Flo said. "Maybe you can understand that."

Yes, she could, and maybe some other things, too, so that it was only after supper, when the big square kitchen windows were black with night, that Leslie finally got to the topic that had taken over her dreams and driven her north.

They'd done the dishes and wiped up the kitchen. Aunt Flo was ready to go through and turn on the TV, but Leslie stood looking out the window. In the building's security light, she saw a neat lawn and a small garden with what looked like rows of lettuce and onions already started. "I understand what it's like to want a baby," she said. "I really do. I can understand that now."

"I suppose you do." Aunt Flo's voice was soft and wary.

"But still, there's something I've got to ask you," Leslie said. "I've got to ask you about my parents."

Aunt Flo looked up quickly, wounded. "Mac and me were your parents more than twenty years."

"And you were very good to me. I know that and I'm grateful. But I'm talking about my parents before you and Uncle Mac."

"I told you, you were my brother Will's girl." Leslie could tell that she spoke without real conviction.

"You told me that Uncle Andy brought me and that my parents were dead."

"That's right."

"My mother," Leslie said, "what did she look like? Or my dad? You know, I've never seen a picture of either one of them. They don't have much reality for me."

"Will was thin, kind of brown hair. I don't know what she looked like. I never saw her. Your Uncle Andy was the one who'd met her . . ."

"But it wasn't Uncle Andy who brought me, was it?" When her aunt hesitated, Leslie added, "I'm pretty sure it wasn't."

Aunt Flo gave her a sharp, angry look. "That's why you've come all of a sudden, is it? Or was that why you didn't come before?"

Leslie shrugged, determined not to feel guilty. "I have a right to know." In the silence, the kitchen clock gave a dry click like an electronic cricket. "I'm not a child anymore, and it wasn't Uncle Andy."

"No, it wasn't Uncle Andy," Aunt Flo said after a moment and sat down wearily at the kitchen table. "But I don't know about your parents. I never did know anything about them." Her face was pale and sad, her dyed hair accentuating the yellow tinge in her cheeks. "I knew you'd find out one day. I knew you would even before you went and became a reporter."

"Maybe I always knew."

Aunt Flo shook her head. "You didn't remember anything. Never spoke of them. You came and settled in. Now that I think back on it, it was amazing how you settled in."

"Memory's mysterious. You know my memory for names was damaged with the surgery. Too much anesthesia or something. But now I've started to remember other things. Important things from far back. I'm beginning to think my memory was damaged twice."

"What sorts of things?" Aunt Flo asked cautiously. She seemed half curious, half resigned.

"I remember a meadow. A big meadow with wildflowers."

"I don't know anything about that," Aunt Flo said.

"And I remember the man in the brown suit. Very thin, very pale, very nervous."

"Ah," she said. That was all. Just a soft intake of breath.

"Do you know who I mean? You remember him?"

Leslie could hear the tension in her voice, and her aunt looked at her with sad curiosity. "I thought you might understand now. When I saw you sitting there on the porch today, I said to myself, she knows but now she'll understand. I wanted a child. He brought one and I . . . I just did what I thought was right at the time."

"But what about me? What about my parents?"

"That's what Mac said. Mac said, 'What about the parents?' But I couldn't worry about them. I tried to, but I just couldn't. And then you might not have had any parents. They might not have wanted you. They might have been dead."

"You told me they were dead. You told me that. How could you tell me that?"

"It seemed best," Aunt Flo said. "It seemed best to set your mind at rest. They weren't going to show up."

Leslie digested this for a moment. In one part of her mind she was astonished that she had been right. That her fantasy, her intuition, her one moment of conviction had, after all, been correct. "You knew him," she said. "The man in the brown suit. The man with the car."

Aunt Flo nodded. "Yes, I knew him."

"Who was he?

"He has nothing to do with you now. He never came back."

"He changed my whole life! He picked me up one day and took me away from home. He was . . ."

"I know what he was," Aunt Flo said quickly.

"He was a relative," Leslie guessed. "A cousin? An uncle?"

"He was my brother," Aunt Flo said.

"Your brother!"

"What was I to do, Leslie? I'd helped raise him. He was a salesman when he was well. A very good one. Very persuasive. He traveled for a dry goods firm. It was when he wasn't well that there was trouble."

"Trouble?"

"He took irrational spells."

"Spells of abducting little girls?"

"Not before. Not that I knew of. I thought he was all right. He was working, you know. He had a responsible job."

"I think he picked me up somewhere out in the country."

"That's quite possible. I couldn't get the whole story out of him, but he was never aggressive. I expect he offered you a ride and you took it."

"What time of year was that, Aunt Flo?"

"It was in October. October twelfth."

"October! It was spring, early summer. There were roses." There had to be roses. The roses, the scent of roses, the meadow in bloom—those were the landmarks, the survivors of memory. Without roses, everything was uncertain again, her memory unreliable, the Edens coincidence.

"Maybe he'd been traveling for a while with you?" Aunt Flo suggested indifferently. "Maybe not. You said you couldn't remember."

"I can remember bits and pieces, that's all. That's the worst, just bits and pieces. He was frightened, though. I remember that."

"Yes, he was always frightened. When he took a spell, I mean." Aunt Flo got up for a pack of cigarettes, and though she'd already had her ration for the day, shook one out and lit it. "He thought the black people were going to take over that year. That was the of Watts. The Watts riots. That was the first thing he said to me: 'Flo, it's all over. They're going to take over the city.' I had to ask him who and what city." She looked at the smoke twisting up from her cigarette in a loopy braid. "And then I asked him about you. I think I was already hopeful. The porch in Syracuse was high, remember?"

Leslie nodded.

"I looked down and I could see you sitting in the car. It had been raining and the trees had already turned—that's another reason I'm sure of the date, because the street was reflecting yellow and brown from the leaves. I said to Willie, to my brother, 'Who's the little girl?' He was surprised, you know. Like he'd forgotten. Then he said, 'That's my little girl. She doesn't want to go home.'"

"He said that?"

"Willie was never realistic. I couldn't get anything out of him, not your name, nothing."

"I told you my name," Leslie said quickly. "I told you!"

"Did you? We called you Leslie from the first. That's the only name I ever knew for you. You didn't say much. You sat on his lap and didn't say anything."

"There was a little girl missing from Connecticut that summer, dark haired, the right age, taken from a rural area," Leslie said. "Had you called the police . . ."

"We didn't know anything about missing children. He was my brother. He sat in our living room and told me he'd saved you from the radicals and niggers. That was his state of mind. Everything had come apart for Willie. I know what would have happened if we'd called the police."

"What happened to him? Where is he now?"

Aunt Flo drew on her cigarette then took a minute flake of tobacco off her lip. "Do you remember what I promised you?"

"You promised me he'd never come back. So long as I was 'Leslie.'"

"Yes. You were a clever girl even then. That's what I promised you. And I promised him I'd take care of you and tell no one provided I never saw him again. Never ever. He was to die rather than come looking for help from us. He left the same night. Sick as a dog. I could see that."

"There might have been other children," Leslie said, moved and horrified at Aunt Flo's ruthless devotion.

"I never heard. I'd pretty much raised Willie. Mother was sick. Dad was a drinker. You didn't know that. Willie was the little one—he got the worst of everything. It wasn't all his fault, Leslie. I just couldn't do it. I couldn't call the police. He'd been my baby and then I lost him and got you instead."

"No one suspected?" Even her years as a reporter had not given Leslie this conviction of society's capricious unreliability.

"Suspected what? I said you were my brother Will's girl, and that they'd been killed in an auto accident, very sudden. The only one who knew was Andy, Uncle Andy, and he wasn't around much. Beyond that, I was careful."

"And Uncle Mac went along!" Uncle Mac. So kind, so jovial. He *couldn't* have gone along with such an idea! Never. But he had, and so her parents were lost, her name and her old life erased.

"Mac knew I wanted a child more than anything in the world. He knew how it would be the moment he saw you in that car. He knew I'd risk anything. Everything."

Leslie felt suffocated by fearful, contradictory emotions. She had been loved by Flo and Mac, who had deceived her. And her parents, her real parents, what about them? Had they loved her? Had they deceived her, too, in some way? And was it even true that she'd "settled in amazingly"? Leslie's heart was jumping, for nothing was reliable. The surface of the world had become porous, unstable, and behind all that she thought she knew lay deception and uncertainty. She pushed herself away from the table. "It was all a lie," she burst out with cruel desperation. "I was never your child."

Aunt Flo's face was drawn and white. "You're gone now. I've lost you now. But I had my girl for all those years. If you are lucky enough to have children, you'll never think about me. But if you don't, you'll maybe understand."

Part | Two

Summer 1990

3

The first letter came on a Tuesday. The first letter from Leslie Austin, that is. Ross Eden had had other letters over the years, the very first ones the year of Ruthie's disappearance. Those were from the psychics, the sympathetic busybodies, the cranks. Other letters, from troubled or imaginative adolescents, commenced a decade later when Ruthie would have been fifteen. Lately the correspondents were troubled or opportunistic adults, looking "to find" themselves and, just incidentally, financial as well as familial support. Ross knew all that, and still each letter, handwritten or typed, formal envelope or small pink stationery, momentarily stopped his heart.

He flipped through the mail again: a phone bill, a circular from the garden center, and the letter with the typed Florida address, a woman's address. It was one of those letters, he'd known that at a glance. He should have expected them after the "anniversary" story ran. He'd been opposed to that, had called Tompkins at the local paper and stopped it there. But a wire story, Tompkins said, was beyond his control.

Yes, he could expect some more letters, Ross thought, and he stuck the envelope into his pocket, half intending to throw it away.

He remembered the letter when he was at Peter and Cindy's, on his standing Tuesday night dinner invitation. "Are things going all right, Grampa?" Cindy asked.

"Fine, fine," he said, though he knew she meant the time of year. She was a sweet girl, Cindy, blonde and plump, and not the worse for a few pounds, either, in Ross's estimation. She was a great peacemaker, a great soother of quarrels and differences, a good mother. Ross liked her, praised her cooking, and approved of her handling of the grandchildren.

"No cranks?" Peter asked. A fine set up man with fair hair and brown eyes, Peter was Ross's oldest child, the most like him in appearance, but quick and energetic like his mother. He'd been quite a good baseball player, and he was a good business manager, a competent person with only some rare, disturbing flashes of a passion that was like Kate's. Ross and Peter got on well, and Ross and Cindy and the children got on better.

"No cranks. No, I lie. I had a letter today. Florida address. Know anyone in Florida?"

Peter shook his head, frowning. He was sensitive about his sister's disappearance. As a child he'd been terrified by her loss. Ruthie's disappearance had punched a hole through his world; first, Peter had feared that void and, later, whatever might fill it. As an adult, he hated any publicity and despised the importunate seekers after identity. "Who's it this time?"

"Don't know. I just stuck it in my pocket, I was running so late."

"Too late at bowling last night," his daughter-in-law said.

"Must have been." Ross winked at her. The family did not officially know that Ross spent Monday and Thursday nights with Sheila Murray, a charming woman who was pastry chef at the fancy new restaurant in what had been the Wilkersons' old hay barn.

"Throw it out," said Peter, who did not have his wife's impulse to avoid tender topics. "I get so mad at these vultures."

Ross raised his eyebrows noncommittally and changed the subject to the new line of imported cider that Peter had persuaded him to try. When they'd settled the importance of lighter beverages to their complete professional satisfaction, Ross kissed Cindy's cheek, clapped Peter on the shoulder, and went upstairs to say good night to his grandchildren.

Markie was asleep but Jenny was sitting up in her bed, fair and solemn, looking out at the last of the sunset. Something in her small, serious figure reminded him of Ruthie, who'd been a quiet, secretive child with a flashing energy that was forever taking her out of bounds. Ruthie had been the odd one, he realized, and he felt the familiar pain. Ruthie had been his favorite; he had adored the child from the first moment, almost against his will, as if, by some quirk in his nature, his love must flourish on uncertainty.

"How's my girl?" he asked Jenny. "What are you doing up so late?"

"Watching the pretty clouds." She pointed and smiled a little, secretive smile.

"I see one like a bunny," he said.

"I see one—I see one like a whale."

"And what's that one?"

"It's like a lamb."

"That's a good girl. Time for bed now. Mommy sent me up to see if you were asleep."

The child put her warm arms around his neck and kissed his cheek, then slid under her quilt. Ross ruffled her hair and said good night. At the door, he felt a stab of anxiety; Jenny was four, a vulnerable, dangerous age. For years he'd told himself that

Ruthie was dead, or, if alive, lost beyond recovery. But his granddaughter reminded him so strongly of her sometimes that he felt his belief challenged: Ruthie was still so vivid after all those years and didn't that mean . . .

"The kids asleep?"

"Markie's asleep. Jenny's on her way."

"That kid never quits," Cindy said.

"We should have some of that energy," Ross said, putting on his jacket. He stood for a minute in the doorway, exchanging shop talk with his son, then walked to the car. He felt the letter as he took out his keys, and when he got home he poured himself a beer, sat down at the kitchen table, and opened the envelope.

"Dear Mr. Eden," he read, "I've started to write you a dozen times, but this week I learned something that makes me think I should definitely contact you. I am thirty years old, and I work for the local paper here, the *Sun Coast Times*. In the course of editing wire copy, I came across the story of your daughter's disappearance. One paragraph struck me very forcibly: the description of the meadow where she was last seen.

"Mr. Eden, my earliest memory—indeed, one of my few childhood memories—is of standing in a meadow picking flowers and of being frightened by the woods behind me. For years, that was an odd, unimportant detail, but recently I learned that I was abducted at about the age of five. I was raised by a couple who pretended to be, but were not, my father's sister and brother-in-law. They also claimed that my parents were dead, but there were never any documents to prove this nor pictures that might substantiate the relationship. No photos were taken of me—or were ever allowed to be taken of me—before I was in junior high school.

"For reasons of my own, I have suddenly become curious about my background, and I was interested enough in the story of your daughter's disappearance to send to Woodmill and to the state paper that covered the case for further information, including photographs. These I found suggestive for reasons you may perhaps understand from the enclosed recent photo of me. I am five feet nine inches tall with dark hair, a fair complexion, and brown eyes. My teeth have been poor since childhood, and I have a scar of unknown origin on my left hand. As a youngster, I was quite good at sports, especially softball and basketball; I dance well and can carry a tune. I am slightly farsighted and now need glasses for reading.

"I feel silly telling you all of this, and yet, after so many years, I realize that any trifle might be important. Working for a newspaper and having covered cases involving missing children, I know only too well how intrusive the public can be and how many people recklessly (or hopefully) claim to know something and thus impose on a grieving family. That is why I've hesitated to write you. But, Mr. Eden, I remain troubled by what I can— and what I cannot—remember. Though I have very little hope, perhaps there is something you could tell me, something not included in the many news stories, which would make it clear that I am not Ruth Eden—some mark, some detail that might set both our minds at ease.

"If you have such information, I should be very grateful."

The letter was signed in a firm but jagged hand, "Leslie Simpson Austin."

Ross folded up the letter carefully and opened the second, inner envelope. There were two pictures, one of a serious-looking teenager with long dark hair seemed to Ross completely anonymous and unrevealing; the other, the recent photo mentioned in the letter, was disturbing. It showed a slim, dark woman with a thin, angular face and wavy brown hair, holding a yellow cat. Leslie Austin was smiling at the camera, a nice smile, quick and open like Kate's, Ross thought, before caution took over. This woman was slimmer than his wife, lightly, even delicately, built.

Five feet nine—that was tall for a woman; Kate had been no

more than five four or five five. He was six feet even, the boys a inch or two either way. Possible. The hair was right and the eyes—his were blue but Kate's brown—and the teeth. The teeth! He had a sudden memory of Ruthie screaming in the dentist's chair, of her accusing eyes, dark with anguish and fear, and of his futile attempts to comfort her.

Ross ran a hand over his face and realized that he was taking the letter seriously, as he and Kate had taken the first ones, those terrifyingly ambiguous, gut-clenching missives. "We have to try everything," Kate had said, "everything."

Her energy and determination had been frightening. Heartbreak exhausted him, but she'd been tireless, driven by grief and despair—and what else? Remorse, Ross thought. He thought remorse, though he'd never been sure, had never asked, had never encouraged any discussion or confession, had never wanted to know. Knowing could never be kept secret in a small town, and revelation might have made life impossible, insupportable. She had said in her statement—and to him in the car in those terrible minutes when they searched the road, stopping to call at every break in the hedgerows, those terrible minutes when life took them by the throat and ended youth and innocence together—she'd said that Ruthie had been playing on the swing set in the backyard. For years afterward Ross could scarcely bear to look at it, averting his eyes as he passed with the mower yet reluctant to give it away as if its absence might prevent the child's return.

"For God's sake, weren't you watching her? What the hell were you doing?" he demanded, his voice taut with fear, though he'd known Kate was capable and devoted.

"Paul brought the specs for the costumes. I looked out while I was fixing him a cup of coffee. She was right on the slide then."

Ross inwardly cursed Paul and his arrival, too. He'd never liked Schott's bony face and smart-ass remarks. Paul was clever in ways Ross was not, adept with his hands and with mathematics, a good trapper, a tireless runner, but these triumphs could have been forgiven. What Ross had disliked even when they were schoolboys was a quixotic, idealistic strain in the younger man's character. He had seen Schott as a prig and a fool, the more dangerous for being clever. Later, Ross had resented him as a rival, because Kate had dated Paul during her last years at high school, and Ross got his chance only after Paul left for college and mysteriously broke off the relationship.

Ross poured himself another beer and thought about his wife and when he had begun to love her. As he finished the glass, he looked through the letter again. Then he fetched a piece of stationery from the desk and wrote the single line, "What reasons of your own?" signed it, and stuck it in an envelope.

"Of course, you were right to ask," Leslie Austin wrote back without preliminaries. "Reporters forget the normal courtesies: that's called 'professionalism.' All right, two things . . ."

Ross slowly read her account of the hospitalization and its aftermath. "I am haunted," she continued, "by sharp but incongruous memories: a meadow, a car, a thin man in a brown suit. He, incidentally, has turned out to be real. And, increasingly, I find myself preoccupied with your daughter or with my idea of your daughter.

"That sounds crazy, doesn't it? I seem to have lost some essential foundation, but that's what they've all written, isn't it, all the women who thought they were your daughter?"

Ross smiled when he read that. Leslie Austin was either more sensitive or more subtle than the others. The others had all been convinced that they were the real Ruth Eden; they hadn't the slightest doubt about his paternity or even, in one case, about the availability of funds. In contrast, he felt that Leslie Austin might almost be as happy to be told that the connection was impossible. Approving her caution, he responded at slightly greater length, and thus they began an exchange of furtive, almost clandestine letters. Sometimes Leslie Austin wrote about her husband. These references were alway affectionate, although, reading between the lines Ross sensed that Doug disapproved of her investigations. When Ross cautioned her not to trade a good husband for an uncertain father, she wrote back that she was not looking for a father but for the facts. Sometimes, she did hint at misgivings; these she put aside, even as he did, and Ross was soon intensely curious. Still, his native caution and indolence made him delay and hesitate, and it was only when she mentioned Mr. Eddie that Ross decided she must come north.

Leslie arrived on the Friday after the Fourth of July. It had been dry and blazing hot for a week and a half, and Ross had been running the two window air conditioners in the store full blast from eight A.M. When he got home after work, his neighbors had already lit their barbecue fires, and he smelled the passing perfume of their steaks, burgers, and chickens and heard their kids splashing around in the big aboveground pools.

How much the area had changed! When he and Kate built the cottage, it had been quite isolated, too much so for his taste, though Kate had liked the wood and the fields. The wood remained, slightly shrunken, and the far pasture, but the fields along the road were now a double row of neat houses with flowering trees and foundation plantings. Ross wondered what they would suggest to Leslie Austin, what memories? Maybe nothing and maybe that would be best after all. Though Ross was rarely nervous, he was nervous now, in part because he realized that he hadn't told the boys. When Carol Olson asked him to stay for supper, he thanked her and made excuses: He was expecting Leslie Austin's call.

He crossed the lawn—dry enough lately to spare the mowing—and unlocked the door. He'd had the floors refinished a year before and some new furniture a couple of seasons before that. For years he'd lived with Kate's taste and their old assemblage of furniture, then everything had seemed to wear out at once. Now he had a plain leather sofa and two chairs combination and a big square coffee table that he could eat dinner off when he wanted to catch *Cheers* or watch a ball game.

The cottage was bigger, too. When the boys were small, he'd needed an extra room for Mrs. Goff, who had served as babysitter, housekeeper, and counselor in residence. The solution had been to connect the house and the garage, making a good-sized room; later, he'd added another bedroom in the garage loft. That the once diminutive cottage now looked solid and substantial was a source of satisfaction to Ross, who'd built the original house on a precarious mortgage in order to impress Kate's folks and to make things sure with Kate; he remembered that. Even then he had been coolheaded and had known how important it was that everything seem decided and final. The house had been a gamble: The down payment had taken every bit of his savings, but, with it, Kate had seen the inevitability of their marriage and consented. He'd managed her cleverly, all right.

With that thought, Ross slammed down his car keys and stalked into the kitchen. The worst of this business was the way that it undermined all his assumptions by suggesting completely different perspectives. He wondered why he'd answered the damn letter in the first place. He'd been up and down like a yo-yo all week, one minute desperate to see Leslie, the next indifferent, the next, like now, irritated almost beyond endurance. And underneath it all, like a pool of oil, lay the desperation and anguish he'd first felt when he'd picked up the receiver and heard Kate, breathless with fear, say, "Ruthie's disappeared." Oh, he'd been a fool ever to awaken such misery, even for Ruthie, even for Kate.

He'd have dinner, he decided, and pretend it was a normal night. It *was* a normal night, damn it, nothing would change, but when the phone rang as he was unwrapping a small steak, Ross felt his stomach clench.

"Hello?" she said before he could speak, and he knew that she was nervous, too.

"Leslie?"

"Yes. I'm at the motel on the state road. I wasn't sure of the directions. I'm sorry I'm so late; Jersey was endless and there was so much weekend traffic."

"Have you eaten?"

"No, but it's all right. I'm told the diner in town will be open. If you like, I can come by your store tomorrow."

"No, no," Ross said, suddenly feeling that the wait would be unbearable. "I'll put on another steak. You can be here in ten minutes." He gave her directions and put down the phone.

When Leslie pulled into the drive, the hot red sun was almost down, and the big oaks and maples darkened the house and shaded the man who came out and waved to her.

"Any trouble finding the place?" he asked. His hair was white now; she had examined the yearbook pictures and the news photos so intensely that she had almost forgotten they were twenty-five and thirty years old.

"Perfect directions." Leslie shook his hand, took off the floppy sun hat she was wearing, and looked around. She was still too nervous and excited to take anything in, but she felt that he was waiting for some reaction. "Of course, everything's been built up, hasn't it?"

"Not so bad as some towns."

"The center's very pretty. Picture postcard New England." If she'd been in New England before, she'd forgotten everything.

"Convenient, too," Ross was saying. "We have just about everything we need."

"Is that your shop on the corner? With the beautiful old sign?"

"Been there fifty years—it was my great-uncle's originally."

Leslie smiled, though the shop had been as impenetrable and unrecognizable as the newer houses around them, as Ross Eden himself. She looked at the cottage and at the narrow strip of pasture and, behind that, still catching the last of the golden light in the topmost leaves, a wood. Surely it had been bigger, Leslie thought, and the pasture much wider.

"We enlarged the house a few years ago. More than a few, come to think of it. Must be getting on for twenty. I needed the room when the kids were growing. Peter and Lyman. They both live nearby."

Leslie admired the house and murmured compliments, although it suggested nothing, and her eyes kept wandering back toward the field, toward the wood.

". . . the original house," he said, pointing, and Leslie tried to visualize the building without the garage, without the breeze-waylike connection and second-story dormers. Ross Eden began to speak about his boys and then, abruptly, as if nervous, too, as nervous as she was, he broke off and said, "Come in, come in, you must be tired and hungry."

"I am. Washington on up is a long haul, and the Garden State's a high-speed parking lot."

Ross smiled sympathetically. He had, Leslie thought, a pleasant smile, and though the low light revealed fine lines under his eyes and a pair of furrows on either side of his round chin, his trim physique and solid, tanned arms might have belonged to a much younger man. Leslie easily recognized him from the old pictures; time had been kind to him, more than kind. The boy's bland good looks had developed into a face of interest and character, but his fine, even features touched no chord, stirred no memories.

"You're feeling better?" he asked as they walked toward the house.

"Much. Getting back to work helped. And writing to you, this trip, both have helped a lot."

"Busyness," Ross said. "Busyness helps. Let me tell you, I know."

"Yes, it gets you through the day, doesn't it? I was scared for a while that I'd have to leave my job, that I might not be able to work in journalism again." They looked at each other awkwardly for a moment, then Ross held the door open and motioned her inside.

"Ah, it's cool," Leslie said. "I've been barbequed ever since I left Florida air-conditioning."

"We're hotter than Florida at the moment. And smoggy. You couldn't pay me to live down in the city."

He moved as if to enter the living room, visible through the wide doorway at the right, but without thinking Leslie walked straight ahead down the short hallway into the kitchen. There was a table set with china and place mats, a stove, a refrigerator, a big upright freezer, patterned wallpaper, a sink, and over the sink a window where Leslie stopped and looked out.

She rested her hands on the counter and looked, not outside but at the window itself, aware of her heart beating, aware not so much of memory, for there was nothing exact enough to be called a memory, but aware, as she rarely was, that recollection should be possible, that there should be a past, a long past.

"Something used to hang in the window," she said.

"A plant?" Ross asked.

Leslie shook her head.

"Kate loved flowers but we rarely had indoor plants."

"Not a plant," Leslie said. She suddenly knew it was not a plant. An image hovered in her memory, bringing a mixture of anxiety and triumph. "It was a witch on a broomstick. A kitchen witch. That was it. I remember a kitchen witch."

She heard him draw in his breath and knew she was right. But when he spoke, his voice was casual. "I think you're right. They're pretty common, aren't they?"

"Oh, yes. One of our friends had one. One of Aunt Flo's friends. I had one, too, in our first apartment. Silly how you think of things."

When she turned from the window, the room was ordinary again, pleasant but unfamiliar. Leslie sat down on one of the kitchen chairs. "It was awfully kind of you to let me come." She didn't know how to say more, how to thank him for at least considering what had to seem a nebulous and disturbing proposition.

"I'd better put the steaks on," he said. He didn't know exactly what to think of the shy, high-strung woman sitting at his table.

"Can I help?"

"No, no need. I'm all organized."

Leslie could tell that he was anxious to be moving around.

"How do you like yours?"

"Rare, please."

"The only way to eat steak."

"That's what Doug says."

Ross closed the broiler. "I hope your trip didn't cause problems with him."

"Not problems exactly." Her mind ran to tension and awkwardness, to poignant attempts at reconciliations for buried, even unspoken, quarrels, for her own stubbornness. "He was afraid it would be . . . would be too much for me to handle. With being sick, you know. But I just felt that this was something I had to do."

Ross gave a tight little smile. He looked as if he wanted to say something and then changed his mind. "What about salad? There're some rolls, too."

"I'm not too hungry," Leslie said. "To tell you the truth, I'm pretty nervous."

"Me, too. Tell you what. I'm going to have a beer. Would you like one?"

"Please." She got up to get the glasses and went to the right cabinet without being told. What did that mean? If she had a real memory, she seemed condemned to recollect only trifles. "It's odd, isn't it?" she asked as she set the glasses on the table. "If we knew one way or another, this would be quite pleasant, I mean, it would be an ordinary social occasion. But as it is . . ."

"We're trying to size each other up."

"Yes. Every little thing seems important." She realized that her hand was shaking.

"The others," Ross said reflectively, "the others were sure. Absolutely convinced. Obsessed. Even a couple who were clearly wrong. Wrong age, wrong coloring. I had to take a blood test for one."

"I wish I was sure." She folded her arms and looked around the kitchen. "Because this feels nice," she said. "Happy, even. Like a happy home."

"I was lucky," Ross said. "I had the best kids in the world."

"You raised them yourself."

"Yeah. Me and Mrs. Goff. A saint and a genius—a former one-room schoolteacher. She'd taught me, in fact." He turned over the steak and shut the broiler door. "It was hard on the kids. Ruthie's disappearance, then their mom's death. We had our rough times, but yes, they came out all right. I learned that what is important is your kids, your family."

She smiled without responding and looked around. She noticed snaps of young children pinned up on the wall. "Grand-children?"

"Yes. Those are Peter's two. Markie and Jenny."

Leslie picked up the girl's photo and studied it carefully.

"She reminds me sometimes. She reminds me of Ruthie—and of Kate. The boys, not so much. They took after me in appearance."

"Handsome men," Leslie remarked.

Ross smiled.

"Do you see them often?"

"Every Tuesday for dinner at Peter's and lunch after church with Lyman. He just got married, Lyman. A year ago in February."

"We never had any relatives except Uncle Andy. Aunt Flo's brother. No one else. Uncle Mac's people were still overseas. Or dead."

"I was an only child, too," Ross said. "The Edens weren't a big family. Dad died in his forties, just before I graduated. That's why I started right in the liquor store. But there you have it: It's suited me okay. And as you say, we've been happy here. Think this is done enough?" He cut a slit in the steak and Leslie nodded.

"Lovely."

"Local beef, all grass fed," Ross said.

He served the dinner and they ate in silence for a time, until Leslie became aware that he was studying her. She wanted to ask him what he saw, if there was any resemblance, if her features suggested anything. Instead she asked, "And before? Were you happy before?" She saw his face change and said, "Oh, I'm so sorry. I'm not doing this well. It's just that what I remember was, not unhappiness exactly, but tension. Tension over me in some way, a way that was upsetting, frightening. Maybe I wandered off because of it. I don't know." Her long hands were eloquent.

Ross shook his head. "Kate was a remarkable woman, you know that? Without doing anything remarkable, she was remarkable. Do you understand what I mean?"

"Her personality," Leslie said.

"She had a lot of energy. That's what I remember. She was full of energy. She wasn't pretty, she certainly wasn't beautiful—a bit on the chunky side by today's standards, which I don't agree with. Give me a woman who enjoys her food, any day. But when

Kate was around, any number of pretty girls faded out of the picture. They just went flat. Kate had . . . an appetite for life. She took living seriously so that what was important to her seemed genuinely important. And she was fun," he said. "She loved the children; she knew how to keep them busy and happy."

Ross compressed his lips and stared out at the dark window, where Leslie could see their reflected images emerging with the night. It struck her that he had not really answered her question, and she wondered why not. What wasn't he telling her? Then she thought, I'm being unreasonable, a suspicious reporter; it's obvious that they were happy.

"She was always doing something," Ross said after a moment. "Me, I know how to be lazy. Kate was full of pep. Out in the garden or painting the house or rounding up the kids to go somewhere or do something."

"Aunt Flo was a bit like that," Leslie said and saw Ross's expression momentarily darken. Of course, he would hardly be interested in Aunt Flo, not if Leslie was Ruth Eden. "A real worker," she concluded lamely.

"Ahead of her time, too" Ross said without breaking his train of thought. "Kate was one of the first girls to become a lifeguard here. Quite a novelty. In fact, the first time I remember noticing her, she was sitting up in the lifeguard's chair at the town pool." Ross smiled. "She had a black suit with her Red Cross patch on it, and she was wearing a baseball cap. Best-looking guard we ever had."

"Was she a good athlete?"

"Yes, pretty good. She played all the girls' sports. The thing was with Kate, she had enthusiasm. She never lost that enthusiasm," he said, but his face darkened and he was silent for a moment. "When Ruthie was lost, it just about drove her crazy that there was nothing she could do."

Leslie nodded.

"She was a fighter, my wife. She couldn't stand to lose. Not ever. And Ruthie . . ." He shook his head.

Leslie bit her lip. "I'm sorry," she said. "Intellectually, I knew this would be hard for you, but I'm afraid I just focused on how hard it was going be for me."

Ross gave a little laugh, his serious mood broken. "We're none of us saints. What about some peach ice cream?"

"I don't think I need anything more."

"Who said anything about need? This is local stuff. Real cream."

"All right."

"That's the spirit. You need a little indulgence."

"Aunt Flo was always big on character, you know, character building."

"I've always thought happiness helped build character."

"A comfortable doctrine."

Ross smiled. "But one I believe. Try this." The ice cream was a very pale pinkish yellow, and Leslie was surprised by the intense fruity flavor.

"The real thing," Ross said. "No artificial color."

"Delicious."

"I know the farmer. They've gone into ice cream now that the bottom's dropped out of the milk market. Anything to stay afloat."

Leslie had done a piece on the cattle industry in Florida, so they were able to talk about cows and ice cream and rural economics, and then about her house back home, renovations, the expansion of the cottage. It was after ten before they began the dishes, and when they were finished, Leslie said she thought she should go.

"You must be tired," Ross said.

"It's been wonderful to see you, but I am tired, and I need to call Doug. He'll be worried if he doesn't hear from me."

"Do you want to come by tomorrow and see the village?"

"Oh, yes, if it's convenient for you with the store and all."

"I can get away tomorrow morning. The store's not too busy early. Say, nine o'clock?"

"I'd really like that. Shall I meet you here?"

"At nine," he said and shook hands. He walked Leslie to her car and stood on the drive waving. His light shirt was visible for a moment in her rearview mirror, then the lights of the neighboring houses winked through the trees, and there was only the woods and fields and the big summer moon squatting behind them, losing its size and orange tint as it rose. Leslie could feel her heart. In the house, she'd been calm, calm talking to Ross, calm eating dinner at the kitchen table, but the shock she'd felt walking toward the kitchen window, the overwhelming sense of déjà vu, seemed to have been waiting out in the car for her. As soon as she was alone she felt it again, that uneasy excitement, that dangerous sense of conviction.

Coming over a rise, Leslie saw the glow of a car on the state road and, farther on, the scattered lights of the village. Her own headlights formed a dusty cone, illuminating bushes and trees, before something low and dark ran into the road, and she stabbed the brakes, as a possum shuffled into the undergrowth. Leslie brought the car to a stop, shaking. Around her were the night songs of insects and frogs, and for a moment she felt nothing but her heart and her breathing. Then she straightened her back and caught her breath: It was only panic and muscular tension. Or was it something else, something farther back, some fear? She was sure that she had been unhappy as a small child, and there might be things that she was afraid to face.

Leslie shook her head, angry with herself. Ross's memories were different, and if he *was* her father, then this momentary anxiety was nothing except fear of discovery, the ignoble fear of the future. She fumbled among her cassettes for Bob Segar, for "Hollywood Nights," for good driving music to ward off the evil spirits of the past, the unworthy fears of the present. She glanced in the mirror, then pulled away, driving slowly and carefully. Her heartbeat began to calm and, with a sudden surge of excitement, she let herself think, I've perhaps met my father.

Perhaps. Leslie was sorry now that she had done so much research, sorry she'd ever looked at the school photos—though how would she have decided if she hadn't? But it would have been better to have come, if that had been possible, totally unprepared. To have stopped by accident in Woodmill would have been best. To have stopped, perhaps to ask directions and come to his house and known, suddenly and without doubt, that this was the place. Instead, reality: a mix of evidence and circumstance, probability and coincidence. She remembered the window with the kitchen witch, but she didn't remember happiness, she didn't remember the sort of home Ross Eden did, and she didn't remember Ross at all.

What came to her were vague, dim images of a tall man, of being called, of him lifting her onto a swing. His face was gone, forgotten, and in its place was Uncle Mac's, broad, coarse, and jovial, the square pug nose, heavy brows and broken tooth, the wonderful smile and the raspy, throaty voice with the guttural Glasgow vowels. Uncle Mac took up all the foreground with his jokes and his Harry Lauder songs and his low, expressive voice. She remembered how he would say, "Now Leslie, lass," and felt tears in her eyes. Uncle Mac had been fun and patient. From Uncle Mac she knew how to grow vegetables, nursed tenderly in the sunny backyard in Syracuse, and how to whistle through her fingers, and how to make beer. He'd taught her to ride a bicycle and, later, to drive a car.

And now here was Ross Eden, handsome and kind, the sort of father she'd imagined, whom she liked and admired and who made her feel disloyal to Mac and Flo and the life they'd had together. She hadn't expected to feel divided. One part of her was frightened, half regretting the whole business. The other was exhilarated in spite of uncertainties at Woodmill and problems at home, which included a second absence from the paper and arguments with Doug. When Leslie reached the Hunt Club Motel with its overgrown flower beds, white flagpole, and little cast-iron grooms, she went straight to her room to call home. The phone rang a long time, and Leslie was nervous as well as excited before Doug answered.

"Dear, did I wake you?"

"No, I just got in the house." No explanation, she noticed.

"Late on that restaurant job?"

"That and out to dinner. You know I hate eating alone."

"I know. I'm glad you're still up. I just had to call; it's been amazing. I saw Ross tonight."

"Yeah?"

"He's great. Really nice. And when I got in the house, I remembered where the kitchen was, even that they used to have a kitchen witch in the window. It was almost scary. Just for a moment it was like I knew."

"So is he the one?" Doug asked, but he did not sound particularly excited, and Leslie felt her joy begin to diminish.

"We aren't going to jump to conclusions. Ross is going to show me around town tomorrow, and we'll see how that goes. The big thing is that I feel I'm going to know. One way or the other, I'm going to know."

"Good, that's nice. Listen, Leslie, the paper called you again today."

"What did you tell them?"

"That you were resting at your aunt's."

"Good. That's the kind of thing Harvey'll buy. He's from the leisure class."

"This can't go on, Leslie."

"The *Sun Coast Times* will survive. I left them two features. I'll bet they haven't run the update on school antidrug program yet."

"No, but the Pelican Man story ran. Front page of the second section."

"Oh, good. Phil got some terrific pictures, pelicans feeding and one with its leg in a splint. That should hold Harvey for a day or two."

"And then what?"

"I'll be back midweek, of course."

"Of course?" he asked.

"What else, Doug? Woodmill's pretty, but it's the end of the world—not a mall for twenty miles. No baseball, either, no winter Sox," she added, trying to tease him into better humor. "But I couldn't come this far without meeting Ross, not when I can know for sure."

"I don't know," he said. "I don't know what you want anymore."

"I keep trying to explain to you," Leslie said. She wanted terribly for him to understand—and to approve. "I seemed to lose so much all at once, that's all. Big bits of the past just disappeared."

"Just watch you don't lose other things. We need your job at the paper. Without it, you know I'm always slow paying the suppliers."

"Yes," Leslie said, "yes." But that was not it. After she hung up, she knew that was not it. Doug's business was sound and thriftily managed, and though her salary allowed him certain economies, that was not the problem. She'd thought it was, but sitting in Woodmill's only motel—rather elderly, smelling faintly of mown hay, gasoline, and pine scent air freshener—she saw something else: This was the first time they'd disagreed about anything important. And why did he oppose this trip and Ross and Woodmill? She thought it was just out of habit, a habit she'd liked. She'd liked him deciding the important things, being the responsible one; she'd depended on him.

And that was funny, too, because at work she was considered tough and determined, willing to dig for information and to stand by her stories, even if the paper took some heat. There'd been hell to pay when she'd written that a prominent construction firm had been responsible for shoddy concrete work up north. The company's good political connections and the anticipated boost to the town tax base couldn't change the fact that one of their building projects in New Jersey had collapsed. A construction worker had been crippled by the accident, and when Leslie started digging, she learned that wasn't the only disaster, either. After the story ran, the company had threatened to sue for libel, and although Harvey had been up the wall, Leslie had all the facts and knew it and wrote several follow-ups. Eventually, the firm backed down and the *Sun Coast* won a commendation in the state journalism awards.

But the Leslie Austin who wrote bylined stories was the public side of her character, the one, she supposed fashioned by Uncle Mac and Aunt Flo, that was tough and hardworking and ambitious and sensible. She'd showed more of the other, hidden, side to Doug, the side shaped by abduction and the man in the brown suit, by Woodmill, perhaps by the Edens. That was the Leslie Doug loved, diffident, even insecure, and now he wanted her to come home before she was sure, because when she was sure, she might be—would be—a different person. Leslie hadn't seen that, but Doug had. Because he had trouble expressing his feelings clearly, she sometimes underrated his perceptiveness. Leslie grabbed the phone and punched in the numbers. "I love you," she said when he answered. "Please remember I love you more than anything."

It was only after they'd hung up that she realized permanence might be impossible to guarantee, a thought that brought her restless, frightening dreams and carried over into the next morning as nervous anxiety.

4

Although it was a lovely, fresh morning, green and wet with dew, Leslie woke up feeling exhausted. The trip and the accompanying emotional tension had tired her out, and she kept yawning during breakfast in the motel. Beyond the bay windows and red gingham curtains of the dining room, yesterday's green countryside seemed completely alien, and Leslie's stomach grew unsettled at the very thought of Ruth Eden. When she glanced at herself in the car mirror, she was so pale that she was not surprised when Ross asked if she was feeling all right.

"Just a little tired from the trip," she said and changed the subject to the welcome break in the heat.

"We do get some nice summer weather," he said. "Why don't I drive so that you can look around?"

"Great. It's hard to see much when you're driving."

"Yes, though I like to drive," Ross said as Leslie rolled down the window in his big gray sedan. "Just so long as it's a Buick. I've always had Buicks. First to last, they're a reliable car."

He began to reminisce about his first one, thirdhand from an uncle, and Leslie nodded politely and studied the roadside. At the juncture with the state road was a field with a few Holsteins grazing beyond the barbed wire, and when she turned to look at Ross, he nodded without being asked. Leslie looked back toward the wood, now a thin screen before the little development and wholly innocuous, then they were speeding down the state highway, past a nursery, the town pool, and a little country store, before a group of sizable houses and a sharp bend announced the main street.

"I thought we'd park at the old school and walk from here," Ross said when they stopped at a handsome, buff colored Victorian building. "Riding's not the same."

"This was your school?"

"Yup. The old town school."

"I've seen the yearbooks, the school pictures. I think I told you I'd sent away for them."

"This was all elms once. They were cut down twenty years ago and replaced by maples. That's the library, we enlarged it a few years ago—big fund drive."

As they walked down the street, Ross waved to friends and now and again stopped to chat, introducing her always as a distant relative, a reporter on holiday. Everyone knew him and knew his history; the town was cozy to the point of claustrophobia, but not static. Ross pointed out the changes between interruptions: the old soda shop that was now an antique store, the renovated newsstand where, Leslie remembered, Kate Eden had once worked. The men's shop, too, was under new ownership. Ross disapproved of the changes there as "too smart, too many Italian jackets," and when Leslie checked the trendily decorated windows, she felt that she agreed.

But there was nothing for her, no tremor of recognition, and she was beginning to feel disappointed when she saw a two-story wooden building set back from the sidewalk with a cluster of mowers and lawn tractors parked in front: the hardware store. Inside, it would be dark and old-fashioned with high display racks, little bins of metal parts, a glassed-in case with a sticky rubber gasket around the face and . . .

"Do you want to go in?" Ross asked.

Leslie realized that she had stopped smack in the middle of the sidewalk.

"Yes," she said. His face was unreadable, but she could feel the tension. A bell clanged as they entered, and Leslie saw the racks, not as high as she'd remembered, but steep, worn, full of little compartments with nuts and bolts and screws and washers, a giant version of Doug's supply bench. She looked up at the fans and the old acorn-shaped lights hanging from the high tin ceiling and then down at the wooden floor, worn to a dusty gray-brown.

"Wood floors," she said.

"Not many changes here," Ross said.

Leslie bent down and touched the curiously soft boards. The top fibers, unprotected, had worn to a nap, and that cellulose fuzz awakened first a tactile sense and then a fleeting image of bare legs, white socks, the edge of a red dress, and her own small hand exploring the floor and picking at something lodged in one of the cracks. The clerk came over and gave Ross a look. "Lose something, miss?"

Leslie stood up into a present that seemed somehow more ambiguous than that brief, vivid recollection. "No, thank you," she said awkwardly. "You have a wonderful old shop."

"Good enough not to change. Introduce me, Ross. Not too many pretty girls like hardware stores."

Ross smiled, though he knew that once Artie had an item, the news would be around town before noon, and he regretted again that he hadn't warned the boys. "A distant relative" always triggered speculation, but Artie became animated as soon as Leslie mentioned her town.

"I know it! Damned if I don't, and I read the *Sun Coast Times* every day on vacation. Sand Castle Motel on the beach, always stay there. I'm telling you that heat is so great for my arthritis that if it weren't for making a living, I'd move down there in a minute. Am I right, Ross?"

Artie laughed, and Ross and Leslie smiled politely. She could feel her heart again; she'd been here, she was sure.

But the bank, the post office, the diner, the closed-up movie theater, the condominium that had once been the hotel suggested nothing. Perhaps she had come from a town something like Woodmill, some neighboring place with a similar hardware store. Ross must have thought that, too, because he mentioned taking the kids to cartoon matinees at the old theater and for Sunday lunch at the diner. They walked on without saying anything more, and they had almost reached the end of the village and were approaching the green and the war memorial, when, quite causally, Leslie glanced up one of the small side streets and saw the Woodmill Garage sign, a faded oblong of red and white.

"Oh! It's Mr. Eddie's! That's Mr. Eddie's sign!" She knew it without a doubt. "That's the man I tried to tell you about," she said. "The man who was so disfigured. Half his face was all scarred and distorted. I was just terrified, and Mother, it must have been my mother, said, 'That's Mr. Eddie. He's a special friend of mine. You call him Mr. Eddie, and you never mention his face.' It is his, isn't it?"

Ross had to take a deep breath and then another, before he could say, "It was his. It's his son's place now." The words felt strange in his mouth, hope felt stranger yet, and he realized that, despite all his nervous anxiety, he had been almost totally unprepared. "Eddie owns the car dealership on the state road. It got to be too much for Eddie's hands to do mechanical work."

"His hands were damaged too! That's right. I remember him giving me a lollipop and my being afraid to take it. Oh, God, it's true! I couldn't have read that."

"Eddie's face was never in the paper," Ross said.

Leslie put her hand over her mouth and walked rapidly toward the green to hide her confusion. When they reached the trees, she stopped and faced him. "I've been here before," she said. "I was here as a child. At the very least, I know that."

"It's more than that," Ross said. His voice was hoarse, and he figured his blood pressure had gone stratospheric. He sat down on one of the benches to let his mind absorb the shock: This stranger from Florida was his child. After all his searching and hoping, after giving up, his baby girl had been returned, courtesy of Mr. Eddie, as this shy, intense, coltish young woman. Mr. Eddie! In how many strange ways was his life connected to Eddie Vincenti's, just as Eddie's had been connected to Kate's and Paul Schott's. Ross took a deep breath and gestured for Leslie to sit beside him. When he found his voice, he said, "Eddie was a special person for my wife. An old friend, not a boyfriend, but a real friend. That wasn't as common then as now. I mean, good friends of the opposite sex."

Leslie nodded. The customs of a generation ago were scarcely believable.

"He looks different now," Ross said reflectively. "Modern plastic surgery is quite amazing."

"But years ago?"

"Years ago, he was seriously disfigured, and kids were frightened of him at first." Leslie saw the pain and fear and hope in his eyes and laid her hand on his shoulder. Ross took a breath and went on. "I remember Peter, that's my oldest boy, not wanting to go to the garage, and Kate saying, 'That's Mr. Eddie.' That's just how she handled it. 'That's Mr. Eddie, who is Mom's special friend.'"

He turned and she saw his tears before he said, "Oh, Ruthie!" and pulled her into his arms. Leslie held him close for a moment; she could feel his warm, shaved cheek, the strong line of his back, and his leaping heart banging his ribs and hers indifferently. Then he sat back, wiped his eyes, and looked at her.

"The last time I saw you, you were wearing a little red sweater and blue overalls. That was the last time. You always came to the door to wave good-bye in the morning. I'd kiss you, go out to the car, and wave as I left the drive. Every day from the time you could walk, you'd always come to the door." He swallowed hard and looked off into the distance for a moment before he said, "If only poor Kate could see you. If only she could be here now."

Leslie took his hand.

"It broke her heart. The suspense, the waiting, the imagining, the not knowing. She was such an active, determined person that she couldn't endure helplessness. You have to understand."

Leslie nodded.

"She'd given up hope." He shrugged slightly. "I don't know if I had or not." He took a deep breath and said, "I've got to call the boys. It'll be around town that you're here and all, and I want them to know. I want them to know we've found Ruthie."

"You're sure?" she asked. "You're really sure?" She'd lived with her belief for so long, a belief so intimate, so personal to her alone, that she was almost shocked to find Ross sharing it, to find that, yes, she was Ruth Eden, Ruthie, his lost child.

"As I can be. As soon as you mentioned the disfigured man in one of your letters, I thought, maybe."

"It feels right," Leslie said. "You know, it feels right." But she sat as if stunned. He wanted to call the boys, to whoop and holler; the news took her differently. "The kitchen witch and the hardware store and Mr. Eddie. Is that enough?" she asked. "Is that enough for you?"

He saw her hesitation. Her conviction had started everything and carried them this far, but Ross sensed her fear, her doubt. He understood that, at this particular moment, everything was up to him, that she needed his help, that his was the decisive voice. "There'll be more once you're here for a while," he told her. "You'll see." In his happiness and relief, he assumed she'd be staying. "And when you meet the boys! You have two brothers."

"Yes," she said, biting her lip. "Brothers, father, place of birth. I can't believe it."

"It's all right," he said, putting his arm around her again. "It's all right to cry."

"From the moment I saw the story, I thought that could be me. The idea came all at once."

"Like Eddie's sign."

"Yes," she said. "Yes, I must be Ruthie."

Ross jumped up, unable to sit still. "Come on, we'll call the boys. They've got to know! We've got to celebrate! We'll have them all over for a cookout, and you'll meet the kids. You've got a niece and a nephew, cutest kids in the world."

"Yes," Leslie said, although she was suddenly nervous about meeting them, of declaring herself, of embracing the past she had sought so long.

Ross gripped her shoulder. "It'll be all right, you'll see. Things are going to be all right now."

They went back to the house for lunch, grinders that Ross bought at the sandwich shop. He opened a couple of beers, called Cindy to invite her and Peter, and left a message for Lyman at his answering service. Then he went into the living room and returned with a stack of padded brown, green, and blue leatherette volumes. He opened one and laid it in front of Leslie. "There you are," he said, and she looked up and smiled. It was a small, sharp photo of an infant in a blanket.

"Seven pounds even," Ross said. He turned the page to a snap of a woman holding the infant. "My mom. Was she pleased—she'd always wanted a girl."

"Is she still alive?"

"Died two years ago in September. I'm afraid we're not a long-lived bunch. Healthy for the duration, though. Kate's folks, now, are still going strong. The old man's—what?—eighty-three, and Mama's a year younger. He still keeps a couple of cows, if you can believe that."

Leslie turned another page.

"Kate," Ross said.

"Am I at all like her?" Leslie asked without looking at him.

"Thinner," he said. "Not so vivacious. You have her hair and the eyebrows." And now that he thought about it, something about the assertive line of her hip. Was she like Kate? Yes and no. And like him? He couldn't think, but Ruthie had always been Kate's child, quick and dark. "The day you were baptized." Ross looked very young and blond in the photo, very handsome; Kate looked serious, almost worried, Leslie thought.

"Was she religious?" she asked.

"Religious? Oh, she went to church, but my wife was a practical woman."

"I only asked because she looks so solemn."

"She wasn't too well after the birth. Odd. The other two she was fine, healthy as a horse. Carrying you, too, she was okay—Kate was meant to have children—but after, she wasn't so good. Postpartum depression, they said, though that didn't last too long. Here, this is a better picture. What do you think?"

Kate looked relaxed, smiling at her alert, fat-faced baby. "She was very attractive," Leslie said.

"One of those people pictures don't do justice to," Ross said.

"You, now, were always handsome," Leslie teased.

"So they said."

She turned the pages, a slow-motion movie, watching the chubby baby acquire hair and sleeper suits, a ball, a kitten, then spindly legs, a short, neat bob, a tricycle. Ruth Eden clambered about a swing set and posed with her big brother, who frowned in manly disdain at the camera.

"This one was taken just before," Ross said, pointing to a

snap of the child sitting on the ground, a fuzzy crown of daisies on her head.

"I'd remembered them as dandelions."

"You remembered that?"

"Not long ago. I suddenly had this image of sitting on the grass like that, of learning how to make a chain of flowers. With a woman with dark hair."

"That's the last," Ross said and made as if to close the book.

"Can I see the others?"

"Sure. I've got stacks. I used to be very fond of taking pictures. Kinda let it slip for a while once the kids got older. They get to that stage of not wanting their pictures taken. Now, of course, there're the grandchildren. Grampa is indulged about that."

"Could I see some more of the grandchildren?" Leslie asked.

Ross produced his most recent pictures, Markie in a striped T-shirt at the Memorial Day parade, Jenny dressed for church in a pink dress. "She's not usually so neat," Ross said. "A live wire."

"She looks like . . ." It was hard to say "me" and equally hard to say "Ruthie."

"Yes, the same sort of bright, active child, though she's quite blond. And here's her dad."

Leslie smiled and slowly examined the photos, going back and forth between the grown men and the skinny boys that Peter and Lyman had been. Her brothers, her family. She could see everything falling into place.

"You know, I was so afraid to write you the first time," Leslie said. "I was afraid of bothering you, of being wrong, of—I don't know—just of the unknown."

"Of remembering more?"

"Yes, that, too. I think I knew more all along. I probably know more now that just hasn't surfaced yet." She ran her hand over the albums, the piles of loose photographs. "When I look at these, I'm confident. I feel sure."

"And you should, you should be sure," he said and hugged her again so that she felt new and tender, as if just born from these photos and memories. Leslie felt that she was no longer Leslie Simpson Austin or Ruth Eden but an amalgamation of the two, someone different, someone brave and new.

The others arrived at six-thirty. Leslie and Ross had gone shopping for the cookout stuff in the afternoon, and maybe that was the mistake, appearing as his hostess, as a fait accompli. At the time, she was caught up in the fantasy of reunion, of a family so perfect and flexible that the past could be enlarged, with new photos added to the album, another place set at the table, another birthday marked on the calendar. She'd managed to bridge the gap and so had Ross.

Going to the supermarket in the car, they both started laughing at a silly bumper sticker and then talked about cars and Uncle Mac's bus—though that, Leslie saw, was difficult territory, best avoided—and about their early memories. She and Ross had the same whimsical sense of humor, the same pleasure in taking off from the ordinary into silliness, and, though she could remember nothing about him, Leslie felt, yes, I loved him, I must have loved him. In the supermarket, they discovered that they both liked the same kind of hot dogs, the same mustard. This was an additional cause for celebration, justifying the purchase of a cake and a stop at the roadside stand for early corn, late strawberries, and a watermelon.

"The kids like watermelon," Ross said, "and so do I. Like watermelon?"

"My favorite," Leslie said, "supermelon." And he put his arm around her.

"I can't tell you how happy I am."

"I must call Doug," she said. "I wish Doug was here, too."

"Invite him up. Tell him to come. It's about time I met your husband. After all these years." He laughed again easily, and Leslie felt giddy. They stopped for her bag at the motel and went home to start the fire and make the hamburger patties and shuck the corn. Leslie got the plates out and found the cutlery on the first try—everything was charmed. If I don't think, she said to herself, if I trust to instinct and act, everything will be all right. When the cars pulled in, Leslie fussed with the salad, giving Ross time. Then he called and she walked out the back door to the deck; they were waiting on the grass in a loose semicircle. She recognized them from the photos, Peter, tall and blond, exceptionally good-looking, and his wife, also fair, rather plump, with a sturdy little boy clinging to her skirt. Lyman was shorter than his brother, heavier and more muscular looking, his hair darker. He was wearing a T-shirt, jeans, and mirrored sunglasses. Beside him, his wife, Judy, was tiny with short red hair and wide-set dark eyes. She'd been talking to Ross, but she turned at the sound of the door opening, and all the rest looked up.

"Come on out, Leslie," Ross said, walking over to the steps and taking her hand. "This is Leslie Simpson from Florida. Peter and Cindy, and Markie. Say hello to Leslie, Markie. And Judy and Lyman. And Jenny." Jenny extended her hand so formally that everyone laughed, and the tension was broken for a moment. Ross waited until the two children had run off to play in the yard, then he said, "Leslie's been writing to me for some time. Since the story ran about Ruthie."

Peter gave her a sharp, shrewd look. "You saw the story in Florida?"

"I work for a newspaper. The story came up on the feature wire."

"I thought we'd agreed no more articles, Dad."

"Leslie's not here for a story, Peter."

"I see."

"No, I don't think you do. She's convinced, and I am too, that she's our Ruthie."

In the silence, Leslie felt an emotional vibration like a psychic sonic boom. "Holy shit!" Lyman exclaimed and stuck his hand out to her again. He studied her face for a minute then said, "She does look a bit like Mom. Like I remember Mom."

"A lot of people look a bit like someone else," said Peter. "There's got to be more than that."

Cindy took his arm. "I'm sure Ross has good reasons, and Leslie, too."

"There have been a few others over the years," Peter said. "I don't mean to be rude, but there have been others."

"And did I give them a moment's credence?"

"Give Dad time," Lyman said. "So what's the story?"

"Let's sit down," Judy suggested, moving toward the picnic area. "I've been on my feet all day at the hospital."

"No rest for the wicked," Ross told her, and she laughed. Ross sat down in one of the lawn chairs, and the two boys took the benches on either side of the table. Judy perched behind Lyman on the bench. Cindy dropped down on the blanket beside Markie and kindly patted the space next to her for Leslie.

"So," said Ross, "it's this way." He outlined their correspondence, the story, the gaps in Leslie's recollections, the odd things she mentioned in the letters, the crucial reference to Mr. Eddie.

"Mr. Eddie," said Peter. "Anyone who'd been in Woodmill in the sixties would have remembered Mr. Eddie."

"She remembers Mr. Eddie and she remembers being told exactly what your mom told you. Do you remember?"

"That he was her friend," Lyman said. "Though it never bothered me for some reason."

"You're the strong, silent type," his wife said.

"And there's the hardware store," Ross said, continuing. When he finished describing their visit to the village, they all looked at Leslie.

"I know this will sound crazy," she said softly, "but from the moment when the wire story mentioned a meadow, I just froze. I saw this field again, the one I remember, with woods behind it." She told them about the man whose image had come to her so strangely, about how the idea of Ruth Eden had taken over her mind, and how, against all odds and expectations, her unknown abductor had turned out to be real and her memories to be correct. As she spoke, her shyness dropped away. Ross was surprised at the forcefulness in her voice and understood how her conviction had been able to erase so many obstacles. There was something of Kate in her, after all, something more than he'd seen originally: a certain passionate determination. Leslie told them about sending for the yearbooks, examining the old pictures, worrying and trying to decide, and then finally visiting Aunt Flo. "I don't know how to explain this to you," Leslie concluded. "I guess it's like people who claim to see a ghost: It can't be and yet they are utterly sure. That's how I felt, and finally, I wrote to Ross. I really expected him to tell me that it couldn't be true. To mention some detail, some mark, something that would put Ruth Eden out of my mind—"

"The fellow in the brown car," Peter interrupted, "the man you think kidnapped you, he was never arrested?"

Leslie shook her head.

"So there's no police record."

"No," Leslie said. "And I don't remember what my original name was, either. I just know I was told I was to be Leslie."

"You could be anyone," Peter said.

"Yes, and that's what's worried me. But, in fact, there weren't too many missing children that summer who were the right age, race, and sex. Those things are right."

"Unless someone was unreported," Peter said. "An unwanted child . . ."

"Leslie and I are convinced," said Ross, who disliked the tenor of Peter's questions and saw that the quest for confirmation could become open-ended. "Although Leslie doesn't want any publicity. Not yet."

"I heard she was a cousin," Cindy said. "I heard that in the drugstore on the way here."

"I had to say something," Ross said.

"Otherwise worse rumors," Judy agreed. She gave him a look and smiled. She was the only one who knew for sure about the chef.

"I know that this has been a lot to spring on you," Leslie said, "but things got to the point where I felt I had to know one way or the other. That's all I want, just to know. And though Ross and I sincerely believe I'm Ruth Eden, if any of you want to check things out more carefully, I certainly won't take offense."

"Things will work out," Ross said quickly, for, to his mind, the matter was settled: This was Ruthie. She was, after all, his child, her identity his decision. "And you're not to run away so soon, either. I want you to get to know the rest of the family."

"Listen," Lyman said, "if Dad's convinced, that's good enough for me. I say we need a toast. We need a drink."

"Right," Ross said. "Judy, lend me a hand with the drinks, would you? Lyman, why don't you and Peter check that fire. The kids will be hungry."

"Shall I make the burgers?" Cindy asked.

"We're way ahead of you, dear, but you can put them on if the fire's ready. What about the pool for the little ones?"

"Do you want the bother?'

"What's the bother? Markie, Jenny!" He veered off to corral

the grandchildren, and Cindy smiled indulgently. "Come on, we'll get the drinks. Once he's started with the kids . . ."

Leslie got up, too nervous to keep still. "I'll put on the corn. The salad's all fixed and—"

"Cindy knows where the pots are," Peter interrupted. He gave his wife a look, and she got up and touched Leslie's shoulder. "Keep Peter company. I'll see about dinner."

Leslie smiled uncertainly and sat back down. She would rather have been busy in the kitchen.

"You just drove up this week from Florida?" Peter asked.

"Yes. A long drive."

"Some way to spend a vacation."

"Not exactly a vacation. I had major surgery, and I've been on leave recently."

"I thought you said you'd seen the story at your paper."

"I've been working part-time on rewrites and occasional features."

He studied her for a moment. He looked very like Ross with the same well-fleshed, regular features, blond hair, and smooth brow, but he seemed more intense, sharper, maybe, or just higher strung. "You must understand that we've been troubled over the years. The case was never officially closed."

"I know. I've covered missing child cases."

"Reporters don't know anything about it," he said. "Only the families know."

"I suppose the missing children might have an a opinion, too." She jumped up and walked over to the fire. Lyman was standing watching the coals. He smiled and said, "I'm asking myself, am I ready for a sister?"

"This is pretty sudden, isn't it?"

"Dad said you'd been writing letters." There was an unspoken reproach.

"Your dad wanted to be certain. He wasn't convinced until I saw the sign on Mr. Eddie's garage."

"It's made him happy for sure," Lyman admitted.

Judy appeared carrying a six-pack. "What do you say after all this time?"

"What about, 'Have a drink'?" Lyman asked.

"I think I need one," said Leslie.

"Don't let Peter bother you. He's the family lawyer, accountant, general watchdog. Hey, Peter, come get a beer." Judy started toward her brother-in-law, but Lyman stopped her. "Naw, let him walk. He's putting on weight. Come on over here and talk to our new sister."

Peter managed a smile, a professional salesman's smile, Leslie thought, and came over.

"Here we go!" Ross exclaimed from the porch. "Hold on, hold on."

"He's got that damn camera," Peter said.

"Just the three of you," Ross said. He raised his camera and snapped their picture. "Wait, one more with the Polaroid for Leslie's husband and then one with Leslie and me." He put down the 35 millimeter and snapped the other machine, which spewed out a piece of coated film.

"Can I hold it, Grampa? Can I hold it?"

"Hold it still, Jenny. It needs two minutes. You hold it, 'til I get my picture with Leslie." He came over and Lyman took the photo.

"It's coming," Jenny called impatiently.

"Let's see," said Ross.

She ran over, and there they were, the three Eden children, the boys tall and handsome, with Leslie in the center, slim and dark and nervously eager. Ross took the photo from Jenny and handed it to Leslie. "First of the new family pictures," he said, putting his arm around her.

Ross heard a bug rattling the screen with an insistent two-note buzz like a tiny doorbell. The moon was still up, the empty lawn almost white in its light, the overgrown shrubs at the back black as ink. His children and grandchildren had gone home, though he could see that they'd left the cloth and a couple of bottles on the picnic table. Upstairs, Leslie Austin slept in Ruthie's old room. He knew that she was asleep. When he'd gone up to say good night, her light had been out, the door ajar—he'd never fixed the latch properly—and standing in the hall, he thought that he could hear her light breath. How many nights had he stood there when the children were small, checking each of their beds in turn? And after Ruthie was lost, how many nights had he awakened, restless, and gone out into the hall and listened to the now diminished night sounds of the children, or entered her room, hopeful and despairing, as if she might have been miraculously restored?

Now she had been, and although he reserved judgment on both the efficacy of prayer and the immortality of the soul, Ross prayed that Kate knew, that this comfort had not eluded her. Forgetting he'd renounced smoking for good, he got up for a cigarette, then sat down again on the edge of his bed to take off his shoes. He wanted to drive Leslie around the area tomorrow; he thought maybe they'd go to church and satisfy the village's curiosity all at once.

But when he lay down, Ross was still too excited to sleep. Ruthie was home! And perhaps because only now was it bearable, he found his mind running over the terrible moments when he and Kate had returned home after searching the road. She had gone into the yard, shouting for Ruthie, and he had jumped from the car without shutting off the motor and rushed through the house, into the living room and kitchen, down to the basement, back up the stairs and onto the second floor, convinced in some hopeful chamber of his heart that Ruthie was there, had been there all along, perhaps asleep, oblivious to adult panic. The door of her room was closed, the ill-hung door that seemed to swing of its own volition, and Ross had thrust it open on the neatly made bed, the mess of toys on the floor, the crudely crayoned drawing on one wall, and Ruthie's Raggedy Ann sprawled on the chair.

He had looked down from the window into Kate's frantic eyes, before dialing the troopers and stepping into the nightmare of bureaucracy, investigation, and reporters, of false leads and false hopes and devastating revelations of loss. Devastating and unending: the first meal without Ruthie, the first night, the first search party, the first suspect. And then, the start of a long series of holidays robbed of their joy. The Fourth of July was endurable, though she'd loved sparklers and fireworks, but Thanksgiving's very name was mockery, and Christmas was horrible, the more so because he and Kate must feign enjoyment for Peter's sake. So they'd learned deception, and they'd learned it well. They got good at evading the sympathy of outsiders, the sorrows of their parents, even their own expressions of anguish and regret; they knew better than to disturb raw wounds.

In this way life became a long convalescence: Ross remembered his father's illness and recognized the parallels: the fatigue, the occasional terror, the perpetual undertow of anxiety. For weeks after Ruthie disappeared, Ross and Kate did not make love, though they huddled together in bed at night, desperate for comfort. Peter, too, had trouble sleeping and would stay up until all hours or else awaken terrified in the night and wander into their bed. Ross would realize the presence of his thin, bony body with a mixture of tenderness and exasperation and fold his son in his arms. For weeks he called home every afternoon fifteen minutes after Peter's school bus was expected, and he was furious with a neighbor who returned the boy half an hour late from a Scout meeting.

For several days, they'd believed, or pretended to believe, that Ruthie had wandered, that she'd be found, that she was already found and safe but too distressed to make clear her name and address. And then, that she was in a hospital nearby, suffering perhaps from exposure, but safe. In this time of hope and illusion, they listened for the phone. Ross acquired the power to detect the first, faint sounds before the bell, and many times he was there and waiting and had lifted the receiver before the first ring faded. He wanted good news so desperately that he could hear the words running though his head: "Mr. Eden? We have good news for you, sir . . ."

When it finally became clear that the calls would always be disappointing or inconclusive, the phone became an instrument of terror. Ross was especially afraid in the store—he assumed they'd try to break the worst to him first—and at night, when a ringing phone would clench his heart. Some of his distributors ceased to recognize his voice, because each time he lifted the receiver he was tensed for disaster, for the discovery of horror, murder, irregular burial, for an official voice saying, "I'm sorry, Mr. Eden, we have some bad news . . ."

That official voice never came; instead, there was nothing except the sickening suspense of false hopes and false trails and offers of assistance ranging from the innocent to the bizarre. How many weekends did he and Kate leave Peter with the grandparents and drive off to some distant neighborhood where there was a new, small girl, dark-haired, just recently arrived? They met some quite nice people, mostly military folks in transit whose children were not yet familiar to their neighbors. There were other helpers, too, writers who claimed publicity was the only way, and psychics with haunted eyes and bundles of handwritten testimonials. He'd paid a couple; he assumed Kate had, too, while maintaining, like him, a profession of disbelief. In despair, he almost began to wish for the bad news that would put an end to the uncertainty and to the long-running horror show in his imagination.

And in Kate's. When Peter was out of the house, she was frantic, yet she was uncharacteristically impatient when he was at home. She obsessively searched the wood behind their property, then stopped walking altogether and spent her free time working in the garden or calling around the country, following up every rumor, every clue, every "sighting." The phone bill alone was almost enough to ruin them.

Sometimes, anxious, Ross would call the house during school hours and hear the phone ring unanswered. He remembered standing at the counter, receiver in hand, his heart thumping: They had called her first, something had happened to Peter, to her, to them both. Later, he knew the truth, that Kate took the bus into Torrington, and sometimes even the train into the city, to walk the residential streets and haunt the schoolyards as obsessively as a madwoman.

That's what she said to him one night, "You've married a madwoman," and Ross felt the words twist his heart and understood that this, at last, was love with all its anguish. Perhaps he had never really loved her until then, when it was too late for happiness, when all their memories and emotions were colored by Ruthie and her loss. Love and pain expanded his soul and made him imaginative. He had a terrible vision of Kate walking alone on a city sidewalk, her dark hair long and unkempt, her eyes wild, crying ceaselessly and pathetically for Ruthie.

Later on, when the searches had turned up nothing, when there was no word, when all the trails had gone cold and all the clues were useless, he tried to calm her and thought of another child. With a painful effort of hope and cheerfulness, he began to court her again. They resumed making love, without the wild spontaneity that had marked their first years or the dark excitements of the time before Ruthie's birth, and, late in the winter, Kate became pregnant. Her reaction took Ross by surprise.

"We can't replace Ruthie," she cried. "We'll never replace Ruthie."

He saw the naked superstitious fear, the fear that any change might keep Ruthie away, the fear that had kept her room untouched. "Of course not," he said. "No one could ever replace Ruthie."

The idea alarmed her so much that for a time Ross had been afraid she might do herself harm. "We'll have a boy," he said, without knowing where he got his assurance. "A brother for Peter, like you've always wanted."

At last, she had accepted that, but things were never the same. They never recovered the almost childish innocence of the early years of their marriage, when he'd been fascinated by Kate's energy and sexuality, as, he guessed, she had been by his looks and his vigor. And Peter had been wonderful, a fine, healthy baby. Ross had never considered fatherhood, regarding children as an expensive but scarcely avoidable consequence of adult life and, properly, as entirely a woman's concern. He hadn't expected to love the children, hadn't expected the exhilaration of first holding Peter, small and scrunched, bundled in a blue hospital blanket, or the happiness he felt watching the child stalk around his playpen or bounce with strong and supple little legs on his cot. Life was full of surprises: He'd turned out to be a good father, a better father, in retrospect, than he'd been a husband or a lover.

Still wishing for a cigarette, Ross lay down on his bed. Leslie Austin hadn't remembered happiness. He'd changed the subject, denied her memory, and seen her doubt. When had he gotten bored? Not before Peter was born. He was still drunk then, drunk on lust, high spirits, and independence. And not when Peter was an infant, either. That had been a year of peace and contentment. No, it was a year or so later, when, lacking obstacles, passion was becoming commonplace, and to recover their original excitement, they'd had to resort to awkward couplings in the Buick or up behind the dairy barn.

Ross began flirting with customers again, and Kate, who had counted on passion in order to forget love—it was amazing, but he hadn't realized that at the time, hadn't taken her feelings into account—began to be out of the house, doing costumes for the local theater group and attending their meetings. She complained that she'd put on weight, and she used the proceeds of her part-time work at the newsstand to hire a neighbor's girl to watch Peter two afternoons a week. She spent those afternoons walking through the fields and over the old logging trails in the wood, returning home flushed and happy.

She had changed somehow. Ross sensed a new exuberance, an irrepressible gaiety that left her restless. Kate had fits of cleaning, cooking, and canning. Or else she put on her sunhat and worked for hours in the garden behind the house. Ross, who was experienced in romantic affairs, was uneasy, although his jealousy remained without a focus. Kate went to the drama group with their unimpeachable neighbor, Mildred Pawley, and returned the same way. The woods and fields were completely isolated. And yet, Ross was suspicious, and curious, and interested.

He could date the start of the new phase precisely: It was an October day when the trees were just starting to turn and there was a chill in the air, a proper fall feel. As he left the liquor store, Ross heard the sounds of football practice over at the Y and the higher-pitched voices of the field hockey squad. The heavy sky had a faint purplish tinge, and all those things, leaves and football and girlish voices and the first cool breath of fall, combined to make him feel restless and energetic. When he passed the Pawleys' house, he could have stopped to get Peter, but he drove on, impelled by the little hidden vein of excitement that had caused him to leave his assistant to close the shop and that now sent him tearing up over the hill and down the winding road.

The light was fading when he arrived, the house already shadowed. Ross got out of the car and stood for a moment in the yard. He could see that there were no lights on and that Kate's bike was still in the open garage. He took out his key, unlocked the door, and moved softly inside to listen to the scratch of a lilac branch against the front window, the rumble of the icebox, an early cricket. He quickly climbed the stairs. Their bedroom door stood open, the doll with the pink ruffled skirt that held Kate's nightdress placed neatly between the pillows. Ross felt a momentary embarrassment and returned downstairs. He started some coffee and stood looking out the kitchen window. The field still held the suffused autumn light that saturated the pale sienna grass, and then, vivid against it, Kate's red jacket and dark plaid skirt.

From his vantage point, Ross watched her secretly, as if they were strangers, as if he were an intruder and dangerous, a silly fantasy that pleased him, for even from that distance he sensed the gaiety that had suddenly become apparent and aroused him again. Now he thinks, was that all? Was that the only reason, or did he know even then? But these are darker waters, and Ross has learned not to fish for sorrow. That was all, he thinks, just the autumn after summer heat, just Kate's flushed, triumphant face, just the enveloping darkness. He heard her at the back door.

"Ross?" She'd seen the car or sensed his presence.

He stepped back from the window, and the bank of kitchen cabinets hid him.

"I'm here," he said softly and she jumped.

"Jesus, Ross! What on earth are you doing?"

"I was watching you," he said. "I was watching you walk across the field."

Kate laid her hand on her chest. "For God's sake! You could have given me heart failure."

"I thought I'd surprise you," Ross said, "and see if you were alone or if you'd found a boyfriend."

He was joking, of course, and she said, "Fat chance."

Ross touched her hair. It was thick and springy rather than soft, and he fancied he felt a few bits of dried leaves.

"Where's Peter? Didn't you pick him up?" Kate asked.

"We pay her 'til five," he said and stepped closer. A ripple of energy ran the length of his body to begin pounding in his ears.

"Stop it," she said. "I've got dinner to fix and Peter to get."

"Janet will bring Peter." He ran his hands down her back, over the sweet curve of her butt, down the narrow folds of her pleated skirt.

"They'll be here," she said, pulling away.

Her resistance excited him and made him stubborn. "Not for a while, not for a little while. Just a little while," he said. Her thigh was smooth and muscular, her waist supple, newly slim. He could smell the light, clean scent she wore and the feral smell of her hair, and something else like the urgent essence of fall, a compound of dry leaves, frosty air, woodsmoke. "Now," he said and kissed her and lifted her skirt.

Kate tried to wiggle from his grasp, but Ross was stronger, a foot taller. As they struggled, he could hear only their breathing, no other sound, not the clock, or the cranky, perpetually running refrigerator, or the cars on the road or the crows in the field, then he trapped her against the counter and began kissing her, rumpling her blouse, stroking her long, straight legs.

Her hands were against his shoulders, holding him back. She was angry, he knew she was angry, then he felt her muscles relax, felt her forearms fold back against her shoulders, felt her body against his and teetered on the edge of ecstasy.

"Darling," he said, "darling, darling, darling," before he lost control of his voice. She took a step toward their room, but the distance was impossible. He stumbled back into one of the kitchen chairs, pulled her violently down onto his lap and thrust them both, groaning, into the autumn darkness. He remembered that, and the fact the chair got bent and that later, when she untangled herself and picked up her white panties and turned on the fluorescent light, there was a moment when they were dazzled, when every object had a green and violet halo, when they looked and felt like strangers. Kate glanced at him and shrugged, and when he'd reached for her, she'd taken his hand and drawn it all up and down her body, so that he was late getting Peter and had to give Janet Pawley an extra two dollars.

After that, Ross often came home early on Mondays and Thursdays, the days when Kate had Janet to watch Peter. Sometimes he waited in the kitchen, sometimes up in their bedroom, once or twice, senses alert, out of sight in the garage. But he never went down the field to meet her; that seemed to be one of the unspoken rules. The other was the necessity of his insistence, of an insistence approaching violence, that would suddenly be rewarded with the submission and abandonment that excited him. In retrospect, it was all there and clear as day. He had traded honesty for pleasure, and simplicity for corruption, but at the time he had thought only of the excitement, violent, sweet, and vaguely dangerous, which lasted until Ruthie was born.

Or not quite. To be accurate, say that the dreamlike erotic excitement lasted more than a year until the day Kate came downstairs and announced her pregnancy. She'd been excited when they'd discovered Peter was coming; this was different. She seemed nervous, somehow. Unhappy, even. She resisted telling the grandparents and became so grumpy and difficult that Ross finally told her mother on the QT to keep Mrs. Birch from fussing.

"Oh, I should have known!" she exclaimed. "Natural as rain to be upset and touchy. She was just lucky the last time. Kate expects her life to be charmed," she added ruefully. "Though where she gets that notion is beyond me."

Ross smiled at this Old Country pessimism, the pathological caution born of centuries of predestination and frugality. Kate was lucky to have escaped that blight, though she had been quite ill after Ruthie was born. The doctor called it hormone imbalance and prescribed sedatives, but it was months before Kate recovered her vitality and humor. Ross had had much of the work with Ruthie, washed her, fed her, changed her, and that was perhaps the reason he had loved her best.

After Kate was well, they settled into a new routine, less intense, less demanding. Ross had an unserious affair with an assistant to a beer distributor, and Kate continued designing costumes, and sets, too, for the drama group. They adored the children, prayed and planned for them, and asked more for them and less from life for themselves, so that their parents nodded their heads and said that the young people were maturing, settling down. Then came the June morning when Ruthie disappeared, breaking the family circle and leaving them wounded forever.

Now here was Leslie Austin, this unexpected, late-delivered daughter with her shy eagerness, her quick intelligence, her touching—and trusting—candor. Ross found Leslie sympathetic. He saw that she needed a family, that she would blossom with attention, that she could close the circle and heal the all the wounds of anguish and despair. They'd failed the first time with Ruthie, failed despite love and care. Here was a second chance, and Ross was determined to take it. He wanted to keep Leslie with him.

"If I don't go back pronto," Leslie said, "I'll be a former journalist, not to mention, the ex–Mrs. Austin. Really, Ross, I promised Doug last night."

"I hate to see you go."

"And I hate to go. You and the family have been wonderful. I was half dreading this visit, and I certainly didn't expect Woodmill would be so much fun."

"You'll have to come back soon," he said. "You and your husband. You're welcome anytime. Anytime at all."

"I know that, dear. We'll come."

"We'll set a date," Ross said. He was an inveterate planner and organizer. "What about Labor Day?"

"That would be great," Leslie said wistfully, "but I'm not sure I can get enough time off. It's a long drive and over a holiday . . ."

"I'll send you a plane ticket. Fly into New York and drive up to Old Ashfen. We always go up around Labor Day to close the beach place we rent out. It's a nice-sized house, really. It used to belong to my great-aunt. How about that holiday weekend?"

"Oh, that's very kind, but it's really too much,"

"Not for my daughter," Ross said.

Leslie bit her lip and blushed with pleasure. "All right. It's a date."

She had, Ross thought, a truly radiant smile. That was something new—since she'd been in Woodmill. "Good," he said. Good she would visit, good she would be at the shore, good they'd all be together. "And you'll write?"

"Every week."

Ross laid his hand on her shoulder for a moment. "We'd better get going, then, if we're to see the old people."

"Do I look all right?" Leslie asked.

"Lovely as always," Ross said. It was true. Though Leslie had initially struck him as too thin and nervous, quite unlike his bluff, confident sons and grandchildren—and not much like his lively and vigorous wife, either—her personality had grown on him during the past week. On closer acquaintance, he found Leslie Austin a charming woman, attractive and sensible, who was handling a delicate situation with considerable grace and tact. "This town suits you."

Leslie took his arm. She felt that they understood each other.

"Grampa Birch is a little deaf," Ross said in the car. "He doesn't say much. Don't take it the wrong way. It's just him."

"What did you tell them?"

"Just that I had someone I wanted them to meet. See those silos? That was the farm Peter Birch used to manage. Owned by an agribusiness now. Smell it a mile away. He bought one of the tenant houses when the farm was sold and got rid of his place in the village. Felt he'd miss the cows. There, see those heifers? Those are his. Course, I don't think he figured on living to be quite this old. It's a little inconvenient this far out," Ross concluded as he turned into a blacktop drive leading to a small red house and a substantial gray-shingled barn. A dog neither collie nor shepherd nor Lab but with the traits of all three came out barking, and before its tail started wagging a tiny, plump woman appeared at the screen door. "Well, Ross! How are you?"

"Fine, Gram, fine. How was Michael's family?"

"Couldn't be better. And we saw the new baby, too. Such excitement. You'll have to see our pictures when we get them back." She smiled, her clouded eyes enormous behind the thick trifocals, and in that impression of warmth and vivacity, Leslie understood the impression her mother must have made. "Ross and I share a weakness for photos."

"A strength, Gram, a strength."

The old lady laughed. "Now, Ross, you were never one to keep a secret. Who's this young lady? Mildred Pawley's been bending my ear that you've been all around town for the last week."

"I'm Leslie Austin, Mrs. Birch. I'm visiting from Florida."

"Well, very glad to met you, I'm sure." She looked at Leslie, then glanced at Ross as if vaguely disturbed.

"Why don't we go in, Gram, and sit down for a minute? I've got those groceries you needed in the trunk."

"Oh, bring them in! With this heat! I hope you weren't looking to escape the hot weather on your holiday."

"No, I . . ."

"Leslie came up to meet us, Gram," Ross said as he opened the trunk.

"I'll take one," Leslie offered, and he handed her one of the heavy paper sacks.

"Ross is very good about doing shopping for us," Mrs. Birch said. "Peter doesn't drive as well as he used to."

"No need for him to drive at all," Ross said firmly. "The kitchen's through on the right, Leslie. Is Grampa around?"

"He's out in the barn. He'll be coming in. That dog lets him know when a car comes. He's got the eyes and I've got the ears," Mrs. Birch added confidentially. "I'm to go in for a cataract operation in the fall." They heard the sound of a door, and Mrs. Birch nodded. "That's Peter now. You'll need to speak up good or he won't hear a word."

"Hello, Ross, Miss." The old man was tall and thin. He had a good head of white hair and strong features, tanned like leather by eight decades of outdoor work.

"This is Leslie Austin, Peter." Mrs. Birch's voice was pitched just below a shout.

The old man came forward, extended his hand, then stopped with a look of surprise, almost alarm. "Who's this?"

"I told you, this is Leslie Austin. A friend from Florida."

Peter Birch turned to his son-in-law. "Who does she look like?" he demanded.

Ross nodded.

"I'm right? Don't you see it, Joan? Who is this girl?"

Ross laid his hand on Peter's arm. "I know this will be a shock, but Leslie and I both think she's Ruthie. That's what we think, what we believe."

"Oh," said Mrs. Birch, her eyes filling with tears. "Oh, Ross, I don't know. After all these years! We'd given up hope, you know, and after our Kate died . . ."

"Sit down, Joan. Sit, sit. Anything about Kate, the wife takes hard," he told Leslie. "You better tell us what this is all about, Ross."

Leslie studied their faces while he talked. The old man's was craggy and skeptical, his mouth a thin line, his hazel eyes embedded in a permanent squint from low morning light, sun on snow and hot days in hayfields. My grandfather, Leslie thought. I have a grandfather and this is what he's like: tall, thin, severe. Grandmother was just the opposite, short, stocky, warm. The old man sat rigid in his chair, straining to hear; she leaned forward to repeat Ross's words, her eyes darting between her son-in-law and Leslie, the emotions drifting across her face clearly visible in the lines of her lip and brow, in the faded but still expressive eyes.

As Leslie watched them and Ross, she felt the power of the family gathering around her, adding psychic authority and filling in the dangerous blanks of her childhood. This was what lay behind the meadow, behind June roses and motel rooms, behind prohibitions and forgetfulness: not horrors and mysteries, but a plain, square room with a tartan rug and flowered chairs, a tendency toward deafness and cataracts, a love of animals, a crusty stoicism, a friendly charm that eighty years had not erased.

When Ross finished, Leslie explained about her work and

about the news story, about seeing the paragraph mentioning the meadow come up on her screen. Ross flushed with anger as he always seemed to when she mentioned Flo, and Peter Birch angrily shook his head. As soon as she finished, he rose abruptly and left.

"Don't mind Peter," Mrs. Birch said. "Don't take him wrong. Talking about Ruthie—and Kate—always gets him upset. He'll want to think about it for a while. You know how he is, Ross."

"And you, Gram. What do you think?"

"I don't know. I can't see the resemblance except in the most general way. Are you satisfied, Ross? It's you that has to be satisfied in this."

"I am, Gram, I am. Everything fits. I've slept really well for the first time in twenty-five years just knowing Ruthie's back upstairs."

"Twenty-five years! It doesn't seem possible. She'd just had her birthday, her fifth birthday a couple of months before."

"That's right. We had it on the porch at your old house in town."

"I miss that old porch. Though I'd never manage that house now. Have you seen the old house?" she asked Leslie.

"Ross drove me by. It's a beautiful place."

"They've painted it up. Too fancy for me, but very nice if you can afford Lukas—he's the painter around now. Very good, but very high, don't you think, Ross?"

"I get Peter and Lyman to help me."

"And now your girl." The old lady's mouth trembled and she turned away. "Don't mind me," she said, wiping her eyes. "It's true, you get silly as you get older. But I think of Ruthie and then I think of Kate."

Leslie reached out and gently touched her arm.

"There's a good girl," Mrs. Birch said. "Are you staying for a while?"

"I have to go back tomorrow. There's my husband and my job."

"But you'll come back?"

"I've promised for Labor Day."

"There! That'll be nice." She patted Leslie's hand. "You were a real daddy's girl, wasn't she, Ross?"

"Yes."

"You wanted your mom when you were tired. Otherwise, it was all Daddy. He'd take you to the store sometimes, and you'd sit up on the counter and say hello to all the customers. Little devil!"

"That's right. I'd forgotten that," Ross said.

"I have some pictures," said Mrs. Birch. "If Leslie would like to see them."

"Please," Leslie said.

The old lady smiled when Ross brought over a brown leather book with a crumbling binding and thick, soft black pages.

"Recognize her?" A young woman wearing a long, full skirt and thick white socks stood beside a cow with a prize ribbon on its halter. One of the famous heifers, Leslie guessed.

"That's Kate."

"She wasn't anywhere as old as you then. She must have still been in high school. Well, I know for sure she was because that's Dahlia with her. Best in show in Springfield that year." Mrs. Birch turned another page. A dogwood in bloom and a small child in an untidy pinafore. She wore a curious expression, half mischievous, half sulky. Leslie thought that she looked a handful.

"Is that Ruthie?

"Yes. Oh, she could be an imp. She was what, Ross? Four?"

"I think. Gram, maybe I should go out and see Peter."

"Do that, Ross. He'll have some questions. Maybe Leslie has seen enough pictures, anyway."

"No," she said as Ross left the room, "we never had pictures at home."

"Never?"

"They were afraid to have pictures of me. Just in case."

"Your aunt, you called her 'Aunt Flo'?"

"Aunt Flo, yes."

"She was very wicked to have kept you, but she must have wanted a child very much."

"Yes," Leslie said. "More than anything."

"And she loved you?"

"Oh, yes. She and Uncle Mac. They were very good to me. I could never say they weren't good to me."

"Do they know about all this?" the old lady asked.

"Aunt Flo knows. Uncle Mac died three years ago."

"You must miss him."

"An awful lot. It was so sudden, too. Then I got sick—I had an ectopic pregnancy seven months ago—and I don't know what happened, but I started thinking a lot about the past. About what I could remember and what I couldn't and wondering why my memories didn't make sense. I thought first I was unsettled with being in the hospital and all, but underneath I think it was Uncle Mac's death."

"Losing someone you love turns the whole world over," Mrs. Birch said.

"You see, I don't remember anyone but Flo and Mac. Not really. I've never pretended to recognize Ross or anyone else."

"People change," Mrs. Birch said. "Over twenty-five years, people change a lot."

"What I remembered was the kitchen witch and the hardware store and Mr. Eddie."

"Mr. Eddie?"

"Eddie Vincenti who owned the—"

"Oh, that Eddie. He was such good friends of my Kate

and . . ." The old lady stopped and shook her head. "Funny you should remember Eddie."

"It was because he was so disfigured he frightened me."

"You can see the past in Eddie," the old lady said cryptically.

"That's what convinced Ross. When I remembered Mr. Eddie."

Mrs. Birch smiled again, a soft, sympathetic smile. "Go out and see Peter now. He will want to see you before you leave."

"All right. Thank you," Leslie said. "Thank you for showing me the pictures." She bent down and kissed Mrs. Birch's soft, wrinkled cheek.

"Your aunt," said the old lady suddenly. "Don't be too hard on her. People do terrible things to keep children. Terrible for themselves, too." Then she stood up, supporting herself on the broad arms of the chair. "Ask Ross if he could help me for a moment. I want him to look at my sewing machine. Neither Peter nor I can quite see to fix the needle."

"Yes, of course. Unless I can help you?"

"Better ask Ross. He's the pro. He threads my needle for me a couple of times a week, poor man. I can tell you it's an awful job getting old. Go out the back if you want. Right through there."

Leslie crossed a neat, sunny kitchen and walked out onto a little porch. The ever vigilant dog came from the barn, and Leslie watched it run back to Peter Birch and nudge his hand to announce her presence.

"That's a clever dog," she said after she'd passed on Mrs. Birch's request to Ross.

"Like dogs, do you?"

"Very much. All animals."

"This is Kristie. She knows I'm going deaf. I didn't need to tell her." The dog wagged her heavy tail and danced from one foot to the other.

"Ross says you still keep some cows."

"What?"

"Cows. Ross said you still keep cows."

"A few heifers is all. Just to keep me busy." He walked through the open barn and Leslie followed. A half dozen dainty Swiss dairy were grazing in a small pasture on the other side.

"Pretty," Leslie said.

"Good stock, those. I keep one cow for milk. My great-granddaughter, she likes the cows. She's always teasing me to let her milk. Does all right, too."

One of the soft-eyed animals leaned its head over the wire, exhaling steamy, grassy breath. Leslie touched its wiry coat. "In the house, you thought you recognized me," she said. "Is there really a strong resemblance?"

Peter Birch shrugged. "You see people, sometimes. They remind you, particularly if you're always looking. Always remembering."

"Yes."

"Ross is lucky to get his girl back," Birch said, dumping some feed into the trough. "Mine's gone forever." His face was closed.

Leslie said nothing.

He gave her a sharp, shrewd look. "Are you married?"

"Yes. For six years."

Birch studied her for a moment, and Leslie had the uneasy feeling that he was trying to tell her something important. Then he asked, "Did you marry happily?"

"Yes, very happily."

"That's the chief thing, to marry the right one. Nothing but trouble comes of marrying the wrong one."

He paused, and Leslie waited for him to continue, but he shook his head. "I've got work to do," he said abruptly, as he turned to refill the feed bucket from a heavy sack. "Though we appreciate your coming by."

. . .

"How'd you get on with Grampa?" Ross asked when they were back in the car.

"I don't know. I didn't get very far. He's not the easiest person, is he?"

"You said it. But he doesn't say much. That's a blessing."

"She's a sweetheart."

"Wonderful person."

"Did you ever get on with him?"

"To tell you the truth, not really. One of those men," Ross said. "No one would ever have been good enough for his daughter."

Of course, Leslie thought. She'd known people like that herself, and the idea that had taken shape in her mind as she talked to Old Peter seemed foolish. Just the same, she said, "He went on a bit about marriage. I began to wonder if he'd had someone in mind. From something he said about 'marrying the right person.' "

"That's Grampa," Ross said with a laugh that was not quite easy. "He had someone in mind, all right: the impossible ideal."

"And Mother?"

"Down-to-earth like Gram. I can tell you, you'd have to work hard to be unhappy around either one of them."

6

Leslie left Woodmill on a beautiful day. The heat had broken with thunder showers, and clear, cooler air lunged in from the north, dissolving polluted haze and leaving the sky a new washed blue. She put her arms around Ross for a moment, heard him say, "Don't be a stranger. Come back soon," then got into her car before she could start to sniffle.

"Labor Day," she called as she pulled out. "We'll see you in September." He was reflected in her mirror, a tiny waving figure, momentarily blurred with tears, then she tooted her horn and stepped on the gas.

Along the road, the fields had revived with the rain. The dust had settled, and the summer daisies and cornflowers opened their clean blossoms. Despite the emotion of leaving, Leslie was almost unrecognizably happy. To think that she had driven up these same roads with her heart in her mouth, eaten up with nerves and regrets! Now, in some sense, it all belonged to her: this pretty town, the lush pastures and heavy cattle, the old school, the green, the diner, even Mr. Eddie's, now Vincenti's, Mobil. Hers. She had looked into the past and found it good, full of kind, decent people. Ross was just the sort of father she'd have chosen, but Kate's parents were important, too, and Peter and Lyman and their families. Leslie paused at this thought and wished that she could have seen a little more of them, at least, a little more of Lyman and Judy and the grandchildren. Cindy had been nice, too; it was really just Peter who regarded her with resentment. Resentment? Was that right? Or was it suspicion? Or just the sometimes instinctive dislike one feels for a stranger? Leslie wasn't sure. Peter had something of Grampa Birch in him, that same taciturnity and severity. Still, she'd be silly to worry about Peter. She'd read all about sibling rivalry, which was normal and to be expected, "within the parameters," as her old Psych 101 prof used to say. It was no accident that she and Ross, both only children, had gotten along perfectly. She'd been an only child for most of her life, doted on by Aunt Flo and Uncle Mac. And before? Was there a dim memory? Of being chased about the yard, of screaming, falling? Of birthday candles illuminating a blond head, a child—a boy?—blowing out the candles, then the sweet taste of frosting, the metallic tang of Kool-Aid? Leslie felt recollection coming, emerging unforceable but also unstoppable like some biological process. She would remember. And maybe Peter would, too. They'd be a family; they *were* a family.

Yes! There was the road to the school, the new, modern building where she'd have gone to high school. And that bus ahead was the bus into Torrington, where she'd have shopped for school clothes and jeans and tie-dyed dresses, perhaps gone to work, or maybe to attend the local college. Leslie felt that she had a rich alternative life, another, perfected existence, which, along with the family, was a new and surprising source of strength. She was like her mother, it turned out, her mother after misfortune, but still a person of force and charm. Leslie hadn't realized that. She had seen herself along the lines of Aunt Flo, clever and hardworking but not really lovable or appealing; she'd seen herself as someone who would always have to struggle, someone without gifts. Then, suddenly, she had been given the greatest gift of all, the sense of possibility, and with it, Leslie intended to exorcise her ghosts.

The last time she'd left Woodmill, it was as Ruth Eden in an awful brown car with a cruel, sniveling imitation father. Like a bad elf, the man in the brown suit had taken Ross's place. He'd claimed to be her father. She remembered that. "My little girl! That's my little girl," taking over, insinuating himself, blotting out the truth—that was his real vice. "Don't say anything. Remember, not a word. They'll know right away you're lying." She must have denied this story, insisted on the truth. Athough her memory perversely refused to budge, the name must have been Ruthie. But "Ruthie" had been slapped away, dissolved by violence and by the hysterical tears that had shown her that the world was built on sand and lies. The awareness that nothing was safe, that nothing was as it appeared, had overwhelmed the truth and transformed everything. She was the man in the brown suit's little girl. That was how things stood, and, afraid to contradict him, she had said nothing.

Now in some dark particle of memory, the child sees that she was right: It was all deception. The man in the brown suit was weak and evil, but hidden behind him and the car and the motel rooms was her real family, strong and good and handsome. By the time Leslie reached the Florida state line and the "Welcome to the Sunshine State" signs, she felt she'd purged the terrors of that long ago journey. What she'd feared to discover was good after all, and anything was possible.

Even Doug was surprised by the change in her when she arrived home. Leslie swept in bubbling with enthusiasm, reminding him of when he'd first met her at the community college. "L. Simpson" had always looked fresh and athletic, with her short dark hair, slim, straight figure, and long, tanned arms and legs. No detail of her face or body struck Doug as particularly appealing—she was too thin, her face too angular, her chest too flat—but somehow the total ensemble seemed increasingly pleasing. And she was bright, too, almost intimidatingly clever. Later Doug understood that this was her professional personality: competent, witty, politely aggressive. After they fell in love, he saw less of this public face and more of her shy insecurity, her eagerness to please. But listening to her speak of Woodmill and the Edens, Doug had the uneasy sense that her mercurial personality might stretch to new, and unexpected, dimensions.

"It was wonderful," she said. "Marvelous. I couldn't have invented a nicer family."

"Yeah?"

He sounded skeptical, and Leslie wondered why she'd ever thought to say "invented."

"Aren't you glad?" she asked, for she was a person of words, and he never said quite enough to satisfy her. "Isn't it exciting?"

"I'm sure glad to see you," he said, putting his arms around her and nuzzling her neck. "You look well!"

And she felt well, full of energy despite the long drive. After moping around all spring she had recovered; she was really happy at last.

". . . should see the grandchildren. A niece and a nephew. So cute." She rattled on about the children, the grandparents, even the cows. The town was neat, the countryside pretty; she described Ross's liquor store and Mr. Eddie's garage and the family homes of several generations of Edens and Birches. She couldn't stop herself, though she could see Doug was bored.

As soon as he could, he brought up all the bits of family business he'd saved until her return. "I haven't paid any bills," he told her. "I didn't want to mess up the checkbook."

"I'll get to the checks tomorrow," Leslie said as her smile faded. She had so much to tell him, but though she knew he was glad to have her home, touchingly glad, he was not only not interested in Woodmill, but even a trifle jealous of Ross and the

Edens. She knew that intuitively, and, in fact, the time never was right to talk about them. Doug would always murmur a few platitudes and change the subject, so that though they were happy with each other and with her recovered health, certain things Leslie wanted and needed to tell him went unsaid or were shared instead with Betty and Marianne, who were as interested and curious about Ross and about Woodmill as Doug was indifferent.

In this way, her visit north, Ross's weekly letters and all they revealed and represented—a father, a family, a past—were pushed into the background, where they surreptitiously affected the texture of her life—and his. Doug did not want to see this, and his resistance provoked Leslie to raise the subject obliquely yet obstinately. She had embarked on a great adventure and wished company, needed understanding, craved reassurance.

"I really feel like a different person," she said one day. Doug had started making some long-promised bookshelves for the living room and was trapped there with his all boards and tools. "Having roots makes all the difference."

Doug gave a little sigh of irritation. Although he had seen the changes in her almost immediately, he had not wanted to recognize them, fearing, perhaps, that this new, more confident person might want things beyond his ability, might alter an otherwise perfectly satisfactory life. He knew that she was disappointed by his indifference, and the shelves—extra work in a busy schedule—were compensation, a peace offering. He didn't talk about that, though maybe he should have. What he said instead was, "It's not really going to change your life, Leslie."

"But it has! You don't understand. I feel as if I've come up to the surface, as if I've grown wings." She pivoted on one foot, causing Dylan to dig his claws nervously into her shoulder. "All those hidden fears were a weight, and now they're gone, erased."

"I'm glad," Doug said without looking up. He heard the excitement in her voice and realized what was bothering him. It wasn't her happiness—God knows he was glad to see her cheerful—but the nervous edge she had now, as if she was "on" like an actress, as if she was not only happy but acting the part of happiness, as if she, too, had to be convinced. He resumed sanding the board he was fitting. He wondered if she was as sure of the Edens as she pretended, and although he felt vindicated by the idea, he was anxious about her. He decided he'd trim the edges of the shelves and make them extra nice, though it would mean ripping the cherry strips and a certain amount of wasted wood.

Leslie stroked the cat and stifled her exasperation. She could feel her buoyant mood evaporating. "They're going to look super," she said.

"Do you like the cherry?" Doug asked so eagerly that Leslie felt a pang. She understood the shelves and this extra work on the weekend; they were used to communicating indirectly.

"I had just a little left from that restaurant refitting. I think maybe there'll be enough to trim the shelf edges, too." He stood up and traced a line around the frame. "I can use plywood for the shelves themselves so we can have nice deep ones."

"They'll be beautiful," she agreed. Doug had nice taste; he made all the important decorating decisions.

"Cherry is worth a small fortune now," he said.

Leslie smiled a trifle sadly. There was no way to say that she'd rather have had his attention, his endorsement of Woodmill, his interest in Ross. "I thought we might get some curtains, too," she said after a minute. "Now that wall will be finished."

"Blinds will be sufficient," Doug said, more positively than he'd intended. "We don't want a cluttered effect."

Leslie surprised herself by saying, "We'll see. Ross still has some beautiful curtains Kate made years ago. She was a professional seamstress; she made theatrical costumes. Think of that! I'm embarrassed I can hardly thread a needle."

Doug's silence informed Leslie that he was bored with Woodmill. She shrugged her shoulders. "I'll go down to the office," she said, "and get out of your way."

"You're no bother."

"But I should check some phone numbers. I'm doing a series on environmental hazards. The first part is going to be on septic system failures. You know that trailer park out in the Heron Bay area that's had all the trouble? I've been calling around, finding out how other towns have handled similar septic problems. Plus State Board of Health and so on."

"You didn't mention you were on coverage again."

Leslie detected a hint of reproach. Had she really forgotten to mention the new stories? She felt the now familiar anxiety that accompanied any memory lapse. "This is a special project," she said quickly. "It just came up. But Harvey says if I don't find any difficulties with the septic systems, I'm back on a beat, plus I'm to get to do regular features. They've liked the short articles I've been doing."

"And the names?" he asked.

"I've got my notebook. I just say, 'Let me double-check the spelling of your name,' and they spell it out. I've gotten only one Smith so far." She laughed and drew a faint smile from Doug. "Aren't you pleased you underestimated my value to the *Sun Coast Times*? Harvey thinks I show 'enterprise.' That's the word of the moment." Leslie put Dylan down, got her car keys, then stopped by the front door. "I'll pick up some chicken for dinner. Okay?"

"And ice cream. We're all out."

"I'll remember. The shelves will be great. See you later." She kissed his cheek and gathered up her purse and notebook.

Outside, the lawns were browning under the new water restrictions, and the air lacked the familiar sulfur smell of the sprinklers. Since she'd gotten home, Leslie felt that her powers of observation had sharpened, perhaps only because her perspective had changed. She belonged somewhere else now as well as here. She knew that other standards applied, other ideas were valid. References to Ross and to Woodmill annoyed Doug, because they suggested an entirely different set of opinions. Leslie realized that she'd made a mistake in mentioning Ross's nice curtains. But why not? Doug had too many opinions on trivial matters. She'd buy curtains if she felt like it and maybe today. There was a sale on in one of the fabric shops along the strip; she'd look on her way home from the office. And if she didn't find anything, she could consult with Betty and Marianne on Monday.

It was nearly six when Leslie returned. The worst heat was past, and on the way home she thought that they could go down to the beach after supper. Or maybe take a picnic. Now that she was feeling so much better, they should start getting out and doing things again. "Do you want to take the chicken down to the water?" she called as she dumped the assortment of boxes and containers on the counter.

"No. I want to collapse for a while."

The living room smelled of sweat and sawdust. Doug was sitting with a beer, looking hot and flushed. He was still in his work shorts, boots, and T-shirt.

"You finished the bookcases! I didn't think you'd manage all that today." Leslie admired the tall, well-balanced cabinets outlined with neat pinkish strips of cherry. She was always amazed how a formless pile of boards could be cut and arranged to form cabinets.

"Once I started, I wanted to get them finished. I still have some trim to put on. I'll maybe get to that tomorrow. I've got so many kitchens to do it's been hard to make time."

"They're perfect," Leslie said, "and I got the nicest curtains. Burgundy and a kind of browny-gold stripe. I know they'll just match the cherry trim."

"I think curtains look hot down here."

"You'll see, you'll like them," Leslie said, going into the kitchen. "I picked up some coleslaw, or do you want me to make a salad?"

"Whatever's easiest. What kind of ice cream did you get?"

"Ice cream? Oh, shit! I forgot the ice cream. Let's get cones on the way to the beach. It'll be cool there after supper."

"I don't know why the hell you can't remember a simple thing like ice cream," Doug said.

"I'm sorry, I left my list on the table."

"What's the point of making lists is if you don't take them?" Doug asked, and Leslie saw that he was really cross.

Once that would have upset her. Now she said, "So I forgot. I'm sorry, but it's no big deal. It's just ice cream. Death to the arteries."

"It's just something I wanted," he said, "but I see that's not important." He got out of his chair and went to rinse out the beer can.

"Doug, we can get some later. I'll go out after supper if you don't want to go to the beach."

"I don't know how you manage," Doug said, his irritation mixing with anxiety. "You can't seem to remember anything."

"I'm doing all right. You're just annoyed because I ordered curtains."

"Curtains were an unnecessary expense."

"But I want them. I've decided I like curtains and I can pay for them, too. What the hell's wrong with that? Just let's forget them and stop this silly arguing. I'm sorry about the ice cream, but don't go on about it."

"It's not the ice cream," he said. "It's that I worry about you."

"Then don't keep harping on my memory," Leslie said, angry in turn. "If you really worry about me, just shut up about my memory." She started setting the table, banging the plates down and rattling the cutlery.

"All you remember lately is stuff no one is interested in, like how things are done in Woodmill. I'm sick of the whole business."

"I suppose you never mention your family? I suppose I haven't heard Uncle Al's stories about the old farm in Pittsfield for the last hundred years. I suppose I haven't spent every holiday since we were married with your nearest three dozen relatives. You get sick of mine awfully easily."

Doug took a deep breath; he'd known this had to come, though he'd hated the thought of it. "That's just the point, Leslie. These people aren't your family. You've convinced yourself they are and convinced them, too, but it's all fantasy. It's just a fairy tale."

"What do you mean a 'fairy tale'?" Leslie cried. "What more do you need?" The humiliating realization that he'd never really believed, that he'd only been pretending, sent a hot pain running under her heart and up into her throat.

"How can you ask that when you're a reporter? You don't have a shred of proof. You got coincidence and some sort of family resemblance. What the hell's that?" Doug asked, his voice rising.

"I remembered Mr. Eddie. I knew the sign right away," Leslie said, regaining confidence as she spoke. "I've definitely been in that town. Definitely. And what I was told about him was just—"

"A few unreliable memories. None of those would ever stand up."

"You're talking as if this is a court case," Leslie said. She could almost laugh it was so absurd. Legalities and proofs had nothing to do with Ross and the Edens. She *knew*, she just *knew*.

"It could become one," Doug said, for the intensity of her emotion made him uneasy. He wanted her to face the situation. To be realistic. "Suppose this Ross dies. Which he will one day. You'd be an heir."

"I'm not interested in money, Doug! You know me better than that."

"Suppose he leaves you something anyway. Then you'd see how convinced your 'brothers' are. You'd soon find out."

"Maybe they are convinced," Leslie said, though his words stirred anxiety. "Ross believes. Lyman doesn't seem to have any doubts."

Doug shook his head. "I'm trying to protect you, Leslie! I see you building yourself up, I see how happy it's made you, but there's nothing behind it. Who is this guy? He's been looking for his daughter for twenty-five years. You show up. You 'remember' certain things . . ."

"God! You never listen! You've never wanted to hear, have you? I've tried to tell you about my trip. How many times have I tried? The kitchen. I walked into the kitchen and I knew, I knew what had hung in the window, I knew where the glasses were kept. I don't remember everything—who does?—but everything I remember fits."

"That's nice, but there's no proof. And Leslie, no one's going to trust your memory too far. It's not your fault, but your memory is no longer reliable, and anyone who wanted could soon prove that."

"It's good enough for me to work. I notice you don't complain about that," Leslie said. She touched her pocket and felt the car keys.

"I hope that will be all right for you," he said more gently. "You don't know how much I want for that to be all right."

She started toward the door.

"Now where are you going?"

"I'm going to get the damn ice cream."

"Never mind that. I'll do without ice cream. Sit down and eat dinner."

"I'm not hungry," Leslie said. "I'm not the least bit hungry now."

She slammed out the door and drove off. Near the park, she pulled over and wiped her eyes and blew her nose. Once she'd have started to cry at home and precipitated apologies and reconciliations. Now she drove to the store, bought the ice cream, and returned home dry-eyed. They'd never been in conflict before, mostly because pleasing him had trumped everything else, and she'd relied on him to fill up the emotional gaps in her life. Now she had an alternative. She wanted Ross and the Eden family, she wanted memories of her mother and of the past, and she was stubbornly determined to have them, though she could see that the price was going to be miserable quarrels over curtains and forgetfulness and ice cream.

It was after one of these disagreements that he told her she was different, that she wasn't the same at all. Leslie saw the justice of his remark. She wasn't the same, not the same as before she took ill, or the same as before she met Ross and the other Edens. She was different, for better or worse, and when the curtains arrived, very pretty, though perhaps more formal than was needed, she hung them up without a word. They framed the window between Doug's elegant bookcases, and every time Leslie looked at them, she thought of Ross and of her mother and of being different.

The tickets Ross had promised arrived in mid-August, and after supper one night, Leslie laid them out carefully on kitchen table. She'd carried them in her purse for three days, savoring the confirmation they represented and thinking how to convince Doug. "Our flight's to Providence," she said, as if they'd agreed on the trip long before. "Ross says going from Providence south is an easier drive than coming up from Long Island."

"You're going?"

"Of course, I'm going!" she exclaimed with the nervous gaiety he now recognized so well. "You know how I've been looking forward to this. And to your meeting the family. It's only for four days. Marianne says she'll stop and feed Dylan and bring in the mail. I know you can get away."

Doug looked dubious, although he could see that she was all set, with arrangements in place. He'd been dreading the trip and had secretly hoped something would arise to prevent what he feared could be a disaster for her. "I have two kitchens on order for just after Labor Day, and I think that new convenience store wants refitting."

"Please, Doug," she said, putting her arms around him. "I want you to go with me, please, for me. When you meet them, you'll feel differently. I know you will. You'll see for yourself why I'm convinced. Four days. It's not too much to ask, is it?"

"I want you to be happy, You know that, don't you?"

"I know. I've never doubted that, and I know you've been worried. But you've got no reason to worry. You're wrong about this. That's why I want you to go with me so much."

"I can't bear to see you get hurt." And that was true, although there were other emotions he would own less willingly.

"I just know you'll like them," Leslie insisted. "You'll see. I just know you will."

What he saw was that she would never give up; she had unsuspected reserves of persistence. What made the situation poignant was that he really wanted it all to be true for her. He could see that the discovery of the Edens had given her confidence and lifted her spirits, and eventually, he found himself agreeing, but on one condition. "If this doesn't work out, if for some reason you've been mistaken, that's it. Promise me that if you aren't Ruth Eden you'll accept the fact."

She kissed him, her mercurial spirits restored. "Of course," she said. "All I've ever wanted was to know the truth. But I don't have the slightest doubt. None at all. I just know you're going to like them; I just am so sure you're going to be convinced."

7

"It's a hell of a thing," Lyman Eden said. "A hell of a thing." But whether it was a good thing or a bad thing, he couldn't decide. He had feelings both ways, for it was the curse—and blessing—of his nature that he could see more than one side of an issue; in consequence, he was slow to make up his mind. Unlike his wife, Judy, and his brother, who were quick thinkers, counted as perceptive, Lyman was considered solid. If never brilliant, he rarely made mistakes, and, unlike the quicker members of the family, he usually knew when he didn't know enough to make a decision. Now he shook his head reflectively, looked over the salt meadow to the river, and said again, "It's a hell of a thing."

Peter raised his eyebrows, bit back his impatience, and took a drink of beer. Lyman was as bad as the old farmers at the corner store who could chew on an idea for a week.

Peter, Lyman, Cindy, and Judy were out on the back lawn after finishing the annual postrental cleanup. All the trash had been trucked to the dump, the beer cans and bottles sorted for recycling. Pastel towels and bedspreads hung half dry on the line, the old flower-pattern china had been counted, and, at last, the pots and pans were clean enough to pass Cindy's inspection. Before they left, they would put on the storm sash, drain the lines, and make everything tight for the winter, but, for the moment, all was in order. Ross had taken Jenny shopping with him, laying in some last-minute things for the party. Markie was asleep on the big porch lounge, and the grown-ups were standing out on the back lawn relaxing with a beer and waiting for Leslie and her husband to arrive.

"It would be worth our share," Cindy was saying to Judy, and Peter turned and glanced back at the two-and-a-half story weathered shingle structure: the "beach shack" of his great-great-aunt, the family gathering place of an earlier generation of Edens, now a piece of prime shoreline real estate, very rentable and very salable. His wife had her eye on it for a few weeks next summer, and if he weren't careful, she'd try for the whole season.

Cindy loved the water, felt the beach was good for the kids, and anticipated the cachet the holiday would give her with the other distributors' wives. Judy saw the drawback, namely the decline in the summer's three-way profits unless Peter and Cindy paid the going, and admittedly astronomical, rate. They were discussing this, amicably but persistently, going round and round, trying out the arguments they'd make to Ross. Cindy rested heavily on the benefits to the kids, who were, of course, nearest his dad's heart, but, with just the right degree of uncertainty, Judy was raising the prospect of more grandchildren, providing she and Lyman could afford a house. The necessity for their down payment nicely balanced the beach for the kids, and unsure which way the old man would decide, Peter took another sip of beer and caught his brother's eye.

"You know I've got the goods," he said, and Lyman shrugged.

Lyman hated arguments. He'd told Judy to handle the business of the beach house herself if she had any complaint. He was planning to tell Peter the same thing about Leslie Austin, though in fact his brother had already been taking care of that, "doing some background," as he put it, which made hiring a detective sound almost commonplace.

Out on the river a little sailboat tacked upstream, its blue and white sail floating mysteriously over the high marsh grass. Lyman wondered why his brother was so alarmed, so protective. "It's made Dad happy," he said after a moment. "Can't you see the difference in him, Peter?"

"You sound as if you don't care whether she's Ruthie or not."

"Do you?" Lyman asked.

"Of course I care. Do you want some stranger . . . ?"

"Anyone would be a stranger after all this time," Lyman said reasonably. "I never knew her at all. You were seven. What do you remember?"

"I remember Ruthie, all right," Peter said. "And I remember what happened after she was gone."

"That was hardly her fault."

"I'm not blaming anyone," Peter said, though at some level he knew he did. Someone was surely to blame for the frightening loss of all his childhood security, but he didn't know how to explain that to Lyman. Only he and his father knew about that. "I just don't want anyone taking advantage of Dad."

"Dad's pretty shrewd," Lyman said. "Like you, Peter."

"What's that supposed to mean?"

"Nothing," Lyman said. "Just that he can take care of himself and you'd do well to stay out of it."

"The business will affect us all. Take this place that Cindy and your wife are dickering over. You, Dad, and I each get a third of the summer rental, minus upkeep and taxes."

Lyman nodded.

"Prepare to get a quarter next year."

"If she's Ruthie, she deserves it," Lyman said, though the couple thousand every fall was very welcome.

"If! Now you've hit it, little brother. *If!*" Peter said, raising his voice. Lyman wondered how many beers he'd had and whether he was planning to say anything to their father.

"Dad's convinced," Lyman said, for he had a stubborn streak under his good nature.

"Dad's been looking for Ruthie for twenty-five years."

"There were others. He thinks Leslie's the one. Though she's never claimed to be."

"She's just more intelligent than the others. More subtle."

"He's been waiting for this for a long time," Lyman said, and Peter swore softly, a characteristic reaction. Peter had been nine when Lyman was born. Too old to be a playmate, he had been a frequent guardian and occasional tormenter, scarcely distinguishable in the younger child's perspective from other adults. They had never been close, though their relations were generally friendly.

"That doesn't make her the one."

"Haven't you been waiting for her? Thinking she might show up one day?" Lyman asked, curiously.

"No," said Peter, though that had been one of the horrors of his childhood. Somehow he had always assumed that any "Ruthie" would be alien, a stranger, a danger.

"Never?"

"I've always assumed she was dead," Peter said. His face had gone rigid in the low, evening light, and Lyman felt the shock of a sudden shift in perspective.

"Always?"

"Yes," said Peter, walking abruptly away. Lyman heard him break in on the women's conversation, joshing them both, scattering their polite but determined arguments over next summer's rentals.

Lyman thought about his brother and then turned to study the golden light on the marsh and to wonder why his dad held on to the place. Certainly the property was picturesque and comfortable, even beautiful on a night like this, but Lyman never

enjoyed coming, remembering always fear and grief and the precipitous end of peace and security. In Peter's few words about
Ruthie, he understood that his brother felt the same way, that the
jollity with which Peter "managed" the yearly cleanup was false,
conspiratorial.

Yes, Peter and his father conspired each year to come here;
they brought the family and made a party of it, as, in the early
years, they had made a wake. For what reason? Lyman remembered his father weeping, remembered him, as if it were yesterday, kicking and hurling a red gasoline container across the yard.
Now, though they never used the house but rented it as often as
they could, they returned as a family every Labor Day.

Behind him, the women were laughing. Lyman heard his
brother's voice, jolly, lighthearted. Peter had a thousand moods
available to him, which was why people said he was such an
excellent salesman. He was the successful one; he'll be rich,
Lyman thought. And then, clearly and unmistakably, he had the
answer to his question: They'd come here in hopes of Ruthie.
They'd come for remembrance and, perhaps, for other reasons
known only to Ross, but Lyman suddenly knew for sure that
they'd come for Ruthie, and the idea gave him a queer little
chill.

He went over to the group on the porch steps and laid his
hand on his brother's shoulder. "Don't say anything just yet," he
said.

"About what?" Judy asked.

Lyman hesitated, but Peter said, "About Leslie."

"Peter's not convinced."

"This isn't the time, I don't think," Cindy said. "We're going
to have a nice weekend. For Ross and the children." She glanced
at Judy, her opponent a moment before, who nodded without
hesitation.

"For Ross," she said, "the best father-in-law a girl's likely to
have."

"Oh, there's Ross now!" Whenever he took Jenny or Markie out in the convertible, Cindy was on the alert for its return.

Ross pulled the big Buick onto the gravel. Over his shoulder, Jenny stretched her arm out the window to touch the rampant Dutchman's-pipe that grew along the fence. "Leslie's right behind us. We saw her at the gas station. Damn rental car wasn't filled. I told her to follow us back. Come on, Princess," he said as he unfastened Jenny's belt.

"Did her husband come?" Cindy asked.

"Yes, you'll see him in a minute. Got those cookies, Princess?"

"She'll have eaten half of them," Peter said, picking up his daughter and giving her a hug. Her large eyes were close to his, very bright and dark, and he could not help thinking that she was just his lost sister's age. Just precisely. He could smell the sugar and chocolate on her breath, then her sharp ears detected the car, and she scrambled down before it slowed for the drive. His father smiled and waved, directing the rented compact onto the grass next to his own car.

"Just barely room when we're all together," his father said. "No, don't mind the lawn. The summer tenants don't. Hello, dear. Good to have you here. And Doug. So glad you could come."

Leslie Austin climbed out of the car and gave Ross a hug. She was wearing white pants, a blue and white striped shirt, and a white hat that set off her brown face and arms.

"You're looking well," Judy said. Leslie had put on some weight. She looked more relaxed, more confident.

"This is Doug. Judy, Peter, Lyman, and Cindy."

Doug was big and good-looking and very tanned; solid, was Peter's impression, rather like himself, his dad, and Lyman, the same type. But that was coincidence, meant nothing. He nodded to Leslie, shook her husband's hand, and listened while Cindy asked about their trip and about the heat wave down south. Then his father marshaled everyone for drinks and snacks and ordered the fire on.

Peter went over to the tiny brick patio where they had set up the cooker. A little apart from the others, Leslie Austin was talking to Jenny, kneeling down to see something the child was holding, and he heard her say, "We'll let it go, all right?" before the butterfly or moth, whatever it was, rose in a drunken spiral, righted itself, and sailed off toward the marsh with his daughter after it. Peter dumped the briquettes into the cooker and poured lighter fluid over them. Talking about Ruthie and the past had disturbed him, bringing back unwelcome memories of the plague of reporters, policemen, and other, vaguely frightening, investigators who had devoured their hearts. Peter remembered the agonizing suspense and anxiety, and he remembered how he'd protected himself, at last, by deciding Ruthie was dead. The conviction of her death had insulated him from his parents' tragic, destroying hope and kept him sane.

"This is a lovely spot," Leslie said as she came over toward the cooker. "The marsh is beautiful."

"We were lucky," Peter said. "Wall-to-wall marinas farther down, but the Nature Conservancy and the state bought up most of this marsh for wetlands protection."

"Do you come here often?"

"Once a year after the rentals leave."

"I'm surprised Ross doesn't use the house more now that he has an assistant in the shop," Leslie remarked, and Peter realized that she didn't know.

"We used to come when I was a kid," Peter said.

Leslie felt a little twinge of anxiety. "I don't remember this at all," she admitted.

"It was after," Peter said. "We only got the house when Dad's aunt died. Then we came regularly in the summers and for weekends until Mom's death."

"Was she the one who liked the water?"

"Yes," Peter said, poking at the coals. "She died here. Drowned out in the cove." He saw the shock on Leslie's face. "Didn't you discover that in your researches?"

"I knew it was an accident; I assumed a car crash."

"Our local paper can be very circumspect." Peter's faint smile was both sad and unpleasant. "I'd better get the dinner orders. Who wants what?" he called, his voice hearty again. "Hot dogs, hamburgers?"

"Don't forget the bluefish. Fresh today. We don't want Doug and Leslie to think New England doesn't have fish," Ross said, coming over and putting his arm around Leslie.

"I'll try the fish," she said, though the news of Kate's drowning had squelched her appetite and recast the whole meaning of the beach house and of their invitation.

"That's how you stay so slim," Cindy teased.

"We've laid in plenty of other temptations," Ross said.

"I see you and Jenny stopped at the bakery."

"We did. But that's a surprise."

"I hope you remembered some of those citronella candles, too," Judy said.

"Judy hates bugs."

"The mosquitoes were as big as hornets last year."

"A rainy summer, last year."

"The candles are on the kitchen table," Ross said.

"I'll get them, can I?" Whenever Leslie got nervous, she was anxious to be doing something useful. "I'd like to see the inside of the house, anyway."

"It's a fine old beach house," Judy said. "I'll show you your room and the lav, and we'll get the mosquito protection. Where's your bag?"

"I think Doug put it inside." She looked around to see where he'd gone.

"He and Lyman are already into repair work," Judy said. She

nodded toward the garage, which had suffered from the soccer-playing children of the last tenants. The two men were inspecting loose panels on the overhead doors, and both women recognized their expressions of skeptical regret.

"This way for the tour," Judy said, opening a heavy screen door that led directly into a well-proportioned but old-fashioned kitchen. Leslie saw at a glance how spectacular it could be with some of her husband's cabinets, and Judy read her look.

"Potentially gorgeous, right? A million-dollar view over the dinosaur." She slapped an old cast-iron sink, and Leslie took in the dark green linoleum, the gas stove, and metal cabinets.

"Nice pantry, too, but not up to modern standards," Judy continued. "The living room's through there. A bit dark, but cozy at night."

"When Ross said 'beach house,' I imagined something quite simple."

"It was the rich aunt's. Needs a bit now."

"I hadn't realized Kate died here," Leslie said as they went upstairs. "Peter mentioned it rather mysteriously in passing."

"Taboo topic: a boating accident. I don't know if you noticed the little dock on the marsh. They used to keep a rowboat with a kicker. Some of the tenants bring their own dinghies or those rubber things, but Ross won't have a boat around permanently. Not with the kids. You and Doug are in here." Judy opened one of the doors. "You can see just a glimpse of the water from the windows."

The large, square room had a high ceiling and two long windows that looked over the street and the shingled roofs of the neighboring houses to a line of rocks and a blue green sliver of the Sound. "How nice!"

"Spartan but clean. Finally. Kids and a dog." Judy rolled her eyes. "Bathroom's across the hall."

"I'll just get washed up," Leslie said. "And get a sweater. This feels cool after the heat at home."

From downstairs, they heard Ross calling, "Corn to be shucked!"

"We're all disorganized, because we were cleaning most of the day," Judy said. "We never know how much has to be done until we get here." She hurried down the stairs, her sandals slapping the treads. Markie had woken up, too, and was crying for his mother, while out on the lawn, the men were gathered by the garage, drinking and talking over the upcoming election. Leslie stood for a moment, listening to their voices, then went into a bathroom as old-fashioned as the kitchen, splashed some water on her face, and washed her hands.

"The late Kate Birch Eden" was how Ruthie's mother had been described in the twenty-five-year anniversary story that had mentioned "Mrs. Eden's tragic accident some years after her daughter's disappearance." Leslie had assumed an automobile crash; a careful reporter would have checked. Though she'd been quite ill at the time, Leslie knew she should have checked.

But it was odd, just the same. Ross had told Leslie more than once how much he wished Kate were alive to see her. He'd certainly talked about his wife, though Leslie realized he'd never mentioned her death. "A taboo topic" Judy called it. Yet he'd wanted Leslie to come to the cottage. She ran her finger along the stained porcelain of the basin and realized uneasily that she and Ross and the boys were family and strangers simultaneously, with the drawbacks, as well as the advantages, of each.

"They're nice, aren't they?" Leslie asked. The old floorboards creaked under her feet, as she moved restlessly around the room, brushing her hair. She wasn't ready to go to sleep. Dinner had been a great success, and afterward they'd sat around the living room and talked and even Peter had seemed cheerful and friendly. Leslie wanted to memorize the exact texture of the day, the blend of family voices, the evening light on the grass, and now the cool breeze that brought the rhythm of the surf and stirred all the faint evocative sounds of the house.

"Nice enough," Doug said. He did not meet her eyes but concentrated on the old and ornate cornice and on the good oak casework around the windows. "Nice enough."

"Now, you liked Lyman. I saw you two talking outside."

"Knows his business," Doug agreed. "The best of the bunch."

"Except for Ross," Leslie said quickly.

"He's pleasant, too." In fact, Doug had been quite taken with Ross, who seemed bluff and good-natured, a man with both feet on the ground, despite having supported Dukakis. He had enlisted Doug and Lyman for an inspection of the shed and the garage and had listened to their advice as if he might take it, unlike so many clients, who listen with one ear and are deaf to any constraint. A sensible man. A man Doug would probably have liked had it not been for the aberration that had brought them there, the conviction of Leslie's paternity.

"I like Judy," Leslie was saying.

Doug made a noncommittal sound and muttered something about a sharp tongue.

"But friendly. And Cindy, too." The wives, for some reason, had been warm and accepting from the first.

"Mmmmmh," said Doug. He was not a talker. His ideas took a different form altogether: perfect angles, neatly cut dovetails, matched veneers, smoothly rolling drawers, a certain balance and proportion.

"Don't you think Cindy's nice?"

"Better her than her husband." Peter Eden, with his bland expression and calculating eyes, was trouble. Doug wasn't sure whether Leslie saw that and refused to admit it or had just closed her eyes entirely. But Peter Eden was an enemy, and that disturbed Doug, because, basically, he agreed entirely with Peter: The whole dubious business should never been undertaken.

"He's cautious, that's all. He wants to protect his father. And Peter was there when Ruthie disappeared."

Doug noticed Leslie didn't say, "I disappeared." Though she was convinced, he could see that. She was convinced, but she kept everything compartmentalized, before as Ruthie, now as Leslie, so that no contradiction would appear.

"I'm sure he'll come round," Leslie said. In the euphoria of the evening, she was willing to overlook her uneasiness with Peter. "He seems a fine person."

"They're all nice, all fine people," Doug said. "Nobody's saying anything else."

"I know I don't look much like them. I took after Kate. But you've seen the pictures. You know."

Doug let his eyes slide along the molding. All one piece; he'd checked. Today that would be custom work, five, six dollars or more per foot.

Leslie came and sat down on the bed, and Doug realized she needed an answer.

"Sure," he said. "There's a resemblance. If you're satisfied, I'm satisfied."

"I'll never know the family as they know it, of course. From the inside."

"You know another family," Doug said.

"There's too many of yours," she said, half joking.

"I meant Flo and Mac. You knew them."

Leslie stretched her arms over her head. She didn't want to think about Flo and Mac. She felt grief for Mac and a disturbing mix of resentment and remorse for Flo. No, she wouldn't think about them; she intended to start fresh. "I don't want any more big secrets," she said. "You know, I was always afraid. Afraid of being noticed, as if I was the one who'd done something wrong and had something to hide. I was afraid that the man who claimed I was his little girl would come back. I always felt I had to be so good to keep him from coming back."

"The Edens will have their secrets, too," Doug said.

Leslie was silent for a moment then said abruptly, "Kate drowned out in the cove."

"Drowned? What happened?"

"I don't know. Taboo topic, Judy tells me. That's why they rent the house. Bad memories."

"But they come back every year. Right? This is the policy, back to close the house?" He already knew the answer. Lyman had described the once-a-year cleanup and family get-together as "a serious favor for the old man."

"This annual family party is important to Ross for some reason." As she spoke, Leslie understood that Ross had wanted her to come north because there were sad memories that she was to counteract. The fact of her presence was to be set against sorrow, as she set the fact of the Edens against the sinister mysteries of her childhood. Yes, she understood, that was it. "It's important for him that the whole family's together. As it's been important to me."

"And me?" Doug asked. "Where do I fit in with all this?"

Leslie heard his resentment and anxiety but was gifted with the right answer. "You'll have a wife who isn't frightened anymore." She smiled at him and caught the hand that was idly stroking her hair and nipped his fingertips with her small, even teeth.

"Hey," said Doug. He rolled over and put his face against her neck. Leslie felt his warm, strong torso, the heavy muscles of his back, the wide sprung ribs, and the strong, bony shoulders and laughed as softly as a purr. "You'll see," she said, kissing him. "You'll see you'll like them."

"Hmmm," said Doug, and he began fiddling with the buttons of her shirt.

"And Connecticut. You'll like Connecticut."

"I like Connecticut already," Doug said. "I especially like Connecticut."

Leslie laughed again and ran her hands across his chest and belly. This was new. If much in love with him, she had long been shy and nervous in bed, often physically indifferent. Though she'd hidden that quite well, well enough to please him. And perhaps he'd like comforting her, protecting her; perhaps he'd like that sense of power wedded to kindness better than anything, better, even, than pleasure.

8

Outside, Ross could see the dark and light pattern of moonlit marsh, houses, and trees. He heard Markie whimpering fretfully between sleep and waking, the quick sound of Jenny's feet in the corridor and her mother's warning, the murmur of voices from Doug and Leslie's room, someone coughing, then the night sounds of the house dwindled to the soft creaks of old walls and floors. A car passed out on the street with a burst of rock music, leaving behind a deeper silence, gradually filled with crickets, a cicada, and the sound, so soft as to be almost subliminal, of surf breaking on the rocks of the cove.

Hidden during the day under the noises of the house and street, the surf was audible only at night, and though Ruthie was back to show Kate's unquiet ghost that he'd been right not to despair, the sound stirred uneasiness. He'd watched Peter talking to Leslie before dinner, seen her face change, known that Peter had said something unpleasant. Peter blamed Ruthie in some way, Ross knew, yet it was when Ruthie disappeared that their happiness went, and even Lyman's arrival couldn't restore it. Just the same, Ross and Kate had hung on for four whole years, hurting each other with unspoken resentments and regrets, bound together in sorrow and fear, comforting each other, and trying to be kind. And then came the late August day, the day the surf recalled, the day he returned each year to remember.

Ross had felt trouble coming from the moment he got up, just as you can tell a storm approaching by a feel in the air, a change in the wind, the pale undersides of the leaves. He complained that they were short on bacon, scolded Lyman harshly for some trifle, contributed, in short, to the unstable atmosphere that finally broke after lunch.

Peter had already gone off to join the long-running summer baseball game when Kate sent Lyman outside to play, put the last of the dishes in the sink, and said, "This can't go on. It's killing us both."

"Don't make a fuss over nothing," Ross said, though he knew she did not mean the trivial misunderstandings that had plagued the morning.

"I'm thirty-four, you're thirty-seven. It's not too late for us to start fresh. I think we should, no matter how hard it is. For us. For the boys."

"Is there anyone else?"

"Don't be crazy."

"Is it so crazy?"

"There isn't anyone," she said.

She threw the dishrag into the soapy water and sat down on one of the kitchen chairs. Ross could rarely remember Kate being tired, but that day she'd looked exhausted despite her golden summer tan. "I can't go on like this. We're miserable, snapping at each other, at the kids. We've tried, God knows, but it's not going to work. We're always . . . thinking, blaming, wishing. That's not all in my head, is it?"

"No," he said.

"Well, then, that's it. I want a divorce."

He remembered the shock, though he had thought of it more than once, himself. "No," he said.

" 'No,' you won't give me one? I might have grounds. That woman from Mills Furnace you were seeing last year. I'll do it, Ross, I want to get away."

"You can 'get away,' but I want the boys."

"The boys! How can you take care of the boys?"

"How can you support them? Unless there's someone else. In which case, I'm definitely keeping them."

"They wouldn't give them to you! They couldn't!"

"They might. Fitness is important." And then he said the unforgivable thing. "After all, Ruthie was in your care. She was in your care that day when . . ."

Kate jumped up, dead white, and Ross remembered her eyes, wild with grief and anger. "She was gone in a minute! There was nothing . . ."

"There had been."

"Before! Before she was born! I gave up everything when Ruthie was born. Everything in life!"

"So there was someone?"

Kate's voice was bitter. "You knew. And you knew before. It suited you. All along, it suited you. How I despised that!"

Her face was close to his.

"You could have gone then," he said. "If he'd wanted you."

She swung her hand and struck him in the face, hard enough so that he grabbed her wrist to keep her from striking him again.

"You could have said something! You can't blame me for everything!"

"I didn't dare lose Peter," he said.

"But Ruthie was always your favorite. Didn't you ever think that—"

"Ruthie's gone," he said before she could finish. "I'd have settled for Ruthie, but if you go, I'm keeping the boys."

"Never," she said, pulling free. "You'll see." She tore out of the room and ran upstairs.

In the sudden silence, he heard Peter and his friends playing ball in the field beyond the Beamons'. Lyman was in the big, damp sandbox below the porch, sharing his trucks and cars with the little girl from across the street, and when Ross stepped out into the sultry heat, the children were so ostentatiously busy that he knew they'd heard everything.

Furious, he stamped down to the garage, threw up the door, and grabbed the power mower. He jerked the cord and the engine coughed and choked before sputtering out. After several more tries, he thought to check the gas tank, which was empty, as was the can in the garage. Swearing under his breath, Ross felt for his car keys, before remembering the container in the rowboat. He'd filled the kicker the previous day, and there should be plenty for the engine until they could get more gas.

He took the container out of the boat, filled the mower and tugged it to life, then engaged the gear and swept toward the house, around the sandbox, across the wide lawn and down toward the weedy patch that bordered the marsh. The harsh sound of the machine scattered the neighbors' cats as he descended and, along the bottom of the yard, flushed redwings from the reeds. Ross shifted the motor higher and turned back toward the house, the deafening racket apt for his anger.

It was only when Lyman stood and waved that Ross looked up from the two-toned green swath he'd been cutting to see Kate throw the oars up onto the dock and start the engine. She was just turning the boat when he remembered the gas can and gestured toward where the container sat near the garage. Kate did not slow up, but pulled away in a rolling wash and disappeared onto the river. When Ross completed his circuit and reached the house again, he called to Lyman, "Mommy say where she was going?"

"To see Nancy."

Nancy and Hal Fairchild lived on the far side of the cove. Hal was away all week in the city, and Nancy and their three children often went swimming with Kate and the boys.

"Uh-huh," Ross said, but he was thinking that Nancy Fairchild was a meddling bitch, that she'd paint him in the blackest hues, that she was the sort who'd know lawyers and have advice. This was all her influence, her fault, and when four o'clock came and then five, Ross felt his anger building. At five-thirty, he announced that they were going out to the Clam Box to eat, and it wasn't until the metallic sky darkened, the wind got up, and big round drops of rain rattled down on the windshield and sidewalks, that he began to feel uneasy. Lyman had been fussing about eating without Mommy and now his anxiety was transferred to the rest of them. As soon as Ross got the kids home, he called the Fairchilds, but the phone rang unanswered. They've all gone out to eat, he thought. He kept calling every half hour or so, anyway, and when Nancy Fairchild picked up the phone at eight-thirty, he heard the anxiety in his own voice.

"Nancy? It's Ross Eden."

"Oh, Ross! Did Kate get home all right?"

"That's why I'm calling. What time did she leave?"

"Five. A little later, I guess. Don't tell me she's not back!"

"Did she take the boat?"

"I wanted to drive her home, but she said she'd be just as quick by water. It didn't start to rain here until six. I was sure she'd have gotten home all right."

"I'm afraid she may have run out of gas, and she left the oars on the dock. I'll get the car and take a run along the cove."

"Better come get our boat," Nancy said. "If she's run out of gas, that'll be the best way. And bring the kids over if you want."

"Yes," Ross said. "That's a better idea." He thanked her and put down the phone, recognizing the stiffness, the mental slowness and distance that signaled disaster. He remembered that from Ruthie, but desperate to evade fatality, he bustled around with the kids, bundling Lyman into his little yellow slicker and sou'wester. "We'll go find Mommy. She'll be as mad as a wet hen in that boat," he joked.

Lyman had never heard the phrase "mad as a wet hen" before. He repeated the phrase three or four times, stamping around the kitchen in his shiny rubber boots and laughing. Peter's face remained white and still, and when Ross put his arm around the boy, he felt him draw away.

"Your mom will be okay," Ross said. "A little rain won't have bothered her. She's good with the boat."

When they got in the car, Ross drove fast, sending up sheets of water from the narrow, poorly drained streets. The main road led north to the highway that crossed the river a couple of miles upstream. On the bridge, Ross looked south into the gray sheets of rain, the murky river, the slate band of the Sound. "See anything?" he asked. Their breath fogged the windows, and Ross felt his bare arms slippery under his rain gear. He rolled down the window partway, bringing in a cool gust of rain and wind.

After the bridge, he turned south, peering through the water sluicing off his windshield for the track that ran along the river's edge to the cove. Ross slowed the car so that they could watch the river's current roiling slowly but powerfully under the rain.

"Are you watching? Are you looking for the boat?" Ross demanded. "I've got to keep my eyes on the road. You guys have got to help."

"We're looking, Dad," Peter said.

"I'm looking for Mommy!" Lyman's voice mixed defiance and despair.

"We're going to have to look around the cove," Ross said.

What a fool he was not to have called the Weincrouses and the Potters. They lived right on the cove. And that red-haired woman, Sue something. Kate knew her as well. Maybe Nancy would know. Ross felt rain and sweat running down his face and rubbed his sleeve to clean the condensation off the window. "When we get to the Fairchilds', you call some of the people around the cove," he told Peter. "You know them all, don't you?"

The boy nodded.

"She may have stopped somewhere along there when the rain started."

Peter didn't reply for a moment, then said, "She would have called."

"We were out. You know the phones around here. In bad weather." He gave his son an anxious look, but the boy was staring straight ahead. "Watch the water, for God's sake! I can't do everything."

"I'm watching the water, I'm watching for Mommy," Lyman cried from the backseat. He started to sniffle, then thought he saw the boat so that Ross's heart lurched before he and Peter realized that it was a much larger powerboat. Even that was rocking and bouncing, and the chop would be worse on the cove.

Ross stepped on the gas and raced through the little crooked roads that wound around the headland to the Fairchilds' house. Nancy was on the porch with an umbrella when he pulled up, and she stepped off to shelter Lyman and Peter.

"I feel so bad I didn't call," she said. "We went out to eat right after Kate left. I never thought."

"I'm going to get Peter to call some of the people along the cove," Ross said. "She may have gone in."

"Oh, she might have! Along the other side there. Is it the Bremans? In the white house?"

"I think so. Nancy, can I take your boat?"

"Yes, I told you so on the phone. But in this?"

"It's wet but not that rough. If she ran out of gas, she'll be drifting around the cove."

"And the Coast Guard? Should we call?"

"Not yet," Ross said, hating the thought of real seriousness: He was still half envisioning Kate stuck with the empty motor on the cove "mad as a wet hen."

"If she's drifted farther out," Nancy said, "we'd better to call at once. If she's drifted into the Sound."

"All right, then, call them. But I want to take the boat out now."

He felt it would be unendurable to be in the house, to listen for the phone ringing, to feel Nancy Fairchild's mixture of sympathy and suspicion. He hugged Lyman and touched Peter's shoulder. "Make those calls," he said and walked down through the long, wet grass and wild scrub roses to where the boat was tied up at a concrete jetty.

Ross bailed out the bottom, half full of rainwater already, lifted the rock anchor, and set the oars. He'd pick up Kate and tell her that he loved her, that he thought they could go on, that they owed it to Lyman and Peter. They would row back together, and all would be well in the end.

But with the rain running down his face and blowing in his eyes, Ross soon realized that without a motor his search was crazy, that visibility was nonexistent, that he could pass within yards of Kate without knowing. He rested on the oars and began to shout her name against the wind that was blowing and swirling over the water, bringing now the wet, shishing sound of rain on water, now the boom of surf on the rocky islets at the head of the cove. He shouted until his voice was raw, then came back, drenched, to face dismay and desolation. The Coast Guard had been alerted, and Nancy had thought to notify the local police, one of whom, stopping for a quiet smoke on the south bank access road, finally spotted the boat, drifting out toward the Sound. When they brought it in to shore, the boat was found to be empty; the kicker out of gas.

"Was there no auxiliary supply?" the policeman asked Ross.

It was ten minutes to midnight. The rain had finally stopped, leaving the sandy road wet as a sponge, the air close and dank. He and Peter were standing shivering at the water's edge, talking to the patrolman and to a plainclothesman who'd been called over from town.

"I borrowed the can for the mower. I didn't know Kate would be taking the boat out."

Police lights illuminated the sandy track strewn with sodden tissue paper, the occasional bottle, the varied debris of fishermen and lovers. Across the mist and darkness of the cove, the Fairchilds' lights twinkled faintly. Ross had left Lyman asleep on the couch, and he had a vivid image of the child cocooned in the orange light, wrapped safe from all worldly harms in Nancy Fairchild's purple afghan. He wished that Peter were there, too, safe and asleep.

"You said Mrs. Eden went to see Nancy Fairchild. Where is that?"

"Seven Seaview Lane." Ross pointed. "Almost straight across. But she should have returned by going upriver and crossing to our side."

"She might have," the patrolman said. "The boat was drifting."

Peter spoke for the first time. "She left the oars. She was in a hurry and she left the oars on the dock."

"Could your wife swim, Mr. Eden?"

"She was an excellent swimmer, a strong swimmer," Ross said. The fear he had first felt rocking out on the cove returned, redoubled. And then he thought, as all the others including Peter must have, that an impatient woman who was a strong swimmer would not have sat helpless and soaked in a stalled boat but would have chanced the water.

Kate was found the next morning between four and five o'clock. A fisherman returning upriver saw her body washing against some barnacle-covered rocks not far from where the boat had been discovered. Her face was flayed on one side, the cheekbone and the double line of molars laid bare. Her bluish flesh was bruised; the thick, wavy hair plastered straight and stiff with salt. When the morgue attendant rolled out the gurney, the first things Ross saw were the damp spots on the sheet and the little pool of seawater that had collected on the table. The attendant turned back the sheet and asked Ross if he recognized her.

The figure before him was at once so familiar and so alien that he could scarcely understand the words. He felt that nothing was real, not the black and green checkerboard floor, not the glaring lights, the gray walls, the gleaming table, especially not the wet, dripping thing wrapped in khaki and seaweed that had been Kate. He wanted to deny that it was Kate, that it had ever been Kate. He had expected this with Ruthie. He had seen the steel table and the broken body in his worst nightmares and had dreaded the call that would summon him to them. But he had worried in vain; horror had waylaid him from another direction and taken him completely by surprise.

"Mr. Eden?"

Ross nodded. He reached out and brushed away a reddish strand of seaweed from her cheek. His fingers trembled over her cold, bruised hand, then he turned away. Out in the stuffy corridor, Ross sat on a bench and took deep, gasping breaths. He rubbed his hand over his eyes and looked up to see the detective.

"Her face?" Ross demanded. "What happened to her face?"

"We won't know anything until the autopsy, Mr. Eden, but she was found against the rocks."

"The current," Ross said, remembering the steady tidal pull on the oars. "Why the hell didn't she take that damn boat upstream?" He wanted to take her shoulders and shake her, he wanted to go back to that terrifying table and demand an explanation. Why hadn't she called, shouted? Why hadn't she taken Nancy Fairchild's offer of a ride? And why, it came out now, irresistible as the tide, hadn't he decided to get gas from the station not five minutes away? Reluctant to leave Lyman alone, Kate would have delayed her visit. When he'd returned, they would perhaps have talked; everything might have been different. Change one thing, one trifle, and all history can be altered. The morning Ruthie disappeared, even: Had Kate looked up instead of down or run first to the wood instead of to the road, their daughter might have been found. For the first time, Ross understood what had tormented and changed Kate and driven her half to distraction; it seemed to him now that their small lapses had been punished with ridiculous severity.

"Mr. Eden?"

He realized that the man was speaking to him, had been speaking to him for some time. "Yes?"

"We have a few questions, sir. If you are able."

"Yes," he said. "Questions." He meant his questions about motivation, destiny, and providence. The officer, a thin, sallow-faced chain-smoker, had questions of timing, proximity, intent. It took Ross a while to absorb their import, but when he did, he was surprised but not offended. Deep inside he felt guilty, though he could not have said precisely where his culpability lay.

". . . were on good terms?"

"Yes," Ross said.

"Do you know why she went over to Mrs. Fairchild's?"

"We'd argued," Ross said. "She thought she wanted a divorce."

The officer's eyes were skeptical and sad. "I thought you said you were on 'good terms.'"

"We were. But after we lost our daughter—she was kidnapped five years ago this June—after we lost Ruthie we weren't happy. We lost the ability to be happy." He gazed around the room, surprised at water pipes and window shades, at a calendar, an office typewriter. "She thought we might be better to start again. She wanted to get over the past."

"And what was your reaction?"

"I said I didn't want a divorce."

"Did she accept that?"

Ross shook his head. "I said I would fight for the children if she left. I said I wanted the boys."

"And then?"

"She went upstairs, and I went outside to mow the lawn. As I told you."

"She didn't mention going out somewhere? Going to see someone?"

"No. I didn't know she was going until I saw Lyman, our younger boy, waving. I turned around and saw her in the boat. It's a big lawn with shrubbery, trees. I didn't notice her walking down."

"I see," said the policeman. He lit another cigarette from the one dangling, half finished, between his lips.

Ross shrugged. He did not see. He remembered Kate saying that she'd given up everything in life. He'd let that go by. He hadn't, to tell the truth, wanted to know exactly what she'd meant. So the remark had slipped away like a branch in a stream, and, sitting there under suspicion of many sorts, Ross thought that was the one thing he should have grabbed on to, the one thing that might have kept them both from drowning.

Of course, Ross didn't drown; he was cleared, completely. The neighbors had heard the mower, he was seen at the Clam Box with his children. The autopsy report attributed death to drowning, probably while unconscious. Kate had run out of gas, the official account went, found herself drifting toward the Sound, and, being a fine swimmer, had struck out for shore.

She was near the south side of the cove when either she hit a strong current, or the storm, which had produced sporadically powerful gusts, intensified, and she was washed onto the rocks. Any other motive or intentionality lay with the beholder, and, after all, only Ross heard the cries of the madwoman in the night surf, the madwoman with hair undone who wandered the city streets crying for her child.

The funeral was in Woodmill with the coffin closed. Ross remembered the service as a series of sharp, unreal images, like photographs of some stranger's affairs. He did not believe it. Not then in the Federated Church, not at the pretty cemetery just outside town, not in the condolences of friends, the tears of relations. It was only later, nursing pain and confusion and anger—anger, too, at Kate's stupidity, at her carelessness, at, darkest yet, her despair—that he began to believe, and then he realized her loss, not through ceremonies and formalities, but in the mysteries of daily life. The capriciousness of their leaky washer, the eccentricities of the family pets, the maddeningly difficult coordination needed to produce even the simplest meal, the endless dirt, mess, and clutter produced by two small boys and their friends—these were the things that revealed Kate's loss. Harassed and depressed, Ross longed to escape—from the boys, too, with their sulks and tantrums, their muddy shoes and fussy appetites, their night terrors and morning squabbles. Ross drank too much and was tortured by stabs of fear and regret.

One hot, humid evening, Ross was trying to decide how long to cook the sweet corn and whether to start it before or after the burgers, when he noticed first, that Lyman's face was flushed, and second, that there was a small but rapidly increasing puddle on the living room floor.

"Damn it," Ross shouted, "I thought you were a big boy."

Lyman's face contorted.

"You're old enough," Ross said. Hot with righteous anger, he grabbed his son's arm and propelled him toward the bathroom. "Take off those damn clothes while I wipe this up." He got a sponge from the kitchen and mopped the floor with big, angry strokes.

In the bathroom, Lyman stood lethargic and bare rumped, moving the sodden pile of shorts and underpants around with one sneakered toe. There was a big damp patch on the lower part of his shirttail, and Ross's anger focused on this oversight. "Get that dirty shirt off, too! Where the hell are your clean clothes?"

Lyman shrugged and shrank into himself and muttered something.

"What?" Ross demanded.

He took the boy's arm and, when he didn't answer, smacked him. His hand left a red imprint on Lyman's thigh, and Ross felt an instant shame and remorse before Lyman screamed, "I want Mommy!"

The child's face was distorted with misery, terror, and rage, and, overcome with pain, Ross dropped to his knees and took his wet, urine-smelling son in his arms, held him sobbing against his chest, and pressed his face into the soft, damp hair.

"I miss Mommy, too," he whispered. "I'd give anything in the world to have her back for you. Anything." He realized that he was weeping, and realized, too, that he wanted his boys, that the kindly, efficient relatives weren't going to have them. He rocked Lyman slowly back and forth and heard the child's sobs fade to sniffles, then die out altogether in the wet sound of a small thumb being sucked. Ross sat on the tiles with his knees getting stiff and wished that he could comfort Peter as easily.

But he was determined to do it, and over the next months and years Ross Eden "took hold" as they said in Woodmill. He cut down on the late nights, the casual lady friends, the convivial meetings with his fellow dealers and distributors. He became, in some indefinable way, serious, a man to be reckoned with in a community that had previously considered him too much the ladies' man, too pleasure loving and frivolous, dismissing even his long support of his mother as only to be expected of a mama's boy. Ross was revealed as a good father: strict but fair, a man who never missed a game the boys played, a speech they gave, or a part they performed. Peter and Lyman were clean, responsible, hardworking kids, and Ross's high status in the village rested on them, and on the perception that, though tested beyond the normal run, he had taken hold and come through.

There was even a kind of glamour to his sufferings—if you could overlook the children, the casual housekeeping, the precisely timed routine of sitters and housekeepers and liquor store assistants—that attracted a certain type of woman. Ross was besieged by sentimental ladies, but his tastes were as they had always been, and if his pleasures were well spaced and discreet, they were scarcely conjugal. He did not want another wife and never seriously contemplated a second marriage: He was faithful to Kate in his own fashion. Even old Pete Birch, seething with grief and anger and suspicion, had to admit that.

And that Ross had been cleared, not just by the suspicious shoreline authorities but also by clannish Woodmill, which was subsequently embarrassed by any hint of fault. For who hadn't switched gas between one engine and another? Who hadn't forgotten to fill a tank or hadn't run out inconveniently? Disaster was capricious, and the laws of chance occasionally prove malicious. The community agreed to complete discretion: Kate, liked and respected, vanished from consciousness; the local paper called her death a tragedy and provided such scanty details that Leslie Austin, browsing in the files a generation later, assumed Kate Eden had died in an automobile accident.

In the face of this sympathy and amnesia—a sympathy and amnesia that his heart of hearts told Ross was not wholly deserved—he sought redemption as a father. He cared for his

9

Doug and Leslie slept late the next morning, waking up in a pleasant tangle of limbs and sheets, then lazed through the Sunday papers with the other adults while Jenny and Markie ran about the big lawn and played in a sandbox left by the summer tenants. There were some old bicycles stored in the garage, and Ross helped Doug get two of them working well enough so that he and Leslie could go cycling. They followed a curving road and ran along the blue and silver glitter of the marsh before crossing the highway and taking the main street into town.

Ashfen's outskirts were generic suburbia, choked with car lots and fast-food franchises, but the area near the harbor was picturesque. Dark-shingled warehouses and shipping firms had been reincarnated as trendy shops and restaurants with smartly painted shutters and blooming window boxes. Leslie thought them rather pretty, but Doug preferred the few unimproved Victorians and the ancient Cape Cod cottages. "Look at the proportions," he kept saying, "just a perfect human scale, that's what we've lost." As they wheeled their bikes along the sidewalks, he pointed out the fancy butt shingles and the ornate gingerbread on the nineteenth-century buildings and explained the post-and-beam framing that underlay the unpretentious little one- and two-story eighteenth-century houses. Doug had a vast store of information about architecture and cabinetwork. His real intelligence lay in his vision and in his hands, and through his eyes, Leslie saw the world as structure and dimension. She noticed the proportions of buildings, the reveals of windows and doors, the angles of roofs and dormers, and could read, if haltingly, the history of craftsmen and hacks, muddlers and artists in surface treatments, finishes, and designs. Even for an architectural novice like herself, the old seaside town was full of interest, and she and Doug walked along the docks and marinas, enjoying the hazy sunshine, the old houses, and the town's bright prettiness.

Around three, a sea breeze swept up the remaining clouds, and Ross decreed picnic weather. He told the women there was no need for cooking and set off with Lyman to the supermarket deli. They returned provisioned with exuberant lavishness: salads and cold cuts, roast chickens, bread, rolls, fruit, and the pièce de résistance, a cake, sticky with pink icing.

At five, they packed the cars and drove down to a long, nearly empty beach between the salt marshes of the river mouth and a rocky breakwater that signaled higher ground and the end of the sand. They brought out the coolers and hampers, the umbrellas and blankets and mats, all the weighty but useful paraphernalia of the beach, and settled themselves against driftwood logs, white and polished smooth with age.

Judy, Ross, and Lyman swam out toward the sand bar, visible as a lighter stretch of water. Doug went wading for a while, and Leslie climbed around the rocks with Peter's children, hand in hand with Markie and anxious to keep his agile sister from wandering too far out. The low sun that flushed their faces reddened the edges of the marsh grass and glistened on the wet sides of rocks that seemed to be rising and falling in the weedy tide. The children dipped their little golden hands into the stony pools, pulling up strands of kelp and squealing with joy, while Leslie studied the murky, fertile shallows with a kind of tranquil excitement. She felt that she'd really become one of the family at last.

At the sound of Jenny's rubber sandals slapping along the rocks, Leslie looked up: Her niece was heading toward the slippery, kelp-shrouded point. "Not so far, Jenny! You'll fall! Back this way."

Jenny turned and considered, calculating how far she might test this new, and somehow provisional, aunt.

"Come see this," Leslie called. With the prospect of some novelty, the child scrambled back to where Leslie knelt on the sun-warmed rocks. Down in the weedy shallows, a crab scuttled across an open patch of sand. Markie began to crow with delight, and Jenny could barely be restrained from putting her fingers in after it.

They were still watching the animal's angular progress, when there were footsteps on the rocks behind them. Peter's long shadow darkened the pool, as he reached down to hoist Markie onto his shoulders. Leslie smiled up uncertainly at him. "A wonderful place for children," she said.

"Your mom wants to put some sun oil on you," he told the children, without responding to Leslie. "Get on over there before you're burned."

"Can we come back on the rocks?" Jenny asked. "Can we come back on the rocks with Aunt Leslie?"

He hesitated, then said, "Once you have your sun oil."

"Wait for us, Leslie!" Jenny cried and jumped onto the sand, her arms flung out over her head like the seabird wings of her imagination. Markie struggled from his father's arms and ran after her.

Leslie watched them wistfully. "You have lovely children."

"A handful," he said, though he was clearly proud of them.

"Jenny's a charmer."

"Jenny's like Ruthie. Very lively."

Leslie looked at him, surprised. Peter had never volunteered any information about Ruthie before, but his cool glance told her nothing. Under his professional bonhomie, Peter was controlled and remote. There was a lack of spontaneity in him that Leslie both understood and disliked.

"Don't you care for the water?" He was only one who hadn't put his feet in, and she'd noticed how carefully he picked his way along the rocky outcrop.

"I don't like the beach particularly."

"All, or just this one?" Leslie asked.

"This is for the kids and Cindy. And my dad."

"Yet he must have memories, too."

"That's why he comes. That's why he brought you. You know that if it hadn't been for Ruthie, Mom would still be alive."

Leslie drew in her breath sharply; she must never let down her guard with Peter, no matter what. "You said she drowned in an accident."

"She drowned because she ran out of gas. Gas Dad had borrowed for the mower. The evening came up stormy, and she decided to swim back."

"How could that have anything to do with Ruthie? You can't blame Ruthie for"—she might have said "Kate's" but she said, "Mother's death," and he picked up on it angrily.

"Don't presume," he said. "I'm not Dad. She was never your mother, and the sooner you accept that and get out of our lives, the better for us and probably for you, too."

"You might not believe this, but I came up here the first time to be proved wrong," Leslie said, struggling to keep her temper. "I started writing to Ross to put my mind at rest about Ruth Eden, but I've been convinced. On the evidence."

Peter gave a short, sour laugh. "You don't understand. You weren't here, so you've really no idea how things were. You've got this nice image of us, TV perfect, all warm and fuzzy, but

Ruthie was always trouble. There was always tension over Ruthie. And after she was gone, it was worse."

"Ross remembers a happy marriage, a happy life," Leslie protested, though at the same time she felt anxiety as a physical pressure on the sides of her skull. She remembered the night she'd first met Ross and the momentary terror of real memory on the way back to the motel.

"Dad doesn't always face facts," Peter continued. "He wants peace and quiet and everything pleasant. He's always been able to see what he wants and to ignore the rest."

Leslie moved one foot across the kelp at the side of the pool, crushing the shiny little flotation bladders on the dark fronds. "I wondered about that the first time I came up," she said after a moment. "Because, to tell you the truth, what I remembered was unhappiness. I remembered Mom and Dad being unhappy and me being somehow to blame."

She looked up in time to see his face change, to see what might have been a doubt scud across his closed, confident features. "That doesn't make you Ruthie," he said.

"You wouldn't believe anyone was Ruthie," Leslie said with sudden comprehension. "You're sure that she's dead."

"Most likely."

"But what if you are wrong? How would you feel about that?"

"Ruthie's dead," he said. "Ruthie's been dead for years."

"It's as if you wanted her dead," Leslie said, abandoning all caution. "Why should it matter to you?"

"My mother died of hope! Hope of finding Ruthie, hope of knowing. And Dad! How they both hoped and suffered! Do you think I've forgotten that? I had to live in the real world and face the fact that Ruthie was gone, probably dead. Even at seven years old, I understood that there was safety in certainty."

"But you could not be certain," Leslie said. "You didn't know—"

"No, but I made up my mind, and nothing you've suggested and nothing I've discovered has changed that." Peter jumped down from the rocks and looked back at her. "You're a nice enough person, but take some advice. Don't get into this any farther. If you're convinced, fine, just go home and leave the rest of us alone." He turned abruptly and set off across the sand. His children came running toward him, and she saw him stop and pick up the boy and take Jenny by the hand.

Trembling with nerves and anger, Leslie remained alone on the rocks. She'd believed the uncertainties had been erased, the difficulties overcome, but Doug had been right after all. Some layer of her personal history remained inaccessible, even dangerous, although what Peter said fit her memories better than anything Ross had told her. This bitter confirmation helped Leslie walk back toward the family group that had seemed so comfortable, so unquestionable only minutes before.

She reached their colorful archipelago of blankets, mats, and toys with her mind still a jumble, but when Ross smiled and called, "You almost missed dinner! You should have come for a swim," she felt his affection as an almost physical reality. Leslie sat down to begin helping with the food. She told herself that Peter had always been suspicious; it was his nature, nothing more, and she'd be foolish to fear—what? Error, exposure, some terrible mistake? As her anxiety ebbed, Leslie told herself that she had to hold on to what she believed, what she knew: that she was home.

Cindy had already set out the plates, and Judy, Lyman, Ross, and Doug—Doug, too, recognized as a son-in-law: how that reassured her!—were laying out the picnic supper. How handsome Doug looked, smiling across at her! How good to be here, even if there was now a shadow at the edge to her happiness. "Nothing's ever perfect," Aunt Flo reminded her. Not perfect, but good, Leslie thought. She'd settle for good. They poured the drinks and handed around sandwiches, cold chicken, bowls of salad, and slices of bread until their overburdened paper plates began to sag under the feast. The sea breeze sifted a little sand across the blankets, and there was a great brushing of plates and dusting of sandwiches, a close inspection of the drink cups, and the occasional feel of grit between the teeth.

No one minded. The tomatoes were late natives, delicious with a little oil, tasting of acid and sun, and there was a pasta salad with shrimp, and another salad with melon, pineapple, orange slices, and grapes to complement the chicken, store roasted but very tasty nonetheless, the skin crisp, the flesh firm but not dry. The cool air had made them all hungry, and the kids kept reaching sticky-handed for more grapes and pieces of chicken and cups of juice. Cindy worried they'd overeat and be sick, but Ross laughed and said they'd run it all off playing on the sand. "Nobody gets sick at the beach," he said, leaning back on one elbow like a Roman at a feast.

From that angle, the sky looked enormous, a stretch of pinkish lavender, with the golden west menaced to the south by gray and purple clouds, successors to the previous front visible in the darkness on the northeastern horizon. The meteorological world was momentarily quiet, and if, from the shape of the clouds, this must be a brief calm, the shore was still beautiful, the Sound flat and waveless, deep green blue with evening, and the sand white gold.

The breeze died away to nothing; there was only the whisper of ripples hitting the shore. They'd all stopped talking for a moment, one of those strange but companionable silences that sometimes overtake gatherings, and Ross, sitting on the sand with his children and grandchildren, felt a rare moment of exultation and conviction: Ruthie was back and this was the sign. He had no doubt. When Markie and Jenny broke the spell by scrambling up and racing off to play near the tide line, he opened a bottle of wine and passed it around, saying, "This is a special day."

"A toast," said Cindy.

"To Leslie and Doug," Lyman said and raised his glass in a friendly gesture. The others followed, even Peter, last and obviously reluctantly. Leslie met his eyes for an instant and raised her glass in return.

"To you all," she said.

"To all of us," Ross said, and then he said what he'd been waiting nearly twenty years to say, "and to our last Labor Day at the shack. Our last cleanup, our last tenants. I'm sure you'll all be pleased about that."

There was, instead, a kind of surprised silence.

"Well," said Ross, "I see I've kind of stopped the party."

"You're selling the house?" Cindy asked.

"I've had this in mind for some time. The market will never be higher. With the profits, we can rent a place at the beach and relax, instead of working our tails off. I appreciate all your help. I know I couldn't have done it this long without you, but this is the time to get out of the rental business."

"But why now? The market was higher three months ago," Peter said. "A year ago, even."

Ross smiled. "I was waiting for Ruthie."

"I was kind of counting on the beach house," Cindy said, as she folded up their clothes and laid them in the big case. Outside, the stormy sky that had driven them home from the picnic was scattering big drops over the driveway and the cars.

Her husband shrugged.

"You were always in favor of selling it, weren't you?"

"We could educate the kids with our share."

"If it's shared out."

"No problem. That's all in the will. Dad's always been very fair with money."

"Look how damp these are! That's the sea air!" Cindy

exclaimed, shaking out one of Markie's shirts. "So why aren't you happy if it's what you've wanted?"

"I don't like the way it's being done. I don't like the reasons, and I don't like suddenly sharing a quarter with a stranger. That's what I don't like."

"You talked to your dad?"

"He doesn't want to hear anything. He and I have always gotten on great, right? Then comes this woman who thinks she's Ruthie—just thinks she's Ruthie, that's enough—and what do we have?" Peter's expression darkened as he spoke, and when he heard the children calling from downstairs, he said, "Go on down, Cindy. I'll be there in a little while. I'm not really welcome at the moment."

"Don't be that way."

"You'll see. He's stubborn as a mule when he gets his mind on something, and what he wants always comes first."

Cindy made a little face and thought how alike they were, before finishing the last of the packing and starting down the big, dark staircase. The cleanup had always been a chore, but she liked the place, liked the big, high rooms, the substantial porches and imposing gables.

"There's your mom!" Ross said. "Come on, Cindy, these kids are ready for marshmallows!" He and Doug had found some wood behind the shed and built a fire so that Markie and Jenny could toast marshmallows. That, too, annoyed Peter, and when he came down, he complained of the smoke, then fussed because Lyman was already settled with the charging Red Sox on the TV instead of with the Mets.

"Go get the radio," Ross said. "The Mets'll be on the radio. They're a lock for the playoffs, anyway. The Sox need all the support they can get." He inserted a marshmallow on a fork for Jenny, then put one near the fire for Markie. "I'll hold it, dear. Don't want you to burn your pitching hand, do we?"

"Is mine done, Grampa?" Jenny asked.

"Not quite. You want your marshmallow golden all over. Just tanned. Not burned black. See how it's getting browned on that side?"

"I want mine perfect," she said, and Ross smiled. So did he. They were all there, all together again, and he could listen calmly to the faint sounds of the wind and surf. He'd erred on the house, though, and he could see that his boys were uneasy with the decision. But nothing was said while Markie and Jenny were around, and nothing, either, after they had been escorted off to bed, their bright faces sticky and sleepy. No, the question of the house came up another way, like the backdoor cool front that had plummeted the temperature and brought the now steady rain.

The Red Sox were losing; the Mets, earlier recipient of the passing front, had been rained out in the third, wasting a good start by David Cone. Ross, Lyman, and Doug were discussing the shed; the others were sitting beside the fire with an ancient Scrabble board. Leslie was doing rather well, somewhat to the previous champ's chagrin.

"Leslie's a good speller," Judy said.

"Copyediting builds vocabulary." Leslie used up a *y* and a *z*, forming *zygote* off a *t* dangling amid a long string of smooth, white tiles.

"What she's really good at is research," Peter said. He added two *o*'s to the *z*.

"Do we allow adjectives?" Leslie asked. She felt nervous, although she'd been prepared for Peter to be unpleasant. He'd given her warning, after all, and the real surprise was that he hadn't started earlier, at the picnic.

"Adjectives are okay," Judy said. "We've got *pretty* on the board already."

Leslie added a *t* to *zoo*. "As in 'zoot suit,' " she said.

"Where'd you dig that up?" Judy exclaimed.

"Fashion page."

"In the sixties archives, maybe?" Peter asked. "Leslie must have spent quite a bit of time in the sixties section of—what do they call newspaper files again? 'The morgue' is it? Your prime research ground."

"I'm a reporter, after all," Leslie said.

"And that's how you found us."

"Listen," said Judy, "I accept *zoot*. We don't need references for a friendly game."

"Maybe this isn't such a friendly game." Leslie had stopped considering the board and was looking directly at Peter, whose even features were as smooth and closed as a mask. "But I told you exactly how I found you and how I did the research—if you want to call it that."

"I do want to call it that. It's funny, isn't it, to think that without the wire story, you'd never have known? You'd never have come to Woodmill, you wouldn't be here tonight. Don't you agree that's funny?" On the other side of the room, Ross picked up his head and frowned.

"Oh, I'd have known, but I'd never have found you."

"I disagree about that," Peter said firmly. "Everything—even this business with the beach house—would have been different without that damn story."

"That's enough, Peter," Ross broke in. "You've been sour about something all day." He got up out of his chair and came over to lean against the mantel.

"I'm sorry, Dad. I wasn't going to bring this up since we're having a holiday party. But with the house and everything, you've got to know."

"What have I got to know?" Ross asked. When he was displeased, the resemblance between him and his eldest son was particularly striking.

"Leslie, here, isn't Ruthie. Never was. She *may* think she was or she may *know* she isn't, but I'm willing to keep an open mind about that."

"Just at the moment, your mind sounds pretty damn closed," Doug said.

"Let's just say I've got evidence, which is more than Leslie has." Peter reached for his wallet, took out a piece of paper, and unfolded it. Leslie recognized a Xerox of her Florida birth certificate, and though there was nothing she could have done differently, she felt her face flush with shame and anger.

"Of course, you know what's on this," Peter said to Leslie as he passed the photocopy to his father.

Had she ever mentioned the difficulties with her passport to Ross? Leslie didn't think so. For God's sake, why not? She hadn't been planning, that's why! She hadn't thought about proofs and confrontations, but innocence couldn't keep her mouth from being dry or her voice from shaking when she said, "According to that, I was born in Orlando, a place I first visited when I was in junior high. I'm sorry, Ross, I should have showed that to you. I told Aunt Flo I wanted a birth certificate so that I could get a passport, and she brought me that a week later. God knows where she got it."

Leslie looked around the suddenly silent room. "A good portion of south Florida is using false documents," she said, but even as she spoke, she knew the words sounded suspicious, just exactly what she'd say if everything were a lie. That she could disappoint Ross, that he might cease to believe in her, was suddenly a frightening possibility, and to her horror, Leslie felt tears of anger and grief in her eyes.

"Where did you get this, Peter?" Ross asked.

"I acquired it. And some other information as well."

"I asked where you got it, and I want a straight answer."

"I hired an investigator."

"You did what?"

"I hired a private investigator. A firm my company uses."

"You hired an investigator to spy on your sister?"

"Dad, I've never been convinced that she's my sister! This

woman's a reporter with access to all sorts of newspaper files. She's told us she got old yearbooks last spring. What else did she do? She could have been up in town a dozen times without your knowing anything."

"For Christ's sake!" Doug said. "Last spring Leslie was just out of the hospital. She could barely drive to work, never mind up here."

"I had someone question this Flo Simpson," Peter continued, ignoring the interruption. "Leslie and her parents were in an automobile crash when she was five. They both died. She survived but without any memory of them or of the accident. It's sad and all and quite natural that she would fantasize about her parents, but that's all there is—just fantasy. I'm sorry, Dad, her story doesn't add up."

Leslie felt a rush of anger: poor Aunt Flo. She could imagine some seedy private investigator turning up on her aunt's porch, flashing credentials and a bogus authority. " 'This Flo Simpson,' as you call her, wanted a child more than anything in the world, a child and her family. That's about all she ever had, and she didn't want to lose them. She protected her brother when he brought me, and she's protecting him now. I'll never blame her for that and you had no right to try to frighten her. Why couldn't you have just asked me for my birth certificate?"

"Let's say I'm not as trusting as Dad."

"Forget the birth certificate," Ross said abruptly, and later Leslie would remember that and love him for it. "The birth certificate's irrelevant, it's crap. I can't even hire a kid to sweep the sidewalk without seeing some damn piece of paper. How would Leslie work without one?"

"You're as bad as she is!" Peter exclaimed. "What I'm saying—" he began, but Doug cut him off.

"You've already said more than enough." Doug's voice was tight. "Leslie's never asked anything from you. If she made a mistake, it was an honest one."

Leslie was hurt that even Doug, who knew the whole story, should think in terms of mistakes, of delusions. That was the power of paper, of official copies and bureaucratic stamps.

"With this house for sale, a sixty- to eighty-thousand-dollar mistake," Peter said.

"You can keep your goddamn house!"

"Peter, you're way out of line on this," Ross said.

"Peter's thinking of the children," Cindy said.

"I warned you," Doug said to Leslie. "I told you I could see you getting hurt."

"Just a minute," Ross said. "I'm sorry I ever mentioned the house. We'll keep the place if it's going to cause quarreling."

"Look, Ross, you've been a prince," Doug said, "but it's no good. I can't put Leslie though any more of this." He stood up and put his arm around Leslie.

"It's not your decision, Doug," Ross said. "It's up to Leslie and me, and as far as I'm concerned, she's my daughter, Ruthie. I know what this is about: You've all gotten greedy with this crazy real estate market."

"Not all of us," Judy said coolly, and the others joined the protest.

Ross raised his voice defiantly. "Listen up: When and if I sell the house, Leslie is getting her share. Regardless of what the rest of you want."

"Please, Ross, no!" Leslie cried, frightened. "I couldn't take the money. I don't want it. I wanted a family! My family, that's all I ever wanted!"

Peter began arguing with Doug and Ross, while Cindy tried without success to calm her husband. It was Lyman, the pacifier, the well-disposed, who said softly, "There is a solution, you know."

When they quieted down, he asked, "Do you remember the woman who came a few years ago? She was heavy, a redhead, older than she said and nothing like anyone in the family. Nothing like you, Leslie," he added kindly. "Quite implausible. Couldn't tell a horse from a cow and wouldn't have known Woodmill from Wichita, but she persisted. God, how she persisted! We finally settled that with a blood test. Dad must still have his results. If Leslie'd be willing . . ."

"No," said Ross loudly and abruptly, "no, we don't want that—"

"But we do," Leslie interrupted. "Why didn't we think of that first!"

"No!" Ross repeated. "We're not going though that again. It's totally unnecessary and humiliating."

"But you already have your tests," Lyman said earnestly. "Only Leslie'd have to be tested. And they're much more accurate now. If you're not her father, that settles it: an honest, even understandable, mistake as far as I'm concerned. And if you are, then we share everything equally—three children. Agreed, Peter?"

"Yes," Peter said. His face suddenly relaxed, his tense expression turned bland and noncommittal. "I'll be more than happy to apologize to Leslie if I'm wrong."

"You're so goddamn suspicious," Ross shouted, careless of the grandchildren asleep upstairs. "Doesn't human feeling count for anything with you?"

"It's all right, Ross." Leslie came over and touched his arm, like a graceful, younger Kate, like the very embodiment of the cautionary and condemning whispers of the surf. "I'm sure. I want to set their minds at ease. I want to do this."

"You don't have to," Ross said. He was quite white. "You don't have to and I don't want you to."

"I so want us to be a family," Leslie said, pathetically trusting and eager, her face pink with relief and hope. "I want us to know. Please."

Ross gave her a sad smile, put his hands in his pockets, and walked over to stare into the fire. "I think we need to believe, sometimes. I think we need to believe," he repeated, but no one answered.

They were all products of the modern generation, faithless. They had credulity but no sense of the miraculous. Ross felt the presence of their doubt, of their need to be sure, of their faith in tests and scientific proof. He felt very old when he nodded and said, "All right, I'll see if I can find the results."

He caught Leslie's eye as he spoke, but though he could see that she sensed some warning, she chose not to read his expression. For no matter what Ross wanted, no matter what he believed, Leslie knew they had to be certain. That birth certificate meant things would never be right with Peter otherwise. Never.

"You can change your mind if you want," Ross told her. "You don't have to do this for me."

"I know that, Ross. Nor for me, either. It's for my brothers. You'll see," she said, "you'll see everything will work out right."

Part | **Three**

Winter 1990

This is the Age of Ice. Everything is cold and white and gray now. The low sky is lost in a sleety snow that dissolves the clear edges of things and gives houses, fields, shops, and streets the grainy, insubstantial quality of old photographs. Light is uncertain; distance ambiguous; and the mind itself, deprived of memory and foundation, exists only in emotions. The wind shifts veils of snow, and the street lights turn precipitation as opaque as a curtain. Nothing is sure here; information has been erased like a bad drawing. What was it you thought you knew? What was it you thought you believed?

It is hard to remember here in the cold with the sound of the sleet hissing and rattling, with the snow closing off the sky. The world is a projector screen without a picture, and those bright memories were false, the insubstantial and delusive product of wishes and hopes. And lies? There are always lies. And silences, especially now that the voices are gone. The parking lot is quiet. A car passes now and then, and once in a while a truck with chains runs noisily on the slushy main street. But there are no voices, no shouts, not even those subliminal whispers that suggested this place and this past. They are silent behind the snow that falls with an icy sibilance to deaden everything to whiteness, leaving behind not mystery but emptiness. Now the only voice is her own, and she is reluctant to speak. She is not sure what she should say or why she is here or how it was that she emptied her heart and embarked on futility.

10

The snow mixed with sleet around four, the precipitation suddenly pattering against the glass. Ross decided to leave early and let Martin, who lived in town, close up. Ross had planned to leave early anyway and do Christmas shopping for the children. Now the stores would have to wait, and the postponement of that pleasure made him feel grumpy and out of sorts, a familiar mood recently, which he was hoping Christmas would dispel.

"Better throw some salt on the walk," Ross told Martin, "and go home by six if this keeps up." He got his coat and gloves and carried a pile of cartons outside to the recycling bin. He'd have to shop Saturday early if he wanted to get the kids' things that weekend, and he ran over his list mentally as he walked to the car. He had reached Jenny and was wondering whether she was big enough for a puppy and whether Cindy would tolerate the extra work, when he heard his name. He looked up to see a woman with dark hair standing in the sleet.

"It's me, Ross." In her bulky parka, she looked so much like Kate that he felt the shock of visitation before he realized that the parka was thin, and the sweater and pants pastel synthetics too light for a northern December.

"Leslie!"

He was surprised, and alarmed, too; he hadn't wanted her to visit. Their phone conversation after the tests came back had been painful. He'd heard her crying, and, when he hung up, Ross had fixed himself a bourbon and ginger and looked into the fire and wept for himself and Kate and poor Ruthie. Leslie wouldn't know about that.

"I grabbed a flight," she said. "Completely spur of the moment." She sounded excited and nervous and reached out with a tentative gesture to touch his arm. "I had to see you. Please don't be angry."

"I'm not angry. I'm just surprised. I didn't expect to see you again. I didn't think you'd come."

"I wanted at least to say good-bye," she said, and her low voice reminded Ross so frighteningly of Kate's that he again had the uneasy feeling she was an emissary from the past.

"You must be freezing," he said. "You're not used to our cold. Better come get supper and a drink."

"I just wanted to see you," she said uncertainly.

"You've come up from Kennedy?"

"Yes. Slippery all the way."

"Come on. Follow me back. Or would you rather leave your car here?"

She hesitated a moment, clearly tempted, then said, "No, I've made arrangements for the motel tonight. I'll need the car."

Ross nodded. "Be sure to take it slow on the hill," he said and got into his Buick. His chest felt tight, and when he bent to turn the ignition, he had a moment's dizziness: His blood pressure was up again, but that quack Parshal always claimed it was just stress.

Ross took a few deep breaths and let the engine warm and the defrosters loosen the ice on the windows before he got out and scraped off the crust. If he had left at four, would she have come to the house? Or would she have turned around and gone back to JFK? He should have gone away over the holiday. He should have gone on the cruise that Sheila had been after him to take. They could be off Martinique or Jamaica or Guadeloupe or wherever, lying in deck chairs under a thick tropical night watching stars unclouded by mist or smog. Ross glanced into the mirror and saw Leslie's lights following. He could have been away in the sun, swimming and dancing with Sheila, but perhaps even there, on some starlit deck or tropical shore, Leslie would have appeared, sad and resentful, a symbol of his failings—and of Kate's. Ross shook his head at the thought and rubbed his sleeve across the window. This changes nothing, he told himself. Her coming cannot change anything.

At the cottage, he put his car in the garage and unlocked the front door, holding it open for Leslie. "Come in, come in! I'll need to loan you a heavier coat."

She was white-faced with cold, and Ross guessed that she'd been sitting in the lot for a while, waiting, thinking. He put on the coffeemaker and then pulled out the steak. It would just be big enough if he microwaved a couple of potatoes.

"We had steak the first time I was here."

"The resource of the single male."

She smiled wanly.

"So how are things with you?" he asked. He felt better now that he was home. There were always things to do in the kitchen. Pots to fill, meat to unwrap, ovens and gadgets to be adjusted.

She shrugged and was silent for a moment. "I can't seem to settle," she said at last. "I feel so restless."

"And Doug?"

"Doug's all right," she said. "He's staying at his Aunt Mag's for a while over in Palm Beach, doing a big kitchen installation. There's a lot of work in the Palm Beach area."

"I like Doug," Ross said.

"So do I. It's not Doug's fault. It's me; it's all my fault."

"I doubt that," Ross said. "Nothing is ever all one person's fault."

"But one person can make a lot of mistakes."

"That's universal." He glanced at the broiler glowing red and slid the steak under the coil. Nonetheless, he did not ask any more questions until they were finished eating. "How was it you came north?" he asked when he got up to get the coffee. "You said this trip was spur of the moment."

"I was in the mall and passed the travel agent's. I had the weekend free. That was it." That wasn't quite it. She had been considering the trip for some time. It was one reason she'd quarreled with Doug; it was one reason Doug was in Palm Beach.

"I'm not sure," Ross began and stopped. What the hell did she want?

"You'd rather I hadn't come."

He raised his eyebrows. "I'm glad to see you, but I don't know what good it will do us."

"You don't understand. I fell in love with the whole idea, with the whole family." She gave a weak smile. "I was so sure. Did you know that? That I wasn't bluffing, that I was sure? It's important to me that you know that."

Ross remembered her shining face at the beach house, her radiant confidence and trust.

"Peter wasn't convinced for a moment," she said. "He always thought the worst of me. He was sure I was an imposter and faking everything from the start."

"I never thought that," Ross said. "And I don't think it now. We were mistaken, that's all."

"You didn't want the testing done," she said, her voice rising. "You tried to warn me, but I had to agree, don't you see that? With the birth certificate and Aunt Flo's story, I had no choice, and I was so sure. I believed in what a family should be. In what your family was."

"No family is perfect," Ross said. And every family is menaced by the irrational and dangerous, by Ruthie's disappearance, by Kate's death. Knowing he had to be strong if he were to save the rest, Ross pushed himself back from the table and stood up.

"I loved you," Leslie said softly. "You made an enormous difference in my life."

"And I was and am very fond of you. I'd waited twenty-five years for Ruthie. Think how that felt! And Kate! Kate broke her heart over Ruthie's disappearance. Then you came, and everything seemed right."

"That's how I felt," she said eagerly. "Everything seemed right."

"But we were mistaken," Ross said, though his heart sank within him.

"I understand now." He heard her voice flatten with disappointment. "I understand there are always lies."

"There are no lies without proof." Ross hated how cautious, how legalistic that sounded, and Leslie must have hated it, too, for she jumped up from her chair.

He had encouraged her to believe, had wanted her to trust, and now came this cowardly betrayal of all their emotions. "I'm so goddamned sick of everything," she said, looking around wildly for her coat and purse. "What a fool I was to come! What a fool I was to trust you!"

She opened her purse, and Ross felt an instant's fear before she pulled out a photo enlargement of the group at the beach house: Peter and Cindy, each holding one of the children, Lyman and Judy on either side of them, and to the front and slightly to one side, Leslie and Doug. Leslie held the picture out to him, a last entreaty, then tore it diagonally so that she and Doug fell to the floor in one shiny triangular piece. She threw the other half at his feet and went to the door.

"I'm so sorry, Leslie," he said. "How I wish . . ."

"I wished for you," she said, then she was gone, the door

blowing open behind her in the cold wind. Ross heard the car start and ran out into the wet snow. When he shouted, "Ruthie! Ruthie!" Leslie was already pulling away. Her lights vanished over the crest of the hill as Ross stumbled across the sodden lawn, his chest pounding, pressure and regret ringing in his ears.

Leslie slept badly and woke up late, disoriented by the gray semidarkness of a lull in the storm. Outside, plows and sanders passed up and down the state road, and there was the occasional racket of chains against the pavement. She called the airport, which was open but experiencing long delays, and discovered that the only flight bookable was a nine P.M. into Tampa. She made the arrangements with a businesslike efficiency that propelled her through a discussion of road conditions with the motel proprietor and a breakfast of coffee and doughnuts at the diner. When the snow started again, blowing across the road in great, nearly impenetrable veils, she was sensible enough to return to the motel and wait it out.

Sitting watching a morning talk show in her room, Leslie marveled at her composure. She had gambled everything—past, present, and future: Doug, Aunt Flo, Uncle Mac, and the *Sun Coast Times* on the chance of Woodmill, Ross, and his family. It still seemed inconceivable that she had been wrong, that she had lost everything.

By late afternoon, the snow finally let up, and Leslie left Woodmill in the thin light of a red winter sun hanging over the western horizon. Unaccustomed to ice, she drove with great, and what proved to be tiring, care, and by the time she reached Westchester, she was beginning to get hungry. "You have to eat," Aunt Flo always said. When Uncle Mac died and she was devastated, her stomach in knots, Aunt Flo fixed a stew, full of meat and vegetables with a little red wine just the way Mac had liked it. "You have to eat," Flo'd said. "Mac sure wouldn't have let this go to waste."

Surprisingly, Leslie had been hungry after all, the taste of stew beef, onions, carrots, and thyme blending with a memory of cold Syracuse nights, the nights when Mac was on the evening route, and he'd come home to a late dinner and say, "That's the best stew in the world."

It was funny to be thinking about Uncle Mac and Aunt Flo, but her aunt had been in her mind a lot, and now her advice bubbled up, nothing romantic or deep or revelatory but sensible: "You've got to eat." At the next exit sign announcing food and fuel, Leslie turned off; a couple of miles along the secondary road, she spotted a small stone restaurant with a steep shingled roof. The car was frigid despite the heater, and when Leslie got out to walk across the lot, the balls of her feet felt stiff and swollen.

Inside, the restaurant was attractive, even elegant. Leslie chose a side table in the half-filled dining room, and she had just started her soup when a new arrival came over without waiting for the hostess.

"You're Leslie Austin, aren't you? Do you mind if I join you?"

He was a pleasant-looking older man, but there were empty tables all around.

Leslie said, "I don't want company, thank you. There are plenty of other tables."

"But you are Leslie Austin, aren't you?"

He knew her name; she had been too absorbed in her own thoughts to register that immediately.

"I'm Paul Schott," he said. "I think you spoke to everyone in Woodmill except me."

Then she looked at him, really looked at the bony face, the thinning brown hair, the lanky frame. "How did you know my name?"

"You were pointed out to me at church, and you look so much like Kate Eden, I couldn't have been mistaken."

Leslie drew in her breath and gestured toward the chair opposite without speaking.

"Thanks," he said. "I expect you'll be on your way home. Dreadful day to travel."

"I'm not used to driving in snow."

"The roads will be better nearer the city."

Leslie took a few spoonfuls of her soup then said, "I remember your picture in the yearbooks. And with Kate Eden in the Drama Club."

"We were very old friends."

"It's not true, you know, that I'm related to her. I failed the genetic tests. I'm not Ruth Eden, after all, and any resemblance is purely coincidental."

"Ah," he said, "so you did testing?"

"We were so sure. I was, anyway."

"But the results were . . . ?"

"All negative. I couldn't possibly be his child."

"I'm so sorry," he said, as if he really was. "For you—and for Ross. It was his great hope to find Ruthie."

"Yes."

"You're a journalist, aren't you?"

"That's right. But I wasn't in Woodmill as a working journalist. My interest in the Edens is entirely personal."

"Some of us wondered," Paul Schott said. "So little is really private anymore."

"Oh, you're right about that! But I know that I was kidnapped as a child, and, oddly enough, I feel the need to protect his accomplices."

"Accomplices after the fact?"

Leslie nodded.

"Life is full of complications," Paul said philosophically. "Complications and coincidences, wouldn't you say?"

"I'm not sure I understand what you're getting at."

"Mind if I order?" he asked as the waitress approached. "Can I get something for you? A drink, maybe, or wine?"

"A little wine would be nice. I've started dinner."

Paul smiled when the waitress left with their order. "I like wine when I'm going to be indiscreet."

He looked away toward the bar for a moment, impatient for his drink or gathering his forces or both. Then he said, "A crash and the sound of metal tearing. That's how you began, in coincidence and physics and disaster. Everything of importance came from there. Everything. In my life, in Kate's, in yours."

Leslie would remember that later amid so much that seemed unreal and dreamlike but, at the same time, as indubitable as a dream: "the sound of metal tearing," the sound, that is, of a car hurtling off a country road to stop with the sound of glass and lives shattering.

"I fell in love with Kate when we were sophomores," Paul said. "Of course, I'd known her all my life. There's something absurd about suddenly falling in love with someone you've known since kindergarten, isn't there? December 1952: the night of the Christmas candlelight service at the Federated Church. The girls of the choir used to march in singing "O Holy Night" to light the candles. Kate was wearing gold wings and a tinsel halo when I fell in love with her. One minute I was a happy schoolboy and, the next, I'd met the great passion of my life." He smiled ruefully and thought about sudden changes of state in physics and in the heart. "I suppose that sounds ridiculous."

"It sounds romantic," Leslie said.

"Oh, it was, it was! Though I was the least romantic kid imaginable. But we were so happy. And so optimistic. You know we were both 'half European.' We were different that way. All our friends were either old Yankee or old emigration. But my mom had come from Germany to work as a cook, and Kate's dad—have you met Old Peter?"

"Yes, though meeting me upset him."

"Well, of course you would upset him! From certain angles, you are the image of Kate."

"A painful coincidence."

Paul Schott's expression became unreadable. "He came from Ulster, you know. He's like my mother was, a pessimist; he believes in fate and doom. Mentally, Kate and I were all-American; we believed in luck and in the future."

He gave a little sigh before continuing. "It was to be able to be with Kate, to be able to drive her around and take her out at night, that I wanted the car. The car that Eddie and I rebuilt."

"Mr. Eddie?" Leslie asked quickly, she could not have said why her heart jumped. "Mr. Eddie who ran the gas station?"

"You know about Eddie?"

"My mother, whoever she was, called him 'Mr. Eddie.' He had the most terrible scars."

"Yes," Paul said, "but not then. Then he was one of the best-looking boys in the village. Madly girl crazy and car crazy. A natural mechanic." He paused. "I hardly know what to tell you about Eddie."

Or, Paul might have added, about anything else. The car, for example: a thirdhand Oldsmobile purchased with the profits of his trapline. The car is the fact, a fat, solid, low-skirted, robin's egg blue coupe, as sleek and splendid as a 4-H steer at fair time. When he remembered the car, he always saw Kate running her hand admiringly along its smooth flanks, and he remembered desire and happiness and undeferred joy. This was the umbra around the fact. This was the value of memory. This is what will be hard to convey to Leslie Austin.

"Eddie had ambitions to beat the gang from the South Village at drag racing. He loved speed and motors. I just wanted to get off the Birches' back porch." Paul gave a wistful smile. "A little way up the county road, there was a track that ran through a stand of sycamores and oaks. There was room to park a car there."

He could tell Leslie Austin that but no more; he was a private man. He would not tell her about the pleasure of having the car done and beautiful, or about the happiness of caressing Kate that summer evening, or about the conviction of a future that stretched endless with pleasure.

But perhaps he didn't need to. Sitting in the winter restaurant, Leslie made the connection and began to notice others and to wonder how she could have been so blind. So blind with love and hope.

11

"It was my fault; I was the one driving. Eddie and I were racing a couple guys in a souped-up Chevy. We must have been doing seventy-five when we came over the hill outside town. We were half airborne, then wham, the windshield filled with light, and we had to veer off the pavement for an oncoming car. Trees, brush, stones, drainage ditch, the car all smashed to hell. I don't know how we both weren't killed. For years afterward, I used to wake to the sound of tearing metal; in dreams, I'd hear that sound and see his face and feel my stomach drop." Paul looked away, because this next was hard to tell, impossible to explain. "I gave Kate up," he said.

That's it: four words, but it was no conscious decision, no formal renunciation. No, it was the revulsion of the flesh, a longing wedded to horror. Sitting on Kate's back step, his arms thickened with bandages, he couldn't make himself take her hand or touch her face. His love remained, but his desire had been twisted with the fenders and flayed with the skin of Eddie's face. He had become stiff and cold, the psychic equivalent of disfigurement.

"That winter," he told Leslie Austin, "Kate began to date Ross. I didn't blame her. I couldn't understand myself. And he was older. Smoother, too, I guess, and very good-looking. In the spring, I heard they were engaged. I remember meeting them in the street when I was home for Easter. The worst thing," he continued after a brief pause, "was that I knew she was waiting for me to say, 'Don't do this. I still love you.' I stood there and knew all that and knew I loved her more than life and said nothing."

"So she married Ross."

"Yes. I joined the army, did my time, and returned to school on the G.I. Bill. After graduation I got a job with a structural-engineering firm. The bookkeeper was a girl from Woodmill." He smiled. "One thing led to another. We were married the next June and went to live in Torrington. But when our twins were born, we needed more space, so we moved into a two-family house my wife's parents owned in Woodmill."

"You'd have seen Kate Eden."

"Not right away. I wasn't—we weren't—looking for trouble. I thought it was over with Kate. I thought everything was square. I suppose I thought one thing balanced the other. Eddie was all right, you know. He married one of his nurses. In fact, he was married and had kids before either Kate or I. Kate was married. I was married. It just happened, that's all."

Paul's face was serious, but there was a ghost of a smile, something in his eyes as he remembered Kate stepping out of a Woodmill store one Saturday. She had a handsome little boy with her, and though she'd gotten heavier, she had the same large eyes, the same quick, transforming smile. On that particular September afternoon, Paul had been foolish enough to think that the woman he had loved, had almost married, had lost, was just another school friend, just someone he had known in another life.

He did not see her again until after he joined the PTA musical in October. At rehearsals, everything between them seemed so natural and friendly that when his costume ripped he'd thought nothing of stopping by to get the shirt mended.

At that time, the Edens' cottage was clear out of town, right on the edge of a big farm. Paul had stepped from his car and stood for a moment, listening. Aside from the tick of his cooling engine, there was a complete human silence, but the air was thick with the persistant trilling of numberless insects. Large sunflowers were staked against the garage, their heavy heads drying, and the last few tomatoes lay black spotted in the garden. He was there all alone and he was glad to see Ross's car was out. Paul felt vaguely guilty for that thought, and though he didn't leave, he immediately held up the shirt as his excuse when Kate came to the door.

"Oh, needs a gusset. I've gotten very good at repairs. Come in. Let me just close this door. Peter's naptime."

"How old is he?"

"Past two. And your twins?"

"They'll be a year in November."

"They must keep you busy. You'd better put it on," she said, shaking out the shirt and inspecting the seam. "I'll need to measure."

He loosened his tie and took off the white shirt he wore at work. Kate hung it over a chair and watched him struggle into the red broadcloth.

"It's not you."

"You're telling me."

"Hold up your arm." She ran the tape measure deftly across his rib cage. "Fortunately, I can match the material; this red stuff never goes out of fashion."

"I wonder why."

She smiled and gestured for him to take off the shirt.

"Shall I pick it up later?"

"If you can wait, I can mend it in a few minutes."

He sat down and watched her sew. The scissors sliced elongated red trapezoids with a clean swishing sound. She pinned them into place, working quickly and efficiently, then threaded the machine and spun the flywheel to start it. Out the back window, Paul could see a faded stand of corn and some crows keeping sentry along a wire fence. He felt a peaceful, unthinking, animal content, as if he'd sat in that plain room with the plank floors, the rag rug, the brown tweed sofa, and the high-backed green chairs with the shaped wooden arms every day of his life, as if he'd lived for years with the dark woman bending intently over her work, as if this was where he belonged.

The machine stopped. She brought over the shirt, but instead of putting out his hand for it, he reached up and gently took hold of her forearms. The red shirt spilled onto his lap, and he stood up into her arms and happiness, as the years of army, school, marriage, and children collapsed to the night when they had parked off the county road under the oaks and sycamores. It was as warm in the sun as on that June evening, the soft braided coils of the rug, as green as the leaves seen through the windows of the Olds, and their love as thoughtless.

Time stopped and then expanded like a balloon to deceive them with happiness. It gave them the musical, and then, for they were not without guile, the afternoons when Paul was out on property assessments, the afternoons when Kate could get the farmer's second daughter to stay with Peter, the afternoons when he would pull his car behind the trees that shaded the summer picnic tables at the highway rest area.

Paul would wait until there was no traffic, then he'd walk into the scrubby stand of hemlocks that bordered the pull off and scramble up the slope, his good shoes slipping on the soft needles. Above were hardwoods, and the wind off the distant blue hills swept down through the empty branches. His feet were noisy on the dead leaves and shattered frail little sheets of ice in the ruts of the wagon tracks.

As he walked, the pulse of the afternoon accelerated and

sharpened his senses so that he picked up the faint, sour, humusy scent of the rotting leaves, the rustle in the underbrush that signaled a squirrel or a deer, and, at last, the sound of Kate's boots on the track. He would stride along the path toward her, his coat open, his face stung with the wind, or, his heart leaping in his chest, step into the trees and stand hidden behind a trunk like some aboriginal spirit.

She always sensed he was there, always stopped, alert and wary on the path, to call his name. He'd stick his gloved hand around the side of the tree.

"Don't do that!" she'd exclaim. Her face would be flushed, and it would seem to him that the nervous pulse of her blood was in his ears as well.

"Never," he said, lying, "never." Her face was cold, her hands under the woolen mittens warm. He unzipped her short jacket and folded them both into his topcoat, so that they could not speak for kissing. Soon the weather was cold enough to freeze the ground hard, as hard as a floor, and there was no mud under the inches of hemlock needles and oak leaves. "Do you want to go to the car?" he'd ask.

She held him fast and shook her head, which pleased him always: Their love had to be madness, oblivion. Were time and passion to fail them, they would recognize the distance they had come in eight years and perceive the folly that was as essential as the wind complaining in the thick branches of the hemlocks, as the cold, like steel along the spine, as the stray stones and roots, as the astonishing, overwhelming pleasure that made them greedy, reckless, selfish.

Paul Schott smiled rather sadly at these recollections, but he smiled nonetheless; he would not disown the great moments of his heart. Across the table in the winter restaurant, Leslie Austin saw this and asked, "How long?" She thought she understood everything now.

Paul shrugged, the slightest movement of his shoulders.

Small towns are full of odd arrangements, of long-running secrets, of compromises between temperament and society. "It was off and on. We did try to do the right thing."

"A year?" Leslie asked.

"A couple of years," he said. "Until she became pregnant."

"With Ruthie?" Leslie's voice was hoarse.

"With Ruthie. With our child."

"And Ross?"

The same gesture, the barely detectible shrug. "Whatever he knew or guessed, Ross loved Ruthie from the moment he saw her. Never doubt that."

"I remember. And I remember I never liked you."

He nodded. "Though you're like me, aren't you? Bookish? Shy? Awkward but persistent? Even our hands." He extended his on the tablecloth so that Leslie could compare the long, bony fingers with her own. "But that was natural," he continued. "I was a danger, wasn't I? Though there wasn't much between Kate and me after you were born. Your birth for Kate was like the accident for me. She discovered that she wasn't charmed or even particularly good. So she broke my heart as I'd broken hers."

"You might have divorced and married each other."

He smiled sadly. "Divorces were harder to come by then. She risked losing her child; I risked losing my daughters. None of us had much money . . ." He sighed and compressed his lips. "We thought about it. We talked about it. But then Lee took sick, and Kate had Ruthie."

"My fault," Leslie said. "I always felt that it was my fault Mother and Dad were unhappy."

"Don't blame yourself. There are unhappy loves. Essentially unhappy loves. Did you go to church as a child?"

Leslie nodded.

"I go for the girls, for Lee. My wife is a good woman; I have been fortunate in my marriage. But I remember one Sunday years and years ago, during the time we've been talking about. The reading was First Corinthians, the letter on charity. Do you know it? 'Charity suffereth long, and is kind. Charity envieth not; charity vaunteth not itself,' et cetera. Our love was great, but it lacked charity. It was destructive; it made no one happy. As I sat there and listened, I realized that the price of reversing time was a love lacking in charity."

"Had you married before, when you were young," Leslie began, surprised that she should want to comfort him.

"That would have been different entirely. We would have been very happy."

"Her father thinks so yet."

"And he's right! But we couldn't go back. That was forbidden somewhere, as if I'd made a bargain that I had to keep and, though we tried, our love came to nothing, to worse than nothing, to disaster."

"You were there the day Ruth Eden was kidnapped." Her voice was an accusation.

"Yes."

"She saw your car. She saw you in the kitchen with her mother." Leslie suddenly had no doubt.

"I couldn't live without Kate. I tried. For her, for me, for my wife. I tried to get another job, to be transferred, anything. But my wife's health was poor and the twins were a handful. Lee needed to be near her mother. Do you see how things work out? I saw Kate occasionally, mostly on PTA musical business. We were doing *Carousel* that year. When I was leaving, I kissed her. I held her in my arms for a moment."

He shook his head, remembering how emotion would flood his brain, overwhelming sense and caution and even decency. What had the kid seen—if not that day, earlier, that other day when she'd awakened early and wandered into the wood? Or merely sensed? Children don't need everything spelled out; they are the most sensitive of animals.

"Then Kate said, 'Where's Ruthie? I'd better call that kid.' That's when I left. I didn't know until the next day. That's how quickly it happened. Of course, that was the end. She blamed herself—and me. She never got over losing Ruthie."

Leslie was silent for a moment, knowing that the story fit, knowing that her faint, suppressed doubts had been right. "Did she kill herself?"

"Kate? Oh, no, never! No, I never thought that! She was a fighter; even in despair, she was a fighter."

"Peter thinks Ruthie's loss killed her," Leslie said. "He thinks that's why she went into the water."

"Peter always sees the worst. He didn't know her as well as I did."

"Did he know about you?"

Paul Schott considered. "Probably. Was he the one who raised the blood test business?"

"He made it necessary."

"Peter suffered when Ruthie was lost. And his mother's death coming the way it did . . ."

"Even Ross hates to talk about that."

"Ross never wanted to look too deep. But I don't blame him. He and I have things in common. We've both suffered from violence and irrationality. We've both become reluctant to assess blame."

Leslie fiddled with her spoon, trying to control her turbulent emotions. She had been right after all. Even if the biology was wrong, Ross had been her father, the father she'd known, the father she'd loved. Everything that was false had turned out to be true, and vice versa. "I was thinking how far I'd come to hit a dead end."

"You just hadn't gone far enough," Paul said.

"I was looking in the wrong place. And maybe for the wrong thing: I was looking for a family."

"But someone raised you. Someone loved you. And did a pretty good job, I'd guess."

"Yes." Yes, she had to admit that, and, somehow, it was easier now.

"So, the ultimate consequence of physics, coincidence, and disaster is that we two should meet on a stormy day in this restaurant."

She smiled then, reminding him of Kate. "This was serendipity."

"And unique. Do you understand why it has to be that way?"

"Yes. Though I think now I'd like to have known you."

"That's more than I could have expected. But you and I, who like precision and facts—am I right about that?"

She nodded.

"We have to be content with surmise and probability. To be sure would mean blood tests and to be friends, publicity. I couldn't do that to my family or to Ross. This is all I can give you."

"I wouldn't ever want to hurt Ross—or my brothers," Leslie added, for it came into her mind that if Peter had guessed, he'd known his own share of pain and deception. Across from her, Paul Schott's face was serious. "I appreciate that you've taken a risk," she told him.

"No, when I saw you, I knew it was my chance. I knew that if we were both here, both alone, I was meant to tell you."

She smiled again, that radiant smile that put him beyond doubt. "I feel sure the way I was when I first saw the story on my computer screen." She told him then how it had happened, what she remembered, the two of them leaning over the table, their coffee cups in their hands, talking earnestly, happily—there'll never be another chance—and laughing, too, for they have a similar sense of the moment, of moments, of time stopping, of the pranks of time.

They shook hands formally at the door of the restaurant, then, almost too late, Leslie leaned forward and kissed her father for the first and last time. She waved as he pulled away, then returned to the lobby to call the airline: She had decided to fly into Raleigh and see Aunt Flo before going to Palm Beach to meet Doug.

There were the usual complications. She was rushed to get to the airport and drop off her car and made the Raleigh connection only because the incoming flight had been delayed. Leslie got into her seat at the last minute, and almost as soon as the plane stopped its precipitous climb over the great city's lights, she fell asleep amid the roaring engines, the bustle of drinks and snacks in the aisle.

She dreamed that she was in a boat. She was small, a child of six or seven, maybe, for the rowboat looked big, and the oars were heavy. The boat was pitching in a choppy dishwater-colored sea beneath an expanse of gray and purple clouds. The boat wallowed in the waves, as the shore, a distant line of trees, rocks, and white and gray houses, retreated at dizzying speed. Leslie was lost in horror and despair, before she saw a woman moving with a strong, perfect crawl toward the boat.

The swimmer cut effortlessly through the waves, buoyant and serene, and Leslie recognized her face, not from yearbook photos or family albums, but from somewhere deep in memory, from a lawn with dandelions where a woman, tall and dark, bent down to show her how to thread the stems.

The woman swam closer to the boat, and Leslie called and waved the dandelions she was holding and watched them fall into the gray water. The woman didn't swerve or answer but headed for the distant shore, and the boat was drawn magically in her wake over the deep water that was calm now and the same pearly gray as the turbulent sky, as the headland shrouded in mist, as the seat back and tray table in front of her snapped into focus with a jerk.

Still half in the strange dream, Leslie realized that she had fallen asleep and listed against the man in the adjoining seat.

"Oh, excuse me," she said.

"These night flights are all alike," he replied pleasantly. "By the time they get off the ground, you're exhausted." He was stout with curly black hair and mild blue eyes under black-rimmed glasses.

"Not much choice at this time of year."

"No, not much. Going home for the holidays?"

Once Leslie would have felt a pang, but somehow now it was all right, even easy, to say, "Yes, an early visit. An early visit home."

12

Leslie arrived in the Raleigh-Durham Airport chilled and tired in the aftermath of powerful and conflicting emotions. As she entered the smoky concourse, she felt nothing but fatigue, tinged—and this was the odd thing—with exhilaration. Exhilaration, she supposed, because at last she knew, not just about her family and the whole sad tangle of hope and lust and love and disaster, but that she had been given a moment of grace. And though this was a strange, secular grace, arriving via Paul Schott, maybe grace came only through the fallible and the human, for, against all odds, she had been given the gift of a past: her mother and father and Ross and Woodmill and Mr. Eddie, and the validation of many vague and formless memories, doubts, and fears. In part, she had accomplished those discoveries; she was a good reporter, better perhaps than she had realized. But the last secret, the key to the whole, had been given, along with a new and less censorious perspective that showed her the role of chance and of accident.

How odd, Leslie thought, that after so many years of ignorance and uncertainty, she'd gained a more precise knowledge of

her antecedents than most people could claim. Paul Schott was
right: She could trace her genesis to the sound of metal tearing,
to a moment of folly and disaster on a country road. Her knowledge was that precise, and the sense that she had been given a
gift, a mysterious, serendipitous gift, had raised her spirits and
impelled her to call Aunt Flo and risk reconciliation.

Hurrying along the glassy corridors of the airport, Leslie
occasionally caught her moving image in the night windows,
reflections as insubstantial and fugitive as her last glimpse of
Ross, dwindling against the darkening swirl of snow. She had
recovered him and all the others in only a relative and peculiar
way. All her proofs were painful, and knowledge did not change
the fact that there was a line in some invisible sand beyond
which neither she nor Ross nor any of them could go, not without betraying confidences and devotion. The truth was, that now
she, too, had a secret. Like Aunt Flo and Paul and Ross and
Kate, Leslie had powerful and disturbing knowledge that could
only hurt those she loved.

She thought about that later, standing in the dank fog on Aunt
Flo's second-floor porch. Leslie heard footsteps behind the bat-
tered, mud-brown door, the rattle of locks and the security chain
dropping, before her aunt's pinched face appeared in the opening.

"Come in, come in." She gave Leslie a hug before caution
took over. "You're that white. Was it cold up north?"

"Freezing," said Leslie, kissing her cheek. "Freezing. There
was a storm, so I didn't get out of Woodmill 'til afternoon." She
ran on about this, about the weather and the cold, icy roads, as
she struggled in with her bag. Thank God for meteorology, for a
neutral topic.

"Don't you remember the cold up in Syracuse?" her aunt
asked so eagerly that Leslie understood this meeting wasn't easy
for her, either. "The storms there! I remember when Mac used to
drive the bus behind those big city plows. They'd go out with the
buses behind them."

Leslie did remember. Moving to the South when they did had kept the North fresh and clear in memory: the early dark and the cold nights with the lights of cars and trucks and buses haloed iridescent by icy, blowing snow as fine and dry as sugar.

"Mac used to say he'd had enough of the snow and cold if he'd lived to be a hundred."

"I'd never driven in snow before," Leslie said.

Flo exclaimed about this, said it was a skill, implored Leslie to be careful, and asked if she wanted some soup.

"I ate dinner," Leslie said. "Have you eaten?"

"I was just getting ready when you called."

"Let's have the soup, then," said Leslie, though it was nearly midnight. "But I won't have anything else."

She put her case away in the spare room and set the table, while her aunt opened a can and fussed around the stove.

"You still have your *Cats* mug," Leslie said. "That was a great trip, wasn't it?"

"Oh, and a great show! We did have a good time. And those wonderful costumes." Aunt Flo paused for a moment at the stove. "You'd never have a boring day if you were sewing costumes like that!"

"And you could have," Leslie said loyally, aware, with a mixture of feelings, that Kate, too, had sewed and been interested in the theater. "You were such a good seamstress." It struck her that Aunt Flo must have had many boring days at the bridal shop, not to mention at the university's food service. "I remember you telling me how some of the costumes were made."

"That's right. But it's opportunity. You can't have everything, you know." Her aunt looked wistful for a moment, then shook her head, brisk and sensible. "We about had that show covered between us, didn't we?" she asked with satisfaction. "I knew the costumes and my girl knew the book. That's the advantage of education." She started ladling out the soup. "There now, Campbell's finest. I can remember when I wouldn't have put canned soup on the table, but I've gotten so lazy. Remember how I used to make soup?"

"The best in the world," Leslie said, just like Uncle Mac. Aunt Flo gave her a quick, wary glance to see if she was being teased.

"It was," Leslie said. "With Mac's potatoes and leeks."

"Oh, he grew wonderful vegetables," Flo said. "He did that."

Yes," said Leslie, realizing that Mac—with his vegetables and his stories, the bus and the cold, working nights—was still holding them together; he was part of a stout web of shared memories and events peculiar to her and Flo and to no one else. It was a web that depended not on big dramatic moments, but on daily sights and sounds and smells and tastes: leek soup and maples turning red behind others still green, wet Syracuse streets paved with golden leaves, slush-covered boots and the smell of damp wool on dark winter nights.

She and Ross had tried to make such a web but, in the end, though they tried hard, they'd lacked the material. They'd had guesses and surmises and good will enough for twenty, but they didn't have the taste of winter soup, or a long-remembered trip to New York, or the sound of Mac singing, or the yellow light of the lamp suspended over the table where Leslie's schoolwork was laid out. They didn't have the ephemera of daily life, all those scarcely noticed instants and incidents, which, when lost, show themselves to be irreplaceable. How ironic, Leslie thought, that Peter, who understood precisely what was missing, had still been jealous.

She and Flo sat down to plates of chicken with vegetable soup. Flo had put in a few extra potatoes, and she made herself a cheese sandwich.

Leslie asked, "Is that enough dinner?"

"I don't cook the way I used to," Flo said.

"You should take care of yourself," Leslie said.

Flo smiled a little. By way of commentary, she talked about

her friend Ronny, who had Meals on Wheels now and was happy enough with them. "Course Ronny's a terrible cook," Flo added, "so you can't go by her."

"No," agreed Leslie. While she'd been distracted elsewhere, time had accelerated and skipped a beat. She was amazed that Aunt Flo was old enough to be considering Meals on Wheels.

"Do you want to call Doug?" Flo asked when they were finished with dinner.

"I called him from the restaurant where I had dinner," Leslie said. "He's over in West Palm Beach at the moment. There's a lot of work there."

"I know," said Flo.

"He called you?"

"He's been a bit worried about you," Flo said in a careful, neutral voice.

"He didn't want me to go north."

"Well, he's protective." Flo sounded a trifle impatient. "Would you want him different?"

"I needed to know," Leslie said.

"And did you find out?" Flo asked softly. Leslie heard the tremor of anxiety in her voice.

"Yes," she said. There was a silence, a long, cautious pause.

"And was it as you'd hoped?" Aunt Flo asked timidly. "Did you find the family you'd wanted so much?" She spoke as if the words were acid, burning her mouth.

"I found the answers, but I lost the Edens," Leslie said, and for a moment her heart rose at the idea. Why should she have to give them up? Why shouldn't her feelings count? Why should she be the one to make the sacrifices and accept the status quo? In that instant, Leslie understood precisely what a love lacking in charity entails.

Aunt Flo shook her head and laid her hand on Leslie's shoulder just the way she had when Leslie had faced griefs and disappointments as a girl.

"I've had such a strange evening," Leslie said, recovering her perspective and her sense of grace. "I stopped at a restaurant—I told you how the roads were slow and bad—and this older man came by my table and asked to sit down. You know what I thought. But I was wrong; he knew me, he was sure he recognized me." As Leslie told her aunt the story, it seemed stranger than ever, stranger even than it had in those unexpected and mysterious moments at the restaurant. Her personal history was as full of twists and turns as a Japanese paper toy.

When she was finished, Flo said, "The child was unhappy. Whoever you were, you were unhappy."

"I had some reasons," Leslie said, bristling. "I had some reasons."

Flo gave the slightest of shrugs. "You were asked, you know." Leslie started to speak, but Flo shook her head. "Not by me. I'd never pretend to that."

"I don't remember anything but your telling me my name was Leslie."

"The only real fight Mac and I ever had was over you," Flo said reflectively. "He questioned you, I know he did, because I got it out of him. I was terrified; it would have killed me to have come that close to a child of my own and then to have lost you. After all that had happened."

"You mentioned a late miscarriage last fall." Leslie was surprised that she had remembered, because at the time she had been totally absorbed in her own emotions. "You lost a baby at eight months."

"Yes. No one talked about such things with children in those days, but we had that stillborn child and three other late miscarriages. The last one about killed me, and I had to stop trying.

"I hated that; I hated giving up; I hated feeling that part of my life was over before it ever started. That was a bad time, let me tell you, but maybe you can understand, now that you've had hopes and discoveries and disappointments yourself. I'd finally resigned myself: I'd given up. And suddenly, like magic, you were on the front porch. A lovely, lovely little girl. Then Mac went and tried to learn your name. I was so furious I threatened to leave him."

Flo saw Leslie's surprise. "I did. Not that I would have, but I said I would."

Leslie stood up and went to the window. The dark yard outside reflected the bright little island of the table and her aunt's strained face, hovering on the very edge of darkness. Leslie thought of her mother and Paul and their long, passionate affair, and of Ross with his love for his grandchildren, and of Flo's great, ruthless love for her. She felt that of them all, Aunt Flo had loved her the most, if not the most wisely or the most kindly. Like Paul's and Kate's, Aunt Flo's was an intense, devouring love, lacking somewhat in charity, but it was the love that Leslie had been given; it had made her what she was.

Leslie smiled slightly at her aunt's reflection. They had certain things in common after all. "I may leave Doug," she said after a moment. She spoke experimentally, letting the words float out over the dark yards and the bare limbs of the trees to the faintly pinkish night sky.

"He's a good man," Flo said. "He's stuck by you. That's important."

"He didn't want me to go north. And I shouldn't have, really. When we went up in the summer, I promised that if things didn't work out, that would be it. But I went anyway."

"We all make mistakes," said Flo.

"He wants to manage everything," Leslie complained. "He's always wanting to protect me. I just had to know, but he didn't understand. You understand, though, don't you?" She spoke with some surprise and turned to look at her aunt.

"No man's ever going to understand you enough," Aunt Flo

said. "It's not in them. And you're never going to understand them; I learned that with Mac. But I'm not surprised, because when I look back, I've done things I can't understand, either."

"Was I one of those things?" Leslie asked.

Aunt Flo shook her head. "I understood that," she said. "I just had to have a child. With you it was something different. For me, it was that child; it was you."

Aunt Flo's eyes wavered behind her glasses, quick and intense like a young girl's, as if age were the scantiest of disguises and the person beneath still young, passionate, and hopeful. Leslie reached out and touched her aunt's shoulder before the moment passed, and Flo stood up, brisk and decisive. "You'll be wanting your bed," she said.

"I'll make it up. You'd better get some rest."

"And what else do I do these days but rest?" Flo asked. She opened the linen cupboard beside the hall and pulled out blankets and sheets. "Not like Florida," she said. "Oh, did I ever get sick of mildew."

Leslie agreed that mildew and dampness were problems, said with Florida everything depends on how much you like the heat, reached, in this banal way, the safe shore of the ordinary where they spent the next three days having a conventional visit. They went shopping, had an early Christmas dinner out, and tried bingo with Aunt Flo's friend Ronny, who won six dollars and treated them both to ice cream sundaes.

On Wednesday, Leslie flew home, collected her car at the airport, and headed south. After the snow in Woodmill and the rain and fog of Carolina, Florida had the almost unnatural brilliance and glare of an enhanced photograph. A white sun filled the sky, and the long, dry reeds of the Everglades were swept by great sheets of wind. Along Alligator Alley, the marshy woods and swamps were bleached a dull olive green, and the pools, ditches, and streams showed slick, dark water.

Leslie was nervous all the way across, uncertain of what she
wanted and uncertain about what she might do. She found it
hard to let go of the Edens, whose loss was like a death in the
family, the more difficult because they remained safe in their
own lives like odd, unreachable ghosts. In her grief and resentment, the idea that had come so unexpectedly at Aunt Flo's, the
idea of leaving Doug, shadowed the back of Leslie's mind with
dangers and opportunities. She could start fresh, abandoning all
her memories, and embark on a different sort of life. There were
moments when this seemed like a satisfying conclusion, a dramatic retribution. But whenever she thought too much along
those lines, she was irresistibly reminded of her determined
mothers, of Kate and, especially, of Aunt Flo. Flo had settled for
too little, it was true, but that too little had been her, Leslie, and
Mac, and how could she argue with that? Leslie couldn't sort out
what she wanted to do, because everything came with qualifica-
tions and complications, and the simplest issues dissolved into
the muddle of human wants and failings. About the only thing
clear in her mind was that neither Flo nor Kate had ever been
timid, and, compared with them, Leslie felt almost tentative and
lacking in spirit. From that point of view, leaving Doug, fearing
troubles, avoiding friction, these vague and experimental notions
were cowardly—unless she really didn't love him anymore. And
if she did love him? If he was still the linchpin of her happiness,
not the lost happiness of Woodmill, but of her present and
future? If she did love him, she had to go after him, despite all
her shyness and fears. Their marriage was in her hands, and
she'd best think of Aunt Flo standing on a porch in Syracuse,
seeing a little girl, and making up her mind once and for all,
whatever the consequences.

Burdened with this jumble of ideas, Leslie turned north at
Miami and headed for West Palm, where Doug had been staying
with Aunt Mag and Uncle Kevin. Leslie knew that Uncle Kev

spent most days at the Irish-American Club and figured that the house would be empty. But Aunt Mag worked afternoons at a souvenir shop, and Leslie found her way to Purple Parrot Gifts, crammed with bins of marine relics, boxes of corals, and a whole menagerie of mysterious little birds and mammals made from shells and pipe cleaners, all under the surveillance of an inflated rubber iguana as big as a dragon. Aunt Mag sold a key ring with a starfish preserved in Lucite and a pair of Party Animal T-shirts emblazoned with beer-drinking alligators. Then she struggled with her memory and checked her little notebook and finally remembered that Doug was installing a big kitchen over in Palm Beach.

"Oh, he's just done so good since he came over here," Aunt Mag said. "He does one kitchen on a street and within a week he's got a list of orders as long as your arm. People with more money than they can spend. The sky's the limit. I tell Doug he's gotta get a helper and maybe someone to handle his calls."

Leslie smiled and nodded, although her mouth felt stiff. "Do you know where in Palm Beach?" she asked.

"I don't know the street number," said Aunt Mag, shaking her head. Aunt Mag had a plump, soft face with round, downy jowls. She was dithery but good-natured, and Leslie guessed that her unfeigned enthusiasm for the Purple Parrot's merchandise was worth more than mere efficiency to her employer. "Doug's been good about giving us the phone numbers, though. Since Kev had his stroke, he likes to know where I am and where Doug is—just in case."

"But won't Uncle Kev be out?" Leslie asked.

"Yes, of course, he'll be at the club by this time. There are no gossips like old men, but don't tell him I said that. They're busy solving the problems of the world, you know. But it's Kev that has the phone number." She smiled encouragingly as if to indicate that everything—which was a muddle as usual—was really organized and under control.

"Do you know what street Doug's on?" Leslie asked, forcing patience. "I might be able to spot the truck."

"Well, Ocean Boulevard," Aunt Mag said as if this were obvious, as if her nephew wouldn't be caught working anywhere else.

Leslie got back in her car and drove east on the A1A over to Palm Beach. At a junction in the old highway, she turned north along a street lined with handsome houses, which grew more and more grandiose until the road veered closer to the water, leaving only a narrow strip of beach and the seawall on the right-hand side. Beyond, the open Atlantic sparkled blue to the horizon, providing a pristine view for the mansions crowding the west side of the street. A few blocks farther, she spotted Doug's truck parked in the walled front yard of a sprawling pink Mediterranean-style villa with several acres of tile roof.

Leslie opened her door and stepped out. Now that she was there, she felt hesitant about going up to that grand entrance and asking to speak to her husband. She was delaying, studying the familiar saws and routers and hand tools set out on a table behind the truck, when Doug came around from the back of the house.

"Hey," he said, "I thought I heard a car." He put his arms around Leslie, at once affectionate and wary. "We didn't expect you 'til tonight. How'd you find me?"

"Aunt Mag had *some* information. She knew you were working here among the rich and famous."

"Unbelievable, isn't it? Come on in and see the kitchen."

"They won't mind? I felt odd about going up and ringing the bell."

"Gone 'til the renovations are over. The caretaker opens the house in the morning, and I call him at night so he can check the place out and lock up. Most of the other staff are off at the moment."

"I like the flowers," Leslie said.

"Full-time gardener. He's a nice fellow. He's been giving me some garden tips. In this way," Doug said, opening the door to a tiled mudroom as big as a good-sized kitchen. "They have dogs."

"All the conveniences," Leslie agreed.

"Wait 'til you see the cupboards." Doug was eager to talk about his work, about boards and wood selection and fittings and styles. "Totally custom-made. I made three trips from home just to haul everything over." As they entered the kitchen, his handsome face flushed with pleasure. To handle beautiful wood, to be entrusted to develop a complete design, to work without any anxiety about cost, that was an enormous satisfaction and a very deep happiness.

Leslie looked around. The Mediterranean architecture with its thick walls and narrow windows made the big, square room rather dark and old-fashioned, but Doug had found an elegant solution. The cabinets were a pale, honey-colored wood in a very simple and beautiful adaptation of Shaker design. There were banks of drawers, too, like Shaker dressers, and two tall cupboards, beautifully proportioned and stained a fine light blue-gray. Leslie opened one of the drawers, admiring its perfect dovetails and satin finish.

"They're beautiful, a work of art," she said. "Really lovely."

"I've had opportunities here," Doug said. "I think I've made the most of them."

"I can see. And you're taking photos, I hope. Are you?" Leslie was always urging Doug to put himself forward more and promote his work, and now she added enthusiastically, "You can't beat this for advertising."

"You don't need to tell me how to be a cabinetmaker," Doug said, though she could tell from his tone that he hadn't thought of photographs at all.

"Sorry. I just meant they were marvelous."

"You're full of ideas for other people," he said.

Leslie knew that she had let him down when she broke her

promise and went back to Woodmill, and now, as a result, her hopes were all threatened. But the moment he appeared around the side of the house, Leslie had made up her mind: He was the man she wanted, and she was prepared to ride out a deal of rough weather to have him. Now she suppressed the urge to say something, to explain herself, to lose them both in the verbiage that she knew he hated.

After a minute, Doug said, "Christ, Leslie, I'm sorry." He reached out and gave her an awkward, affectionate shake. "I wasn't sure you'd come back. Have you come back?"

"Are you going to stay over here?" Leslie asked, in turn.

"I don't know. It's up to you in a way. With your job."

"I'm about through with the *Sun Coast Times*. This last trip . . ."

"Was it worth it, Leslie?" He was suddenly very serious, the joy of his cabinets, the happiness of her return, even his momentary, nervous aggravation, faded.

"I needed to know for sure. That was important. I can get another job."

"And another husband?" He spoke without thinking, regretting the words as soon as they passed his lips, but like Leslie, he preferred to learn the worst right off the bat.

"I suppose so," Leslie said, "but I'd never get another one like you."

She stood in the middle of his beautiful kitchen with her arms folded, and something about the way she looked at him told Doug that, in a subtle way, she had changed again. She had lost the unconvincing vivacity that had worried him so much in the months when she was convinced Ross was her father. She seemed quieter and calmer but without the sadness, the terrible sadness that had led, he saw now, to her trips to Woodmill, to her yearning to recapture—or to revise—the past. Perhaps she really had needed to know, perhaps something desperately important had been missing in her life. Doug felt an interest edged with shyness, as he looked at Leslie, his wife and a pretty woman and a slightly different person.

"I missed you," he said. "I was sorry afterward that I'd come over here."

"I think you were right," she said. "You'd never have gotten to build this at home."

"I meant because of us."

Leslie stepped close to him and put her arms around him. "Don't misunderstand me," she said. He kissed her, once, twice.

"We could go to your uncle and aunt's," she said, bringing Doug a rush of happiness, because she rarely made erotic suggestions. "Can we go to the house?"

He looked over her shoulder to his watch. "I'm afraid Uncle Kev'll be back from the club before we can get home. He starts dinner when Aunt Mag's at work."

"Damn."

"I have a better idea." Doug bent down, unlaced his work boots, and kicked off his thick socks. Leslie unbuckled her sandals, and they padded barefoot down the tiled hallway to an enormous living room.

"Good Lord! We're in the Orange Bowl," Leslie exclaimed. "What is this? Fifty feet? Sixty feet long?"

"High enough for goal posts, too," he said. They started laughing at the room's gargantuan scale, at all the lovely, useless luxury: marble mantels and crystal chandeliers and spotless couches as long as buses with little gilt tables at each end. In the middle of the marble tile floor, cool under their feet and smooth as glass, a Persian rug flowered like a vision of paradise. Doug sat down on it and tugged at her hand.

"The windows," Leslie said. Through their tall arches, she could see a green and yellow tangle of tropical foliage.

"The courtyard's kept locked."

Leslie bit her lip, glanced at him, and felt immensely and pleasantly naughty. "The rich know how to live," she said and knelt down beside him on the soft, exuberant flowers of the magical rug.

That was how they put off deciding, and Leslie sometimes thought they'd still be between the Gulf Coast and West Palm, muddling back and forth and living out of suitcases, if one day she hadn't made her farewells at the paper, canceled their lease, and stuck Dylan in his carrier. Three hours later, she arrived at Aunt Mag's and Uncle Kevin's with the orange cat howling in outrage.

"Oh, I don't know about the cat, Leslie," Aunt Mag said, peering into the carrier where Dylan glared with banshee eyes. Leslie was a bit wearied of him herself.

"We're moving out," she said. "This is definitely the place for Doug's business to grow."

With that, Doug had to stop making excuses and go to look at rentals with her. Once they found the condo, which was nicer than they had expected, thanks to the depressed real estate market, everything was settled. Doug became enthusiastic; he found a good workspace through one of his customers and made arrangements to close his old shop and ship everything to the east coast. He and Leslie moved into the condo, and Dylan, who had been kept confined in motel rooms and the back of the truck, stretched his supple yellow body and slunk off toward the small pond on the grounds to hunt mice and chase lizards. After a couple of weekends spent on painting and papering, Doug and Leslie settled down to make adjustments.

The biggest of these was her pregnancy, unplanned and unexpected, a gift of the Orange Bowl and the Persian rug. They were delighted but anxious. Early on, Leslie had some spotting and had to cut back on her new copyeditor's job. She was well for several months, only to have another scare at twenty-nine weeks when she started bleeding again. This time, complete bed rest was ordered, a difficult prescription for a restless, nervous individual. Over Leslie's protests, Doug summoned Aunt Flo, who arrived two days later, clearly prepared to stay.

The two women started out well if uneasily, each on her best behavior, eager for the visit—and the pregnancy—to be a success. But lying in bed all day drove Leslie wild. She was bored, for one thing, although she read until her head ached and her arms lost feeling from holding books over her head. When she wasn't reading, she listened to the radio for new disasters and problems, or else let her mind drift away on music to things she should be doing or home-decorating projects she didn't dare attempt. Of course, she worried about the baby, and about the difficulties, both economic and personal, of her copyediting job, and about how things would be with Doug if she lost the child. And all the time, while her mind was running like a hamster in a cage, Aunt Flo hovered near the bed, which was bad, or cleaned obsessively, which was worse, especially since she worked to soap operas at full volume. Pretty soon they were having snappy little arguments and long, angry silences, and Leslie said cruel things she regretted so much that one day she said, "You should go home. This is bad for you. This must bring up bad memories."

Aunt Flo gave her a quick, angry look. Coming south had, in some indefinable way, perked her up. She had gotten back her feisty, terrier disposition and now she shook her head. "My girl will be all right," she said. "My girl can do it," just as if Leslie was still seventeen.

Irked beyond endurance, Leslie opened her mouth to say something sharp but heard herself ask, instead, "How can you be so sure? Do you really think so?" before bursting into tears.

"Of course, I'm sure," Aunt Flo said, as if she really was sure, as she'd been sure about so many things Leslie had wanted. She came and sat down on the bed and took Leslie in her arms. "What haven't you managed that was in your power? There's no question about it at all. As long as you're patient and stay in bed."

In the end, Leslie was flat on her back for two solid months, since Alice arrived a week late, weighing seven pounds fifteen ounces—"big enough for any baby" as Aunt Flo put it. She and Doug were in raptures about the infant. Back in her hospital room and half doped with late anesthesia, Leslie held her daughter for a few minutes and then insisted on getting up, getting out of bed, and walking to the window on her wobbly legs. The city glittered in the sun, white and pink and blue and ocher, and beyond the buildings, the lake, and farther yet, visible only in a darkening along the horizon, the sea—an expanse that, after weeks of the four walls of her room, seemed endless, wonderful, a perfect image of the sudden expansion of her heart and spirits.

"Isn't she great?" Doug asked. "Isn't this a great baby?"

The baby was scrunched and red and generally rumpled looking, but Leslie said, "We've got the best daughter in the world."

"A couple more," pleaded Doug, fiddling with his new camera. "The sun's coming in through the window just right."

"She's getting tired," Leslie said, wondering to herself just where the command to photograph was buried in the male psyche.

"She's fine," Doug said. "It's her mom that's getting tired."

Leslie laughed. "I don't know what we're going to do with all of these."

"Aunt Flo never says no to a picture," Doug said, concentrating intently behind the lens. Flo had stayed until her grandchild was a month old; she was devoted to the baby and expected reports and pictures regularly. "Alice! Sweetie! Look this way!"

Instead, Alice coyly buried her face against Leslie's breast.

Doug started to whistle and with wonderful surprise on her round baby face, Alice struggled to sit up. Leslie held her firmly by the midsection, while she waved her arms at her father, sending him into exclamations of delight.

"Great. Great expression. And the lighting's just perfect."

"It'll be dark pretty soon," Leslie said.

Doug stuck out his tongue at her and Alice gave a gurgling laugh. "Isn't Daddy being silly?" Leslie asked her, nuzzling the velvet cheek and the tickly new fuzz of baby hair.

"Oh, darn," Doug said, "that's the roll."

Leslie thankfully unfolded her stiff legs and scooped Alice up, while he rewound the film and got it ready for mailing.

"I'm sure some of these will come out well," he said. "I'm almost sorry we already have the Christmas cards made up."

"I like the Christmas card," Leslie said. "You know you're really getting good."

"Constant practice."

"Seriously," Leslie said later as they sat down to address their cards with Alice supervising from the playpen. "You take better pictures than some of the pros at the paper. This is really charming." She held out the card made from a photo of Alice and Dylan. The lighting was soft, tinged with gold, and the baby, frilly in a white sweater, reached across a wash of umber shadows toward the white-whiskered cat. Doug had caught Alice's eager, delighted curiosity and the cat's reserve. Their expressions made for a lovely example of silent communication.

"Did you do Uncle Kev and Aunt Mag?" Doug asked.

"I've done Aunt Flo and all the Florida people."

"We'll send Flo some other snaps," Doug said. He and Flo were united in their pleasure in photographing the baby.

"I'll let you pick those out. I haven't sealed the letter yet."

"And Ross," Doug asked after a minute. "Do you want to send one to Ross?"

Leslie looked at him in surprise. They had not mentioned Ross or Woodmill since the day she'd returned to Palm Beach, and they had lain on the flowered rug—resplendent but a bit dusty—and looked up at the big crystal chandelier. She had told Doug the story and he'd silently stroked her hair. For once, his reticence had suited Leslie, for she had known then that she had to make the break; she had understood that if she could not accept the present and all it included, Flo and Doug and certain limitations, she would not be able to make a success of her marriage. "I didn't think you approved of all that," she said.

"I didn't approve of you getting hurt. You know I liked Ross."

"He made his decision," Leslie said, meaning he'd chosen his family, his grandchildren, and the Birches over her. The topic was closed. She went to work decisively with their rubber stamps, printing out their home address on the family cards and Doug's shop address on his business envelopes with firm, satisfying thumps. She didn't think about Ross then, or during dinner, or while putting Alice to bed, but only much later that night, when something woke her: a heron croaking its way back from the seafront, or a siren, maybe, or the dry rustling of the palm fronds. Leslie sat up in bed, her heart pounding with the conviction that something was amiss, that she'd forgotten something important. She automatically checked on Alice. That diminutive explorer of sleep was lying comfortably on her back in her stretch suit, her arms flung out, her expression secretive and content.

Leslie walked through the apartment—the stove was off, the dishes out of the dishwasher. She opened the sliding glass door but found their tiny balcony empty: Dylan was away hunting somewhere; it was not the cat that had awakened her. The night air was cool, the cement damp underfoot. Out in the darkness beyond the glow of the town, Leslie thought she could hear the surf. Two and a half weeks until Christmas, nearly a year to the day since she had driven out of Ross's yard and slithered down the icy country roads to meet her father and to discover that perfect families do not exist and that while the past can be explored, it cannot be rewritten.

She stood for a moment, aware as she sometimes was now of the vast uncertainty of things, of the immensity of night and darkness and ill luck and trouble that form the backdrop for all human love and human hope and human life. Children, she thought, make you tired, and then they make you philosophical. She rubbed one foot idly against her leg before going quietly into the living room and switching on the desk light. The cards were still laid out, their dark, shiny faces glistening like the surface of a pond. Leslie lifted one, rejected it, then rummaged in Doug's neat store of baby photos until she found a snap of the three of them taken with his timer and tripod. She got a sheet of paper and sat down to think what she would say. Leslie's first thought was to put their names on the back of the photo and stick it in an envelope. She also considered a short greeting: the traditional *Merry Christmas* was always acceptable. But she remembered the night at the beach house with the wind and rain against the windows, the glare of the overhead light on their faces, Peter's angry expression, Doug's concern, her own sick fear, and Ross saying, "Forget the birth certificate." That was the moment when she'd known he loved her, though she had not realized that he understood the situation, that he perceived how things would work out. She had blamed him for not going one step farther, for not accepting the past, sorrows and embarrassments and all, for not putting her first, loving her best—she was not, perhaps, immune to sibling rivalry, after all. Now that she had a family of her own, Leslie had a slightly different perspective. She understood her father's choices better, and, at the same time, she no longer needed him as desperately as she had that last cold night in Connecticut, when all her hopes had shattered.

Leslie picked up her pen and wrote Ross a note, a note like the very first letters, polite, half shy, friendly. She described their joy in Alice, who was a perfect baby, the paragon of daughters, told him about her copyediting job, which was not as interesting as writing but easier with the baby, and mentioned Doug's fine new workshop. "So things have worked out well for me," she wrote, "better than I had hoped or dreamed. I'm a slightly different person—a slightly better one, too, I hope, and that is partly your doing and your family's. Doug and Alice and I are very happy, and we have too many reasons to be thankful this holiday season for any anger or regrets. I sincerely hope that you and yours are well," she concluded, and signed it, "Affectionately, Leslie."

She wrote Ross's address on the envelope and flicked off the light. As Leslie waited for her eyes to adjust to the darkness, she imagined the letter disappearing directly into the warm Florida night, riding on the current of her thought and affection like a message in a bottle. Though she was confident that she could live with his silence, she hoped Ross would answer, and she thought that he might.

One afternoon just before Christmas, Leslie returned home with Alice after picking up a dull but profitable corporate report for copyediting. She'd gotten Alice changed and into bed for her nap when the phone rang. In that instant, everything shut down, the noise of the street, the rustling palms, even the soft, happy baby sounds from Alice's crib: Leslie lost the periphery and was totally focused on the phone, for she knew who it was even before she lifted the receiver, even before he said, "Hello. It's Ross."

"Oh, Ross!" she said. "Merry Christmas."

"Merry Christmas to you, too, dear. And congratulations. Alice Austin!"

"Yes, yes, thank you."

"Now I want to get her a little something—Christmas and baby present combined—so I'll need her size. They're all scaled up, Cindy tells me."

"Alice takes a six-month size."

"Already! Wonderful." He sounded excited, the way he'd sounded in the center of Woodmill when she'd discovered Mr. Eddie's sign and everything had seemed so simple.

"She is a wonderful baby," Leslie agreed. They talked about Alice for a while, and about Doug, the weather, the impending holiday. The grandchildren were delirious, Ross said. Markie was old enough this year to know what was going on; he'd done and said various cute things.

"Another year," said Leslie. "Another year or two and Alice will be able to enjoy Christmas."

"Yes," Ross agreed and there was a little pause. Uneasy in the silence, they both started to speak at once, both stopped and laughed.

"I'm so glad you wrote," he said. "I've been thinking about you. I've been thinking about you since last winter, to tell the truth, but during this past summer—"

Leslie detected something in his voice, and her heart, which she'd thought immune only a few weeks before, took an extra little stutter beat. "What happened? What's wrong?"

"Nothing to be alarmed at. The old ticker. Yes, yes, I'm behaving myself: eating a low-fat diet, walking a mile a day, not a drop to drink. I tell Parshal my palate will be gone and most of my pleasures, but I'm doing well. Just the same, I got thinking about you and worrying a bit that I didn't know how to get in touch."

"We moved last spring."

"Yes, I know; your old phone was disconnected. I was disappointed and, at the same time, relieved, because I'd had no idea what I was going to say."

"I know that feeling. When I sat down to write you, I didn't know how to begin, either."

"And then your nice letter came and you sounded so happy, so . . . confident."

"Now I'm a normal person who doesn't go looking for lost parents in Woodmill."

"No. Though about that, there's maybe a few things you should have known." His voice was tight, and Leslie felt her throat stiffen in sympathy. "I just couldn't tell you that night. I don't know. I didn't want you to think badly of any of us."

"You had other people to consider. I understand that."

"Still, I was wrong. I decided too late. I ran out into the snow, but you were already gone."

Leslie did not tell him that she had seen him in the mirror, that she'd been too furious, that she'd given into despair. Instead, she said, "On my way home the next night, I met Paul Schott."

"Ah." Ross caught his breath, surprised again at the inescapable patterns of his life.

"At a restaurant off the turnpike. What were the odds of that?"

"Unimaginably high," Ross said, hoarsely. "And so you know—"

"Something pretty close to the truth, yes."

"Truth hurts," he said before he could stop himself.

"It hurts at the moment, but not so much as lies."

"Don't blame us too much," he said. "And please don't blame Kate. You had to know us all, how we were, and what we were like when we were young." He wanted to explain to her, to explain the pattern he'd belatedly glimpsed.

"I know you and Kate loved me; I know you were good to me. Everything I'd believed was really true in the end, and after I'd been angry and mean about things long enough, I realized that I was happy after all. I felt well and lucky and I wanted to write and tell you that." Leslie bit her lip and stared out at the intense blue winter sky that was turning watery behind her tears.

Ross's voice was shaky, too, as he said, "I'm glad you did." There was a pause before he spoke again, brightly optimistic despite the quaver she could detect down the line. "A six-month size. Something lightweight, Florida weight."

"Right. We don't get much cool weather here."

"I know just the thing. And a plush toy. Little girls like those, and I like to buy them."

"That is kind," Leslie said, meaning not so much the promised gift as the call and all that it implied.

"I'll warn you I expect pictures," Ross said. "I expect pictures of Alice every few months."

"I won't forget. Doug always has plenty of pictures."

"Great. I'm looking forward to them." And then Ross added the words she'd not known she desired. "Good-bye," he said, "good-bye, Ruthie."

52,319

FIC   Law, Janice.
LAW
             Voices.

$23.95

BAKER & TAYLOR